GRACELESS

BOOK FOUR OF THE GIFT OF GRACE

FROG JONES

ESTHER JONES

Impulsive Walrus

EXCERPT FROM GRACELESS

"Something's wrong," I said.

Three faces in the van turned to me, all of them exasperated at my stunning ability to state the obvious.

"All right, all right," I said. "My point is ... we might want to take this opportunity to think about plan B. I ... think they're onto us, and I'd prefer not to fight my way out of this if I didn't have to."

"They're not coming back," whispered Andrea.

"What?" asked Thad.

"They. Are. *Not*. Coming. Back," she said again, then tension and volume of her voice growing louder and louder.

"What do you mean, Andrea?" I asked. I turned to her, and risked placing a hand on her shoulder, trying to comfort and steady her.

"I mean," she yelled, "that THEY AREN'T GOING TO COME BACK. They're just going to ... oh Gods."

This book is dedicated to Dustin Jeromy Gross. The smartest man to ever design a ruleset, the most creative man to ever sit behind a GM screen, and the most loving husband to share a home with. You made us all your family, and let us play in your immense imagination. Let any who speak ill of you do so to our faces, and at their peril.

SPECIAL THANKS TO:

Paul Anguiano
Beth Barany
Matthew & Eric Melendez Blegen
Nicola Boche
Nancy Greene
Rhiannon Rhys-Jones
Charles D. Moisant
John "AcesofDeath7" Mullens
Randy Neatherlin

ANDREA

A freezing wind whistled out from the portal in front of me, kissing my cheek and pushing my hair back from my shoulders. I could still taste the musty air, full of dust, cleaning products, and the stench of the old mop buckets from the community college's utility closet. The air's passing sounded an insistent, hissing warning against my ears. No one, especially not my new companions, could find out what I intended to do here.

The gloom of my hiding spot did not help the sudden, oppressive paralysis that gripped me. I gulped for air, scents from the two conflicting worlds reaching me. Ammonia mingled with dry earthiness.

To protect us all, I needed to know Cythymau's endgame. Unfortunately, I could only think of one way to get answers. I had no good options, here. Taking one step toward the portal, I stumbled, my mind frozen with dread.

I hit my thigh with the heel of my hand in frustration. *Move, Andrea.* An open portal meant Visitors could cross, wards could be triggered, all sorts of other-world nastiness could get worse.

If anyone catches you here, whether it's Cythymau or not, everything will be wasted, a small voice in the back of my head said. *You didn't even tell Robert's skinny butt where you're going.*

When I thought Cythymau dead, I'd been content to let his knowledge die with him. But now, I needed it to thwart him. Keep everyone else from him. And I'd do it, too— even if it meant sinking to his level.

I closed my eyes, breathed deeply, and quietly stepped out of this world and into my worst nightmares. Being careful not to create an imbalance between the two worlds, I exchanged air for myself and quickly closed the portal behind me.

I crouched, ready to run, and scanned the horizon for any immediate threats. Just by physically being here, black despair hung over me, like a murder of crows waiting to scavenge fresh roadkill.

The cold east wind rustled through the tall blue grass, shaking the yellow bushes, plastering my "Book-Wyrm" t-shirt and loose yoga pants against my huddled form. The earth beneath the grass was chalky and dry, parched for moisture. Just holding it in my Sense made me feel thirsty, craving water. Dead insects lay mummified in its chalky depths. No living movement greeted my Sense.

It was as if all small, insignificant life had left this world along with Cythymau. That shouldn't be true, though. The whole world hung cold and lifeless in his absence.

Caught in the wind, my long copper hair flowed across my eyes. I flinched, the fluttering movement releasing the coiled terror within me like a mousetrap slamming down on my conscious mind. I froze, panic flash-flooding through me.

"Piss and shit," I muttered, batting the hair out of my face angrily. My momentary fear converted immediately to biting anger. Anger at myself. Anger at this world. Anger at having to come here again. Anger at the demon Cythymau who'd forced me into this position.

Wfft, child. Where do you find this limitless outrage? You chose to tie your life to this long ago. Cythymau's voice, never forgotten, whispered through my mind whether I willed it or not.

Cautiously, I paced toward where I knew the entrance to his cave would be. The wide-open, wild hills where Cythymau's former residence nestled had been covered in weaving grasses and small, pungent shrubs last time I'd been here. Now all that remained were their rustling and rattling skeletons. Brittle and bleached by the sun, their fallen corpses crunched underfoot as I hiked toward the cave mouth.

Maybe I should've told Robert about coming here.

He'd been here before, once as an invader and once invited by Cythymau himself. Reality as most people knew it was just one Weave out of many. And each world, each Weave, had its own creatures, some human, some not. If you knew the correct rune phrases, it was possible to open portals or summon contracted spirits from one to another. Cythymau's home Weave held secrets I wasn't willing to give anyone, even if I had to assume that he gave many of them to his new followers.

I clambered over a rock fall, and carefully navigated around where the hill's gentle slope had fallen away, leaving exposed stones and dirt. I'd purposely avoided the crater marking the spot where Grace nuked herself to let Robert and I escape.

Had all this other damage been done in Grace and Robert's last, desperate fight? I couldn't remember; I'd been, at best, semi-conscious, semi-delirious, and semi-sane at the time.

The opening to the cave materialized over the bend of the hill, and I frowned.

The entrance had crumbled on the right side, debris from a rockslide blocking the opening. It didn't look intentional, and made ingress inconvenient, but not impossible.

I felt around with my Sense, looking for wards or traps, poking and testing the Weave in front of the cave. Surely Cythymau wouldn't have abandoned his old home without so much as a burglar alarm? But discovering none, I worried I would find it totally empty and useless already.

Years, maybe decades *had* passed in this Weave since I stood here. Time flowed faster in this Weave than the one I'd just come from.

But in my experience here, the cave had always remained unchanged. The idea that it could succumb to time just felt *weird*. By using runes and blood as a conduit, I could send my Sense to summon matter, spirits, or forces from across the globe, but to manipulate forces and matter within thirty feet, I didn't need any aids at all. With my Sense, I piled the rocks out of the way with no fuss.

Entropy had taken hold of this Weave with a vengeance. I had yet to meet any small signs of life, let alone any of the large predators native to this Weave. One *can* damage a Weave intentionally, and I had to wonder if Cythymau had killed this Weave before he left.

Past the entrance, clammy, cold air embraced me, coaxing a shudder from my muscles that ran the whole length of my frame. I used my Sense to navigate the gloom, rather than lighting a wall sconce or pulling the flashlight out of my backpack. The hearth lay bare and unused. The damp chill stood testament that no blaze had been lit in this place any time in the recent past.

I walked past the front room, cutting a wide path around the patched hole between this room and where the slab of my imprisonment sat. That was the only evidence of Robert's very first visit to this Weave. *That* time, I hadn't left. Gooseflesh pebbled my skin and my stomach heaved as it suddenly tried to claw its way out of my throat, pulling my mind back to a different day in that room.

THE RUNED STRAPS cut into me, holding my naked body immobile against the rough stone table underneath me. I could feel the sharp edges of the ancient, carved runes on the table digging into my shoulder blades, my calves, too. Blood dripped down my forehead, forcing me to squeeze my stinging eyes shut.

I lay there like a gutted fish, ripped out of my own world.

Pain, grief, and exhaustion weighed me down. I had allied with this strange spirit and won the battle against the Lycaon pack, but I hadn't saved my mom, or my gran. My small commune had been wiped out of existence.

I felt pinned there: cold, exposed, more vulnerable than I would have believed possible before this moment. But too tired from everything that happened, everything that had already happened, to have the emotional energy to protest. *This could be where I die.*

Above me, Cythymau moved, his shadow falling across my face. I tried to squint up at him through the blood matting my eyelashes, tears trailing down my cheeks from my burning eyes. I could barely make out his twinkling dark eyes, surrounded by crow's feet. His face and arms covered in the swirling, runed tattoos, decorating every square inch of tanned flesh that wasn't covered by the archaic-looking, hard leather armor he wore.

In one hand, he held the rune-covered stone knife with which he'd already cut into me several times after the fight, and in the other, he held a different sharp-looking metal instrument I couldn't place. He set the implement down next to my shoulder. He pressed the knife to my flesh, and I gritted my teeth, refusing to cry out.

"Whuft! What a mess you are," he said in that lilting voice, as if nothing was wrong. "There is much to correct here. To reform. This is likely to be truly unpleasant," he told me, as if I wasn't already in agony, "but I did warn you this would not come easily. I do applaud the will you have shown this night. The prospect of pain did not cause you to falter once you set your mind on a goal. That trait is always admirable. So many are surprisingly weak when confronted with their own frailty. Shattering and abandoning their convictions under the slightest pressure."

He continued to carve my flesh, humming slightly as he worked.. Despite the cacophony setting all my nerve endings on fire, I could feel blood trickling over my skin in warm rivulets that still left me freezing cold.

A scarlet pool spread out beneath me, filling the runes carved into the table. When he'd said I'd pay for his aid in banishing the demons with my life, I'd imagined a quick death fighting the Lycaon or right after.

And yet, I refused to beg him to stop. To cry out. To plead for my life. I'd told him I'd give it. And I would.

An intense jolt of agony sliced through me, starting at the top of my head and radiating all the way down to my toes, seizing all my muscles. It finally receded, leaving me suddenly aware of everything around me. I could Sense every curl and edge in the runes binding me to the table, the ones pressed against me at my back, the damp chambers of the cave beyond where I lay. The runes on the stone table thrummed, harnessing that power, pulling all that I was through them, and throwing me, scattered like chaff, out into the Weave wherever Cythymau wanted.

"Now the real test begins," Cythymau said, picking up the curious-looking instrument, poking and pricking my already abused flesh.

"Test?" I finally croaked. "What test is there in death?"

"Whuft, child! I asked for your *life* in return for my aid. I would never offer a such poor bargain as your *death*. No, today we begin a much grander, though burdensome, endeavor."

A much grander, burdensome endeavor?

He continued while I was still trying to absorb what that meant.

"The fates brought us here. Even though you are no more than a small flicker today, together we shall become a force that can spite the universe. With vigilant care and crafting, my *plentyn*, the smallest spark will keep a fire burning for millennia."

That day began a long nightmare, each day blurring into the next. As the demon spent long, tortuous hours manipulating my flesh, my Sense, until I was no more than a husk, a shadow that had once been a person, used for the power I fed Cythymau and little else.

I FORCED myself to look away from that room, away from the past it held, and keep walking. I was no longer that, and I needed to keep my friends from sharing any piece of that fate.

To that end, I wanted the oldest writings Cythymau had. Anything that might give me an edge in defeating him. I'd retrieved the runed stone dagger he used to bind me, to bind his creatures, already. To my shame, I'd used it once. I'd had a good reason, but the thought that I'd copied Cythymau, forced another being to obey my will, made my skin crawl.

The storage room was part library, part demented museum, and a complete mess to my Sense. Rune symbols, sigils, and summons crowded me in a jumbled cacophony. I'd only been here one time before being tied down to his slab; I had no idea how this room was organized. At the far end of the room, the whole wall held scrolls from floor to ceiling. Cythymau had crammed them into their pigeonholes until nothing else could fit. In my Sense, rune emblems pressed together and folded in on each other, a bewildering mishmash. Tomes sat stacked haphazardly on the floor, next to carved slate tablets piled ten or fifteen deep.

I closed my eyes, backing away from the onslaught of information flowing into me from my Sense, until it was far enough out of range that I could think.

From here, I could send scrolls and tablets to Robert's Weave, but the utility closet I'd used to open the portal was absolutely not big enough or safe enough to store all this. And as undefended as this cave appeared to be, anyone who Cythymau sent could put their hands on all the knowledge it represented. In fact, I couldn't think of one person who I'd trust with the contents.

Piss and shit. I didn't even trust *myself*.

I decided to look for a spot away from the cave to ward and relocate the trove, backtracking the way I'd come. I walked up the slope north of the cave until I got to the ridge. The more I walked, the more the barren lack of life got to me. No matter how far I walked, I found ... nothing. Nothing lived except me. The grass rattled in the chilly wind, desiccated and dead, like cadaverous omens.

Usually, I'd already have a couple ideas where I could hide Cythymau's things. But in this surreal deathscape, I didn't trust my previous knowledge.

I clutched the charms on my rune bracelet, swinging my backpack to one shoulder before fishing a vial of blood from an outside pocket.

Flicking it open with my thumb, I bloodied a compounded rune emblem. I sent my Sense outward through the rune to explore, winding myself into the crosshatched warp and weft that made up the fabric of reality. With the summon, I stretched myself out and laced myself through the Weave. My Sense picked up the light and vibrations from the landscape, spreading the world out before me so I could travel through my surroundings, as if it was a giant relief map. I threaded my way forward, zooming in and taking a closer look at anything that caught my interest as I went.

Through the runes, the grass, trees, and rocks looked normal, just eerily dead and silent, not thrumming with everyday life like in the past. The wind continued to blow, bending branches and grasses to the east. Some tension in the Weave led off that direction, following the wind as if snagged. Perhaps something pulled a few of the threads, bending it. I followed that small flaw, probing the Weave as I went. I wound my way down a small valley and over a small ridge.

And looked out into nothing.

The ridge stood on what appeared to be the very edge of the world. As I watched, rocks and dirt crumbled away, slid down the far slope, and vanished into a vast void. That inexorable emptiness crept closer. A wall of destruction that left nothing behind.

I stared at it, transfixed.

I couldn't Sense anything I recognized as an active summon. It didn't feel like the rocks were pulled somewhere else, and nothing materialized, exchanged into the Weave to replace any of the damage.

The Weave beyond a certain point just ... ceased to exist. I tried to wrap my mind around the idea. Was that even possible?

The threads anchoring my Sense to the Weave ripped out from underneath me. The ridge began to crumple and slide downward toward the void.

The Weave around me frayed, warp threads sticking out toward the void like skeletal fingers. The weft I'd wound my Sense around fluttered free, no longer attached. I scrambled to grab the loose warp, feeling like I attempted to outrun a landslide. More weft came loose and flung my Sense forward, trying to find somewhere more stable to anchor my Sense.

More of reality slid into nothingness as I tried to stay ahead of it. Dirt, rocks, and plants that I'd just been part of all evaporated as if they'd never even been.

I tried not to panic. If I got stuck here, I'd be unmade too. I'd never heard of that, but right now, that didn't mean anything.

I tried to scramble back up the threads nearest me, but they vanished like snuffed smoke. A force raked the edge of my Sense, trying to sweep me into nothingness with everything else. I could feel the edge of my Sense fray, starting to splinter. I flinched away, desperation lending speed to my flight. I flung myself back up the warp the way I'd come. I could only hope I'd make it back to some part of the Weave that was still usable.

I needed to get home. Get back to Robert. Stop Cythymau.

I *could not* cease to exist here. Not yet.

I wound myself around the warp, scrambling over the disintegrating weft, trying not to get any more caught-up in its inexorable unraveling.

This Weave was literally disintegrating into oblivion, like in a slow-moving avalanche.

Something had caused it to unravel at a much faster pace than I'd ever believed possible. Someday very soon, the Weave where Cythymau had held me captive would blink out of existence. I couldn't help but think he'd set some kind of self-destruct.

Then I shuddered at the implications of that. If he could undo *one* Weave ....

I kept dragging myself up the warp. My sight blurred, my Sense damaged on one edge. Everything felt unstable, ragged. But I doggedly kept moving away from the crumbling cliff. It didn't matter how close doom was at my heels. It didn't have me quite yet.

I hadn't died during the whole time Cythymau had held me captive here. Piss and shit if I'd give my life to ... Whatever this thing was.

I finally threaded my way back to Weave that felt solid, jagged on the edge. It had not torn free yet. I grabbed onto that familiar texture, relief flooding me. I jerked my Sense back through the summons into myself. My Sense reeled away from the blood and runes and slammed into my body with unexpected force.

My consciousness settled back into place with a jarring dissonance that frizzled along all my nerve endings. I sat breathing for a moment, my head ringing with pain, my skin goose-fleshed and slick with sweat despite the cold. I focused on the chalky ground, firm underneath me, the rattling grass waving above my head. Sour acid filled my mouth, and my stomach heaved. I leaned to my side, losing everything I had eaten for breakfast earlier that morning.

Was I all here? Did I still have use of all my faculties? My Sense felt like maybe it was a hair smaller, or maybe weaker? I didn't want to test it here. I wiggled my fingers and toes. They all moved. My head felt like two tons of wet sand though.

I held very still, waiting until I was sure I wouldn't be sick again. But I had no time to dawdle. I needed to get out of here, and I needed to take anything I wanted with me. Now. Before that giant moving wall of nothingness got here.

I ran back down the slope to the cave and then into the storage room, focused on my new mission.

Once I made a portal, I could push whatever I needed through. But I needed it to be safe from prying eyes. There were very few places I knew well enough in my new Weave to pull that off. And with the time difference between the two Weaves, there would be no coming back. This Weave wouldn't exist anymore.

Anywhere in the safehouse was out of the question. Sharing the space with Robert, Phineas, Thad, Matt, and Amy meant there was no real privacy at our hideout in Shelton. I couldn't store anything there. They still treated me as a convalescent or half-wild. Most days that suited me just fine; but it made hiding anything even more difficult.

Concealing the things at school was also sub-ideal. Any janitor or student who stumbled across them by accident would immediately cause me grief, no matter whether or not they ended up on Cythymau's or the fed's side. Neither would be good for me. And if I set wards that accidently caught someone mundane, well, that would get ugly too.

The summons required to create the kind of warded storehouse across the Weaves would be ridiculously complex, and I wanted none of that. I had to find somewhere to dump them temporarily and then come up with something more permanent. The woods outside our new Grove HQ felt like my only option then. But how to keep Robert from finding it with that ridiculously huge Sense of his ...

~

I STEPPED out of the portal into an abandoned, dusty garage on the edge of the rainforest. Its owners were long forgotten but the structure was still sound enough, and currently stuffed to the brim with all my ill-gotten gains from Cythymau's cave.

Under that abandoned garage, I created my own storehouse. Using my Sense, I dug out a wide chamber underneath, bracing the walls and ceiling with wide beams and fallen tree trunks. The excess dirt I scattered under the leaves on miles of the forest floor.

I ventilated the chamber next, fashioning the air covers to look like slowly decomposing stumps. Lastly I fashioned shelves of stone, driftwood, and cooled lava rock. Preparations complete, I finally started organizing the artifacts onto the shelves I'd crafted. The slate tablets, tomes, and runed odds and ends first, since they could not be compressed or destroyed easily.

I moved the scrolls next, starting with the oldest. Everything filled my new storage room to bursting. But I didn't actually need to stand in it to retrieve anything. I'd just summon whatever I wanted to look at next, after all. If I made the room any bigger than necessary, it would make it that much harder to camouflage, anyway. I already felt paranoid about any prying eyes.

Unfortunately, several piles of scrolls remained when I ran out of room. I looked at them quickly, then stuffed the five most interesting-looking ones in my backpack. With regret, I blooded a rune to set fire to the rest, then watched them burn. I scattered the ash, obscuring the signs of my recent activity.

That done I stepped back out into the woods around the garage, then reached through my bond to Rick. I scouted his current whereabouts while carefully avoiding the big spirit's corresponding link to Robert.

I asked him to come to me, calling him through our bond.

Rick was a thirty-foot plus racoon-hedgehog-ankylosaurus-like spirit known as a Cornuprocyon. He bounded out of the trees, his lips curled up in a sharky grin, his tongue lolling. Happy that I had come to play, his joy buffeted me through our link. He wasn't as happy to see me as he would have been to see Robert, of course—our friendship was on the new side, and I couldn't always keep my wariness out of my interactions with him. But we were coming to understand each other better, we two.

"Look," I told Rick, holding up a hand to pause his headlong bound toward me. "I have time for a short –" the giant racoon bounced, and I shot him a quelling look "–game of force ball, as a thank you, but I need your help in return."

Rick cocked his head at me questioningly, his giant club-tail twitching.

"I need you to guard Cythymau's things, so no one can get them."

Rick gave a distressed whine at Cythymau's name, backing away immediately.

"I know. I don't want anything to do with him either. But I need you to guard these so no one knows they're here."

Rick stared at me.

"No one can get close. We're going to play keep away with everyone else. Do you understand me?"

Rick bounded off into the forest. There was a thunderous crash and thrashing from the direction he'd gone. Rick came back into view, a giant, uprooted fir tree hanging from his jaws. His bounding return was hampered slightly by the tree getting caught on various bushes and saplings.

He slid to a stop in front of me and wagged his head from side to side, shaking the fir tree at me. Just like a dog teasing a human with a toy.

I stared. The massive racoon bounced impatiently on his front paws, offering me the fir's dirty gnarled roots where they poked out of the corner of his mouth.

When I failed to do anything with said tree, Rick whined at me plaintively, lowering his head and rolling one big eye up at me.

"I—no," I said. "That's not what I meant. I need us to play a different game." I sent Rick an image of the abandoned garage, of the things I had crammed into the space underneath it. "These things are precious. Dangerous. This area is out-of-bounds."

Rick cocked his head to the side, confused. The tree hanging out of his mouth hit the ground, bent, cracked, then splintered against the forest floor. He huffed a breath at me. Over the link, I felt his disappointment at me for wanting to stand here rather than play. To his mind, I'd said I'd play a game. So why weren't we playing? Rick was a good boy. He already wanted to play the game.

I changed my tactic, trying again. "You and I *are* playing a game." I told the big racoon-hedgehog-ankylosaur. "We're playing a game of keep away. These things are ours and they're precious. No one can come here." I showed him an image of the garage over the link, and then an image of Robert coming to the garage and being hurt by Cythymau.

Rick whimpered.

"You understand?" I asked Rick, "Our game is to keep Robert and *everyone* from finding here, so Cythymau can't hurt them, okay? If people find it, they die," I said.

Rick enthusiastically sent me an image of Robert over the link, cocking his head, insisting that he should get to be part of our keep away-team too. He sent an image of him and Robert playing force ball over the link, which I supposed meant Rick thought Robert was good at dangerous games. I'm sure he was. I just couldn't trust it.

"Robert can't be on our team this time," I said. "No matter how good Robert is at games, we can't involve him in this one. Cythymau will do bad things and try to kill him. We need to show Robert how sneaky and clever we can be. We're keeping this base hidden from everyone so they don't get hurt. Is keeping Robert—and everyone else —away from here a problem for you? Do you think it'll be too difficult for you?"

Rick shook his spiky coat, clearly put out that Robert would choose to be on a different team than him, but gave a reluctant sneeze that I took to mean no.

"So you'll play my game and help me protect this place from Robert and everyone else? To keep everyone *totally away* from here, so they can be safe?"

The mammoth Cornuprocyon crouched down, putting his chin on the ground so he could stare at me with both big eyes. Finally, through the bond, I felt his reluctant but firm agreement. This was not a task I could leave to anyone else. It scared me that my best protection plan was in the claws of a Visitor with the mind of an overgrown golden retriever. But Rick was by far the best ally I had for this particular task.

"Thank you," I said. And I meant it.

ROBERT

Phineas Brandiole stood with me in the middle of the Olympic rain forest and stared coldly over my shoulder at my pet raccoon, Rick. The former Seattle Grove Director—now a fugitive wanted by not one, but two different governments—seemed less than enthused about the presence of Rick.

Ok, ok. That's not fair. Director Brandiole (I couldn't shake the title mentally, whether it remained applicable or not) probably had good cause to be irritated with Rick. "Raccoon" is a bit of a stretch as well, though I'd begun to call him that more out of a sense of irony than accuracy. Rick should be more accurately called "Cornuprocyon," as he is thirty feet long, covered in reddish-orange quills, and packing a massive, chitinous club for a tail. Rick could also generate kinetic force roughly equivalent to a speeding freight train, and harness that force for basic applications (jumping really high, destroying things/people, and playing catch with freight-train sized balls of force).

He also really, really liked to play. Phineas's cold glare did little to stop the great, chitinous tail from swinging wildly back and forth at our presence, and Rick pranced a bit with his forepaws, eagerly awaiting the moment when we would both relent and play with him.

The difference between a German shepherd puppy and Rick the Cornuprocyon lay in the fact that the shepherd will occasionally shred a blanket playing tug-of-war. Cornuprocyons could level a city block when playing "catch."

Having an *excited* Cornuprocyon on one's hands is, therefore, only slightly less dangerous than having an *angry* or a *hungry* Cornuprocyon on one's hands. It is not the kind of situation where one devotes less than full focus.

Unfortunately, rune work training is much the same thing. Which explained former-Director Brandiole's lack of shared enthusiasm for Cornuprocyon Play Time.

Oh, there's no immediate threat with rune work. But when one actually attempts to *use* the runes, getting something wrong can kill people out of hand. Worse, it can shred the Weave, that barrier between worlds that holds all of reality as we know it together. Which brings a new level of excitement to rune-work.

Director Brandiole had, therefore, paused his instruction when Rick approached. Giving less than my full attention to either was simply not an acceptable compromise. I'd told the big Visitor that I'd be unavailable, but to Rick, the thought of me being *present* but not *available* didn't process so well. He could see me. Therefore, it stood to reason (if one had the brain of a Cornuprocyon) that I was, in fact, available.

"Boy? We talked about this. I can't play with you right now. Give me an hour and I'll come play, no problem."

Rick looked at me, then drooped his head in classic puppy-dog-stare form. It probably would have worked better on a head *smaller* than my torso, but I still found it adorable. I reached out and scratched him between his ears, then gave him a couple of gentle pats.

"Now, buddy. One hour. The sun should be ... here," I pointed at an area of the sky roughly to the west of where the sun currently peeked out from the grey clouds to filter down to the mossy forest floor. "Come see me then; we'll play."

Rick continued to stare at me, head drooping. I sensed him trying to muffle his own excitement through the bond we shared. He loved me—unconditionally and uncontrollably—and the fact that I continued to relegate Rick to the forest hurt his feelings. Now I'd come to where he could actually spend time with me, and still I turned him away. My heart ached for the poor guy, but I'd promised Director Brandiole this session.

"Jesus, look at him," said Director Brandiole. "Like a puppy, isn't he? Still, though, I can't believe you trust him. I saw the reports of what he did to the Spokane Grove. To your Uncle. He's not exactly pet material."

"He's saved my life and my friends' lives more than once since then, though. Uncle Herman's death is on Cythymau, not Rick."

Director Brandiole continued to stare at Rick. After a moment of standoff, the big Cornuprocyon shook his entire body (and the very ground we all stood on in the process), then bounded off into the forest.

"Good," said Brandiole. "Now, back to your runes. They're sloppy; it's like you were taught the basic forms, but you've never perfected them. See this Laguz? You've got the angle—the only angle in the entire rune, I might add—off by about fifteen degrees."

"It's still recognizably Laguz," I said. "What's the difference?"

"About thirty seconds," responded Director Brandiole. "Oh, this will still work, but the goal with runes is to make them as exactly as possible, then put them together as exactly as possible. Do that, and you'll be able to send your Sense anywhere, and quickly."

"Huh," I said. "Grace never took me through any of that." Mention of my first mentor always caused a pain in my chest, though it had receded from a sharp, guilty stab to a dull ache.

"I doubt anyone ever took Grace through it," said the Director. "Grace had almost no Sense range; it barely extended millimeters beyond her own body. Now, range and strength are not the same thing; Matt, for instance, has neither range nor strength. Grace had the strength, but no range."

"So?"

"So?" he said, mimicking my tone. "Well, what's the hardest part of using runes for you?"

I thought about that for a bit, then answered "It's trying to focus on the runes. I can Sense them, but putting my Sense *into* them requires that I ignore everything around me."

"Precisely. Robert, you've got one of the biggest Senses on record. Your own Uncle had forty feet; if you didn't feed a portion of yourself to your pet, you'd be at fifty." At this, he gestured in the direction Rick had run. Rick operated by consuming the Weave-energy summoners used to do their business; I kept him fed by giving him a small portion of my own Sense through our bond.

"Yeah, so?" I asked. "My Sense has helped me through some pretty tough scrapes."

"Not doubting it. But run the numbers for a moment. The volume of a sphere is four-thirds, times pi, times the radius cubed. So a one-foot sphere has an area of about 4.19 cubic feet. A two-foot sphere doesn't double that number, though. Rather it multiplies it by two to the power of three, or eight. Which means the volume of a two foot sphere is 33.51 compared to 4.19."

"Why are we doing math right now?"

"Because, even after you shave ten feet off and feed it to your beast, you have one of the largest Sense ranges on record. *Mine* is thirty feet, and I am considered one of the rare greats. *You* have the sort of Sense that comes around only once in a generation, if that. Increasing a Sense becomes cubically more difficult for every foot you add, because Sense is about *volume,* not radius. Your sense at forty feet contains roughly ..." He paused for a moment before finishing his calculations. "... 286,160 cubic feet of data, compared to my own measly 113,130 cubic feet."

"You did all that math in your head just now?" I asked—I had to admit, I was impressed.

"Sense volume calculations are one of the most basic equations we're taught. You should be able to do them in your sleep—another bit of your training that's been sorely neglected."

I mumbled something incoherent. It's always been my go-to when I'm irritated with an adult, but don't want to start a full-blown fight.

"Anyway," he continued, "when you enter the runes, you have to *ignore* that data. For Grace, that sort of thing came as easily as breathing. Of course, she had maybe a millimeter or two of range, so ignoring the things her Sense showed her came easily to her. For me, there is a mountain of data that flows through me—it's exhilarating, and gripping, and I have to pull myself free of it. You, on the other hand; when you enter the Sense, you're getting two and a half times as much information as *I* am. It must be a rapture." At this last, Brandiole's voice turned almost wistful.

"It, uh, it is," I stammered. The feeling when entering the Sense is an intensely personal one. You don't simply become aware of the things around you; you *become* the things around you.

"And when you work with runes, you have to break free of that rapture. So for you, accuracy in the rune phrase is of extreme importance. Because the more precise your rune construction, the better your phrases, the easier you will find it to enter them and block out everything else. Allow me to try an experiment."

Brandiole unfolded a small piece of paper from his back pocket. I recognized the rune tag as he placed it before me, then offered me a small pocket knife. "I drew those runes myself, using a protractor on a clean surface. They are as precise as they can be. The runes will take you into my kitchen, and should allow you to grab my dinner bag out of the fridge."

"I, um, I didn't expect that we were doing practical work," I said. "I didn't grab any blood from the fridge."

"Good," said Phineas. "I mean, not good that you're an idiot—you think I'd come all the way out to the woods to do book-work? But good that you'll have to use your own blood. Once again ... maximize your connection. Grace could do all this quick and dirty—you need to start doing it with the optimal conditions, and that means your own blood, and fresh." Saying this, he drew a small knife from under his sleeve and passed it to me.

I rolled up my pant leg and drew the knife across the front of my ankle. Here's a fun tip for those of you playing along at home: don't cut from a finger if you don't have to. You watch in movies, and any time they need blood, they cut their thumbs, or the palms of your hands. Well, *you might need those to work later,* so I highly recommend using some part of you less useful than, say, *your thumbs.* Even if you're in a pinch, surely the back of one's wrist is a better call.

Some lessons I'd learned the hard way.

Once I'd spread my blood across the runes, I brought up my Sense. Suddenly, everything around me for forty feet (including Director Brandiole himself) became a piece of me. I Sensed his heartbeat. I Sensed the squirrels in the trees, staring at us in nervous curiosity. I Sensed the insects on the ground under my feet, and the worms in the earth beneath. Everything *became* me, a piece of myself I could move about at will, should I desire it.

And, in my hand, the rune tag. It shone like a beacon, calling, beckoning me. I focused on it, feeling it drawing me in, sucking me down. In a moment, I was through the tag, and I *was* the small paper bag containing a leftover sandwich, a cup of yogurt, and a bottle of flavored seltzer. I grabbed it with my Sense, then moved seamlessly back through the tag to deposit the bag in my hand.

Seconds.

"See?" said Director Brandiole. "Get the forms of the runes down correctly and getting through them gets easier. Grace never had to worry a bit about penmanship, or proper forms, but you're going to have a hell of a lot more study than she did. She spent her time coming up with *ridiculously* complex rune formulas; I'm still a bit baffled as to how she managed to nuke herself, honestly."

I'd never been in and out of a rune set that fast. Granted, it still wasn't fast enough to be truly combat-effective, but faster than anything I'd done to date.

Huh.

"Enough for today," said the Director. "Time to head in. You coming directly home?"

"I promised Rick I'd play with him," I said. "I'll grab dinner elsewhere."

~

I LIMPED up the sidewalk to the front door of Smokin' Mo's barbecue house in downtown Shelton with all the grace of someone who very badly needed a beer. There's always an element of risk when playing with building-destroying forces in the hands of a being with all the intelligence and exuberance of a golden retriever. It's a small price to pay for the love and friendship, but still occasionally painful. No broken bones, but I could tell that I'd be coated not in bruises, but in one massive, more or less contiguous, bruise in not so long a time.

Smokin' Mo's had become something of a refuge for me. Oh, we'd moved out of the original two-room apartment and into a much more spacious home thanks to Matt's financial (literal) wizardry, but sharing a house with the Director and Thaddeus—the man who'd once tried to kill me—always left me feeling tense. I'd made Mo's my place.

The very act of walking into Smokin' Mo's constituted a process of healing. There is a magic moment when you open the door to a very, very good barbecue place, where the smells of smoke and meat roll out of the doorway and embrace you like a long-lost mother. In that single moment, all is well. It never lasts, but for one moment your mind fills so completely with that scent that it has little room to contain any worry or woe. That first breath on walking into Mo's had become an almost-religious experience for me; my saliva began to churn in a Pavlovian homage to the aroma.

"You look like hell," said the hostess with a smile. I'd never caught her name, though I'd been a frequent patron over the last several months. I have to say, becoming a regular at a place is an interesting phenomenon; she'd started out dealing with me as a complete professional, but as I made my appearances in Mo's at least a weekly phenomenon, the professional front had been slowly replaced by a friendly, familiar greeting. And she certainly wasn't above ribbing me for my current state.

"Thanks," I said.

"Take table three, over by the window," she said, and waved me into the seating area. I nodded at her, taking a small card with the number "3" on it, then walked to my seat.

The middle of the area was adorned by a large pergola, set up indoors. Underneath it, a group of people wearing pointy happy-birthday hats sat, eating platefuls of meat in a family-style configuration. I didn't stop to parse which of them was the guest of honor, but I knew I'd be in for a round of bad singing in a bit.

Around the outside of the room, small wooden tables lined the windows. Mo's sat on a street corner of downtown Shelton, and that gave them not one, but two walls of their dining area open to the sun. The corner of the room had been done as a massive, curving wall of glass bricks, and the sunlight filtered through the thick glass, bending and warping its way across the room, almost as if through water.

Each table had been separated from the others by a series of brightly-painted, reclaimed doors ... a clever way of keeping tables separate but also giving a sense of community to the space, almost as though the tables to the sides of you were simply your neighbors, waiting to be greeted.

Yes. I know I'm nineteen. That is to say, *Robert Lorents*, known reality terrorist to the Feds and sworn enemy of the demon leading the rebellion against them, was nineteen. *Timothy Ferronton*, the new guy who just moved in off the North Dakota oil fields, turned out to be twenty-two. Matt had been generous when he made up my cover. Of course, the series of scars and general haggard expression I tended to wear these days helped sell the bit.

So, I looked at Mo's beer menu *du jour*, a large blackboard with the names of the current offerings chalked on. The Pacific Northwest was an amazing place for raft beers, and Mo's always had something new on tap. I wasn't in the mood for hoppy, so I skipped the first couple of IPAs and went to the ambers. The beer showed up quickly, frothy and cold, and I sat back in my chair and sipped it, forgetting about the aches my pet Cornuprocyon had inflicted.

I missed Grace.

Every time I walked through the doors of Mo's, I thought about her. Grace, my former mentor, had been the consummate foodie, the kind of person who kept a log of all her favorite restaurants. I'd been along with her on the occasional gustatory adventure, and she always made her notes and kept her little diary. Some summoners (like, say, Thaddeus) had last-ditch rune sets tattooed onto their bodies to use as a final measure. Grace had one, too; it summoned a plate of duck curry from her favorite Thai restaurant. I'd seen her use it, and in a situation where our living for another five minutes had *definitely* been in doubt.

She would have liked it in Mo's. The smells, the food, the way the ribs showed up with a nice smoke ring and not over-sauced, the homemade macaroni and cheese, the cucumber salad with its vinegary bite to cut through the richness of the meal. She'd have noted it all down, and later formulated a rune set to use whenever she wanted takeout, no matter where on earth she was when she got it.

Me, I lacked that advanced level of rune usage. So I came to the restaurant, instead.

Worth it.

"Thought I might find you here," said a female voice behind me. I grimaced as Francene, my foster mother, put her hand on my shoulder, then sat down across the little two-person table from me. I loved Francene, but I also loved this half-finished glass of beer in my hand, and that's not the sort of thing someone who is *not* actually twenty-two years old wants his pseudo-mother to see.

"How are you holding up?" she asked, pointedly staring at the beer.

"Well, uh. Rick played a little hard today. Ended up having an encounter with a tree at a rather higher velocity than I'd prefer. Other than that, not bad."

Francene nodded, then ordered one of those IPAs for herself. "Hmm. They're all a-tussle about something back at the house."

I quirked an eyebrow at her.

"Oh, you know," she said. "I like to be everyone's Mom, and Phineas is awfully nice, but I try not to pay too much attention to their cabal."

Francene, unlike everyone else in that house, had no summoning ability at all. Zero. But I'd turned her into a fugitive from the government right after I'd managed to get her husband, my former foster father, shot in the head. She'd never blamed me for that, but she'd been unconscious when it happened. I'd gotten to watch, and as a result I'd never let myself off the hook for it.

The upshot of that, though, was Francene had the outside perspective.

"So what's going on?" I asked.

"Matt got his latest batch of information," she said. "I left before it got too deep. But I'm sure they're going to want you back at the house sooner rather than later. Also, don't you have class tomorrow?"

Francene's beer showed up, and she took a draw off it that surprised me with its depth. I drank as well, her willingness to imbibe having overridden her ability to maternally shame me. I polished off the last of my ribs, too, and set about coating my piece of cornbread with honey-butter.

"Yes," I said as I spread the sweet fat over the yellow, fluffy treat. "But when have I *ever* been awake in class?"

"Ro—" Francene began in a chiding tone. I coughed loudly, then stared at her.

"Timothy," she corrected, looking about, "you need to focus on your education."

"Look, Mom. We have a demon and a whole cabal of summoners out to get us. We also participated in a major assault on federal forces. There's two major forces at war right now—and both of them want kill us. Education isn't exactly my priority."

"We won't be stuck in limbo like this forever," she said. Punctuating this, she reached over with a knowing little look and finished *my* beer—I suppose the fact that she gave me a pass on having one at all counted for something—then stood and walked away.

As I sat and chewed the last morsel of my dinner, as the off-key singing rose from the table under the pergola, I pondered those last words of hers. Would we, in fact, be stuck here forever?

Because I sure as hell didn't see anywhere else to go.

ROBERT

THE LIVING ROOM of the house that had become both improvised barracks and command center for our little rogue Grove shone with the evening light. The row of windows let the low sun fill the room, glinting off the polished wooden floor and making the ceiling fan more necessary than the light attached to it.

Matt Harper, bureaucromancer extraordinaire, sat with his back to the window at the dining table. I could hear Andrea puttering about the kitchen, grazing on leftover whatever. I shared a sofa with Francene. To our left, Director Brandiole sat in a recliner along one wall. Next to him, the former director of the Spokane Grove—and technically my former boss—Thaddeus took the other recliner.

Thaddeus Nielsen was a gaunt man whose expression had not slipped from "brewing storm" since he'd tried to kill me over a year ago. Of course, my aborted attempt to have the government execute *him* last fall had not exactly sweetened him up any. I figured I should get at least *some* points for saving him anyways, and maybe a bonus round for getting him out of Spokane with only min—Moderate. Moderate injuries.

On my immediate right, Amy flopped onto the loveseat. A former friend of Grace's and a mediocre summoner, Amy had been a classic case of wrong-place, wrong-time. She lacked Matt's sense for paperwork, Director Brandiole's authority, or Thad's anger. If I'm being honest, she also lacked my recklessness and Andrea's occasional bouts of complete-batshit-craziness. Amy had, however, found herself the mediator of our little group. Put enough arrogant lugheads into a room and someone has to keep the tempers down. At the end of the day, Amy *de facto* occupied that position.

"So," said Matt, "I've been working on this for months. We've been slowly gathering data, summoning in government paperwork, and copying e-mails. The seven of us are pretty isolated, here, and if we're going to start acting, we need to know where we stand. As a result, here's the situation as best I can tell."

He pressed a button on his tablet, and a projector on the table in front of him put a map of North America up on the wall. It had Mexico, the states of America and the provinces of Canada, but it had a much thicker, darker set of lines describing Grove areas.

"Obviously, the PNW is Cythymau-controlled territory." A section of the map including Idaho, Washington, Oregon, British Columbia, the Yukon, and Alaska went deep purple. "Sadly, Ms. Miller worked on the Seattle Grove's political alliances, so the Southwest Groves out of Vegas are Cythymau-allied as well." At this, California, Nevada, New Mexico, Arizona, and Utah all went purple.

"I still don't think we should count Abigail Diaz out," said Director Brandiole. "She and I have been friends for a long time." I didn't know who Brandiole meant, and looked to Matt, trying to figure it out from context rather than look like an idiot by asking.

"Maybe not," said Matt. "But she's no longer running things down there. She's on the run like us, which means it's hard to make contact. If we see the opportunity, if she's got some forces gathered, maybe we can do something; for now, the Southwest is Cythymau territory."

Director Brandiole sighed at that and nodded, gesturing for Matt to continue.

"Now the good news," continued Matt. "From what I can tell,

Director Ahren down in Texas has declared Cythymau an abomination. The Texans have never really been all that happy living under *any* outside influence, and Cythymau is about as outside as it gets. The South is in the same boat as the Texans, though they're being a little more circumspect about it." At this, Texas and every state east of the Mississippi and south of the Mason-Dixon line went green. Thad and Brandiole nodded, accepting this information as a given—I nodded along as well, but inside I breathed a little relief at seeing that much green on Matt's map. Maybe there *was* some hope.

"What about the Eastern Seaboard?" asked Thad, leaning forward in his chair. "The Midwest? New England?"

"Still on the fence," said Matt, shaking his head. "There's a lot of internal bickering that nobody else is supposed to know about; there's pro- and anti- Cythymau factions deadlocking all across the area. On the surface, of course, they're keeping a low profile. Underneath, I think someone's going to murder someone and break this loose."

Amy bit her lower lip at this. The idea of political assassination clearly didn't sit well with her. Thad, on the other hand, asked, "Any particular target that would be to our advantage?"

"Jesus, Nielsen!" exclaimed Amy. "You want to just assassinate someone?"

"Miss Milankovich," said Brandiole calmly. "We are, you may have noticed, in a war. If someone supports Cythymau, then that person may properly be considered a target. And with only seven of us, I do not believe that *pitched battle* is going to be the method under which we prefer to operate. Obviously what Thaddeus has suggested is distasteful, but ... it is worth considering."

"Even if it is," said Matt, "there's a couple of targets, but there's a chance it all blows back on us. And I'm not familiar enough with the tier-two players over there to know *how* it blows back. At the moment, I'm suggesting we attempt to make contact with the anti-Cythymau forces to gain more intelligence, but I think direct action stands a high likelihood of negative consequences."

Everyone in the room seemed to relax, at that. The ethical

quandaries of assassination were a debate for *tomorrow's* version of us, not today's.

"Great Plains?" asked Thaddeus, changing the subject.

"Your former boss Mr. Wilson has never liked Seattle. I'm not sure he's against Cythymau in principle; the idea of fighting the government openly seems to appeal to him, despite some of his earlier rhetoric."

"Wilson's a snake," said Director Brandiole with a bit of acid in his voice. "He'll posture in whatever way keeps him in power."

Matt nodded at this. "That seems to track," he said.

Thaddeus snorted. "You know, I've seen Director Wilson take some pretty principled stands before."

"Ones that weren't politically popular?" asked Amy, a sharp point in her normally conciliatory voice. I knew Grace had some disputes with Director Wilson; it seemed Amy knew more about them than I did.

Thaddeus chose not to answer Amy, but rather turned back to Matt. "Regardless, I can't see Director Wilson subjugating himself to any Visitor, let alone a Demon. I'm guessing he's in the anti-Cythymau camp."

"You guess correctly," said Matt. "Director Wilson strongly supports Director Ahren's stand against Cythymau while pointing out that a summoner-controlled state is not necessarily a bad idea."

"Dangerous," said Director Brandiole with a grimace. "Puts him out on a limb. Those cowards back East aren't going to feel like supporting him if that's his take."

Matt shrugged, then colored the states north of Texas and West of the Mississippi, up to the boundary of the Pacific Northwest Grove, green as well. "For now, he's an enemy of our enemy, and you know what that makes him."

"Our enemy's enemy; no more, no less," I said automatically, referencing something I'd read on a webcomic somewhere. Everyone took a moment to stare at me. I put on a cheesy grin, realizing that I'd spoken out of turn, and sort of waved my hand in an *Ok, let's move on* gesture.

"What do we know about Prince Rupert?" asked Amy hopefully.

"We know that they are *really good* at setting wards," said Matt shaking his head. "Everyone else leaves *some* things unprotected, but those central Canadians are just flat-out paranoid. I can't figure out which way they'll turn at any given point in time. Sorry, but they're just going to be a wild card."

Someone had to say it. And, being the resident smartass, that someone was clearly me. "Is there actually anyone *in* central Canada? I mean, how important is Prince Rupert, anyways?"

Amy chuckled. Francene rolled her eyes. Matt simply stared at me. Andrea poked her head out of the kitchen, an entire log of string cheese protruding from between her lips as though it were a cheap cigar.

"Robert," said Director Brandiole in his best giving-lessons-pedantic tone, "Have you ever heard of a place called Vimy Ridge?"

"Nope," I said in all honesty.

"Look it up some time. But for now, you should assume that those Canadians are, pound-for-pound, some of the most terrifying bastards I know if they decide to get serious. I'm taking their security lockdown as a good thing, provisionally."

"Director Wilson never messed with Prince Rupert," said Thaddeus. "Pac Northwest, sure. Midwest and Southwest, absolutely. But he went after Texas only once I can remember, and it didn't end well. He never even *tried* with Prince Rupert."

This particular view did not sync with my own, admittedly stereotypical, view of Canadians as overly polite, apologetic, and soft. Of course, that impression had largely been formed by American television. Thaddeus and Brandiole agreeing on *anything* happened so very rarely that, when it did, it could be taken as the next thing to gospel. I made a mental note to myself to look up Vimy Ridge.

"Mexico?" asked Amy.

At the mention, both Thaddeus and Director Brandiole snorted contemptuously.

"What?" asked Amy. "The Mexican Grove has more summoners in it than any one American or Canadian Grove. It is, by population, the largest block of magical force. Don't you think it's a little important to know what they're doing?"

Director Brandiole sighed at this. "It's not that I disagree with you, you understand. It's that I already *know* what Mexico is doing, and it ain't pretty."

Thaddeus nodded. "The Grove in Mexico has two threats to deal with. Not only are they up against the government, but they're up against the cartels as well. The drug-runners are of the opinion that *all* illegal activity, including summoning, needs to be run by them first. They want their cut out of the Grove, which means being a Mexican summoner is twice as dangerous as being an American one, and that's with our current ... situation."

Director Brandiole continued, agreeing with Thaddeus for a *second* time in a single day. "Which is why the Mexican Grove has declared themselves in support of everyone who will come assist them. If you're willing to head into Ciudad Juarez and take on the cartels, then the Mexican summoners won't much care whether you're from the green or the purple parts of that map. They'll just be glad to have you."

Matt gestured with an open hand at the two men and nodded. "You've got the basics of it," he said. "Mexico is large, but entirely consumed with its own issues. It won't act until Cythymau directly threatens it, and we can't expect more."

"So," I said, moving things along. "How about the military?"

"Good, because this is where it gets really weird," said Matt in a sarcastic tone.

I cocked an eyebrow at him—I hadn't expected Matt to sound so bitter about, well, anything.

"First off," Matt said, "let's dispose of our neighbors. The Canadian military, what there is of it, and the Canadian police force, are maintaining a business-as-usual approach. They see the war in the U.S. as not something they'd like a piece of, so the Mounties are staying hands-off. That gives chunks of the Pacific Northwest, as well as Prince Rupert and Quebec, a safe territory. Cythymau's moved most of his youth and training programs to a remote location up in the Yukon, and many of his more powerful military assets are currently in Vancouver, not Seattle."

At this, Director Brandiole butted in. "Not Seattle? You'd think he'd want to maintain power there; it's the traditional seat of the PNW."

"And he does. He himself stays there, along with a potent cadre of summoners, including Ms. Miller and Riley Dewing. But any major buildups, he uses Vancouver for. Plays merry hell with the government's ability to get the jump on his people."

"Damn," said Brandiole. "I still held out hope that Dewing hadn't signed on. We could have used Vancouver."

Matt shook his head at this. "Anyways, that's Canada. Mexico is Mexico, no real change there. That leaves what was once the most powerful military in the world."

"Once?" I asked, stunned. Understand, I'm from 'Murica. You can't grow up in this country without getting served a full portion of ass-kicking jingoism. Piss off our country, we bomb your ass, hoo-ra. That "once" came at me hard, a jolt out of the blue. I'm not particularly much of a flag-waver, but the basic, hyper-patriotic pablum dribbled into my ear throughout the entirety of my childhood had left me simply assuming that nobody picks on the good ol' USA and gets away with it. Referring to that power in the past tense undercut a lot of the assumptions that I'd simply taken as a given for my whole life.

"Once," said Matt, nodding gravely. "After Airway Heights and Seattle, the military tried a number of other strikes. The Southwest Grove set up strongpoints as well, and the U.S.A. launched some pretty large-scale attacks. The problem is, nobody over in the Pentagon got it into their heads that they were *outmatched*. They'd fought too many brushfire wars against third-world countries, and tried to treat the Groves the same way. The casualties were ... significant."

"Why haven't we heard about this?" asked Thaddeus. "I'd have thought Cythymau would have bragged to high heaven about it."

"Because Cythymau doesn't care," said Andrea, her string cheese swallowed. "Oh, he talks about oppression, but a victory over a non-summoner, to Cythymau, wouldn't be something to take pride in. Did you brag the last time you swatted a mosquito? No, he'll see the fight with the 'rogue' summoners as the real battle."

"How many dead?" asked Francene quietly. She'd held her tongue during this whole conversation, and for the first time I noticed how pale she'd gotten at the sheer scale we were talking about.

"Reports vary, " said Matt, his own voice solemn, "but it looks like somewhere in the ten thousand range, in the space of a couple weeks. Cythymau may have imposed a communications blackout, but as soon as I started summoning in data from east of the Mississippi, this was the only thing people could talk about. The military is getting its ass handed to it. They're getting smarter about how they fight, but there's a funny pattern to their targets."

"They're all in the Great Plains and Texas, right?" asked Andrea. "I mean: every last one of them are in those areas. And all of them have almost total casualty counts for both sides, but not quite. Did I get that right?"

"Uh ... yeah. Yeah, you did," said Matt, a note of confusion in his voice. "How?"

"Spend a couple thousand years inside a guy's head," said Andrea with a little shrug. She pulled up one of the seats next to the breakfast bar, fully placing herself in the room with us, and spoke with the clear confidence of someone who knew her subject. "Cythymau is feeding targets to the military. He'll give them whatever intel he can get on ambush preparation, then swoop in at the last minute and mop up what's left on either side. He'll leave a couple non-summoners alive, you know, to report back. But he'll kill everyone else."

The room went quiet. I'd never heard Andrea give a speech this long, and it all made sense. I felt my own face draining as I considered the implications.

"Dear God," said Director Brandiole in a hushed tone. "It's almost perfect. He whittles down his enemies simultaneously, then finishes off the remainder. It's a win-win for him."

"That ... would fit with what I've been seeing, yes," said Matt, finally. "God, why didn't I put that together myself?"

I took a moment, dealing with this. If foster kids know anything, it's that there's always another beating coming. Time to react. "If that's his play," I said, looking at Andrea, "he'll draw it out for as long as possible, won't he?"

"Oh, yeah," she said. "If it's not broke, he's not going to fix it. Oo, peanut butter. There's an idea." A jar of generic peanut butter and a spoon simply materialized in her hands, clearly brought there by her Sense. She stuck a spoon deep within the jar and simply began to lick. The thought of eating peanut butter straight out of a jar nauseated me. The sight of Andrea running her tongue along—well, that led down a much more dangerous path.

"Sleep on it," said Director Brandiole. "We've probably got more intel at this point than just about anyone. The question is how to use it."

THE MAGICAL THING about Shelton is the little chunks of the Olympic rain forest that exist within the city itself. On one such, the local alternative school built and maintains a trail running along Shelton Creek. The land runs through a ravine, and when standing (or sitting) amongst the trees, watching the creek cascade about the rocks as the sun barely filters its way through the forest, it is impossible to tell that one is actually in the middle of a city. It's technically a park, and it's named after some pillar of the Shelton community, though for the life of it I could never remember the name. I simply thought of it as "Fern Gully," because it was a gully, it was full of ferns, and I was kind of a nerd.

Usually, I walked the trail through Fern Gully alone. This evening, after our terrifying debrief, Andrea joined me. She wore her typical sweats and sneakers, and her unkempt, red hair cascaded down her back.

My attraction to Andrea had become ... uncomfortable. Oh, it's not as though I still harbored my old delusions of grand romance. Whatever aspirations had survived my former girlfriend's sudden return to dating the basketball star had died completely when a Lycaon had destroyed them both at our graduation ceremony. But Andrea and I lived under the same roof, and she looked so similar to me in age.

Looks, of course, can be deceiving—Andrea had several thousand years on me, most of them bad. I knew how broken she was, how fragile. And I knew that she barely could handle herself at the moment, let alone piling someone else into the mix. I knew the play *had* to be keeping my distance.

Doesn't mean I wasn't attracted to her. They say the heart wants what the heart wants, and that's true. Fun Fact: it's also true of the limbic system.

So one-on-one time with Andrea presented its own special challenges. Fortunately, hiking a trail let me hide any increase in breath rate or heartbeat with physical activity. Hiding one's attractions for another is difficult in the best of circumstances. When the person you're trying to hide from has a twenty-foot Sense that she keeps activated *all the time,* it becomes a nightmare.

"So," she said in a mild tone of voice, "what do you think we're going to do?"

I stopped on the trail, then turned to face her with a flushed face. I knew her Sense didn't let her read my mind, but how was I supposed to know what to do about—

"You know, about Cythymau siccing the government on the Groves," she continued.

Oh. Right. The war. Funny how one can forget the little things when embroiled in one's own personal drama.

"I, uh, don't know. I'm not sure there's much we *can* do, really. There's seven of us. Six summoners. And one Rick. We're not exactly a military organization, here."

"Sure, but who else has this much experience against Cythymau?" she said.

"Well, nobody, but it doesn't mean we know how to take him

down." I looked down at the creek, babbling its way about the rocks like a playful child without a care in the world.

"Grace came pretty damn close," said Andrea.

"Yeah. Well. Grace also didn't survive coming close. Doesn't seem worth trying again."

Andrea stared at me, mouth slightly gaping.

You ever have one of those moments where you say something stupid? I mean, really terribly dumb, but it just flies out of your mouth? Once that bastard is out there, you can't take it back, and you're stuck with whatever happens next.

Never stopped me from *trying* to take it back, of course.

"Wait, no," I said. "I meant, in a 'her-versus-Cythymau' sense. Obviously getting you out was worth ... " I trailed off.

"You know what?" she said. "Never mind." And with that, she resumed walking up the trail at an accelerated pace.

Yes, Grace had died trying to kill Cythymau, but she'd been covering my retreat with Andrea at the time. Our escape from my boneheaded, half-assed 'rescue' of Andrea from her captivity. Andrea's freedom had, indirectly, been the cause of Grace's death, and I'd just rubbed her nose in it.

I followed her, face flushed. Stupid. Andrea tended to be touchy about—well, everything—but especially that. I'd stepped in it, and at this point I couldn't inch myself any closer to mercy than silence.

At the top of the trail, a little bench overlooked the stream below. I sat on one end, and Andrea took the other. The view from the top of the gully, looking down Shelton Creek as it wended and burbled down its merry course, always set me at peace. Andrea looked, too; I could not, for the life of me, tell whether she found any peace in it or not.

"So, I was thinking," she said at last.

"Hmm?" I said, not wanting to stick my *other* foot in my mouth just yet.

"Well, we're in a three-way fight, right? I mean, there's the military, there's Cythymau, there's the rest of us."

"Yup," I said.

"And Cythymau's using the military against the rest of us, because it's great when two enemies kill each other."

"Mm-hmm," I agreed. I had to admit, at this point my attention had faded.

"So, why aren't we trying to get the military and Cythymau to fight instead?"

There's a lesson here for those of you playing the home version of this game. Never take anyone for granted. Andrea had spent a significant time in my mind as the scared girl, the helpless girl strapped to a slab, in a cave, in a distant dimension. I'd been trying to kick myself free of those perceptions—but every once in a while, I had difficulty remembering her intelligence.

Underneath her trauma lay a brilliant mind, and occasionally she would break out a gem like this and remind me that she wasn't my *ward,* she was my *partner.*

I shook off my own idiocy and faced her.

"I'm ... not sure," I finally said. "I mean, the military thinks of all us summoners as the same. To them, they're fighting summoners, and they don't really distinguish. Cythymau's pushed them out of the Pacific Northwest, but they don't see that as crossing any sort of a boundary line."

"So, it seems like we just need to show the military we're different," she said.

"Uh ... do you recall last fall? Because last fall, we tried that. And it didn't work out so well."

"Last fall we—*you*—helped Cythymau against the army. But now they've gotten their butt kicked, a lot. Maybe *they* need some hope, too."

She wasn't wrong. But these people had imprisoned me! They'd tortured me for days! How could sh—

Oh. Right.

I'd been through days of torture. Andrea suffered millennia. Her trauma won out. My protests died on my tongue, and I gave myself a small pat on the back for not choking on my own footwear yet again.

Show the military we're different. Convince an organization who'd spent the last century in a paranoia-fueled, literal witch hunt against the evils of summoning, that I had personally done battle with while standing directly *next* to Cythymau. Persuade them I didn't support that demon in his efforts to take over the world.

Yeah, this was going to take some doing.

ANDREA

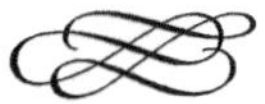

I SLUNK in the far end of the classroom and aimed for a desk at the very back of the lecture hall. No one else was here yet. Good.

I slid into a seat in the corner. The only thing behind me was a bulletin board, rarely updated. Picking the corner seat meant that once the class filled, my claustrophobia would kick a fit, but it was better than the chatty humans deciding to sit right next to me.

Matt had signed me up as a community college student when we moved to Shelton without asking me. Or rather, signed my alias up. When I complained, he'd bluntly said I needed an alibi for my sudden appearance in such a small, rural town. I could pick my own classes, but I had to go, since it was one of the most expedient excuses for moving in. And, he'd pointed out, he'd signed Robert up too, so I wouldn't be out there by myself.

Not entirely reassuring. Robert had turned out to be a mostly good guy, sure. I grudgingly accepted that now. He'd risked his life to save me. He'd rehabilitated Rick. He took such care with his widowed foster mom that it hurt to watch sometimes. But he also got himself into a lot of trouble with his huge ideals. Not to mention that he could be super reckless, because once he made up his mind, changing it turned out to be impossible.

Plus, I'd *already* paid him back for rescuing me. I'd have paid his mentor back too, if I could. But she died trying to rescue Robert from the consequences of his actions. Freeing me in the process, but still. She had gone on to the afterlife, and unlike Robert, I wasn't willing to rip her spirit out of retirement just because I had a few problems that were hard to solve on my own. As someone who'd been subject to another's beck and call for eons, that seemed a horrible repayment of the debt I owed her.

I got out my textbook, then sat my backpack on the adjacent seat. This tended to discourage people from sitting directly next to me. I couldn't do anything if someone decided to sit in the chair after that one ... at least not without being rude. I was going for anonymity here; not to the be that one snooty bitch everyone talked about behind their hands.

Unfortunately, with my Sense, any dirty little secrets whispered around me didn't stay secret, and I didn't want to hear the theories if I managed to attract attention.

Cracking my textbook open, I flipped to the current chapter. A diagram of a human's major muscle groups covered the first page. I flipped to the next section until I found the diagram which outlined the bones in a foot. The first student other than me came in, a girl in a pink windbreaker, with a knit cap pulled down over riotously curly hair. Instead of a backpack, she carried a large tote bag. I hunched farther over in my seat, staring intently at the page and placing my index finger on the diagram, pretending to study laboriously. *Please don't let her decide to sit down next to me.* My breath started to hitch.

The girl sat down in the front row of seats, close to the door, and dug a bottled coffee out of her tote.

The students continued to trickle in. I did my best not to care. I started matching the bones I Sensed as they paced across the room to the diagrams in the textbook. I counted tarsals, metatarsals, the cuboid, cuneiform; I even found a few sesamoids indicating that some of these people's feet had been through some hard times. If I kept myself focused on the book, it made everyone's closeness a little more tolerable. Otherwise, their bodies were a never-ending, overwhelming cacophony, even when they never said one word to me.

The classroom had filled with students now, and the air reverberated with their jokes, their conversations, the movement of their lungs, their hearts pumping with life, their swinging arms and legs. I started naming major muscle groups in my head, careful to observe but not interfere with the mass of humanity I Sensed all around me. I kept my gaze still firmly fixed on my textbook.

The professor finally walked in. I always found her frumpiness reassuring. Here was someone who didn't care about anything except to cultivate excellent students who could go out in the world and kick butt. She dressed practically, in scrubs top and bottoms paired with sneakers. Her hair, greyed and frizzy, had been tied back in a messy bun. The students quieted down automatically as she crossed to the podium. She started passing out graded assignments from the previous week alphabetically. I counted tiles in the ceiling while I waited.

"Andrina Jermaine?" she called.

"Here." I stuck my hand up, and she walked over and flicked the papers onto my desk. One of the dirty secrets that my Sense picked up from overheard conversations was that Matt had been worried I wouldn't remember my alias if I got freaked out. He'd picked an AKA as close to my real name as he could without endangering the whole Grove.

I did appreciate the thought, even as it reminded me of how broken I still was.

A female student hustled in through the door, out of breath, the air rushing in and out of her lungs frantically as she tried to gulp in too much at once. She wore a fuzzy hat and scarf, even though it never seemed to get much below freezing where Shelton was nestled, just off of Oakland Bay. Frost was rare, snow almost unheard of.

"I'm here, I'm here," the girl gasped as she almost fell through the door, her satchel of heavy textbooks swinging like a pendulum behind her. "I'll just sit back here and not be a bother, I promise."

The professor waved her in, saying, "Please be more punctual in the future. What's your name?"

"Miranda Kleyn. So sorry for the bother." She tripped as she said this, her book bag catching on her leg in her hurry.

The professor shuffled through her stack of papers and handed an assignment back to her. Miranda clattered up the steps and sat in the last seat in the row at the back of the classroom— in other words, the last seat in *my row,* blocking my access to exit, since I'd sat in the far corner.

I blew a long breath between slack lips, making a raspberry sound and trying to tell myself it didn't matter. Miranda sat at the end of the row, totally inside my personal bubble. With my Sense, I could still feel the heightened pumping of her heart, the perspiration dampening her forehead and neck.

Miranda flopped her bookbag up on the desk with an audible bang that reverberated in my Sense. She began pawing through her assorted jumble of books as the professor began her lecture. I flipped to the correct chapter in my book and distracted myself by finding all the things illustrated in my classmates' bodies as the professor highlighted them. I gave myself the high score if I could find it in each and every person in the whole class before the professor moved on to the next section.

The Miranda girl at the end of the row gave a low growl of frustration. I shot her a wary look, leaning farther into my accustomed corner. Mistake. She caught my glance with a hopeful look of her own, scooped up her bag, and then slid her chair back with an awful racket. A frantic feeling of impending doom started to press down on me.

She tried to flop herself down in the chair next to me, saw my backpack, and settled for the one next to it. She then leaned far in, stretching her torso over the intervening space between us. My hands curved into fists as I flinched away. Struggling to be calm, I started naming all the bones I could Sense in her chest. Clavicle, scapula, lumbar, thoracic, cervical vertebrae.

"I am so sorry," she said in a whisper, "I can't find my textbook. Can

I share yours? Just this once? Pretty please?" Her hands were already reaching as she asked, as if my answer were a forgone conclusion.

I started to jerk my book away on reflex. She stared at me, her eyes wide with surprise, and her mouth forming a perfect "O."

I had seen other students sharing—I knew that agreeing would be the expected response. Refusing would attract the kind of attention I wanted to avoid. But my skin itched, crawled with the nearness that would require.

Trapped.

If I shared, she would be stuck to me until class ended. I shoved the book across the table toward her, pushing it –and hopefully her— away from me.

"Here you go," I managed gruffly, feeling the exact opposite of helpful.

"Oh, thank you," she let out a long sigh. "Nothing has been going right lately. You're a lifesaver."

I realized that I'd stopped listening to the professor and tried to regain my focus. I started counting fuzz balls on Miranda's sweater, totally unable to change the object of my distraction. My skin broke out into a prickly, nervous sweat. Maybe if I moved the textbook even closer to her, she'd move away slightly. I pushed it toward her, internally begging her to take the hint and get the hell away from me.

"You need to see, too! I'd feel horrible if I made it harder for you to read," she protested in her overly-loud whisper, thrusting the book back at me and scooting her chair even closer.

Unable to take it anymore, I shot to my feet, my chair clattering over in my haste.

The professor looked up in surprise from the point she was making on the whiteboard.

"I'm going to be sick," I blurted, not untruthfully. I grabbed my backpack and coat and bolted around Miranda for the door. I left the damned textbook behind.

I ran down the hallway, outside, and through the campus until I reached the tree-lined parking lot. In the corner sat Robert's empty van. I yanked the door open and clambered inside, then flopped down, lying across the second bench seat. I concentrated on the air going in and out of my lungs, on the warm asphalt under the tires of the van, on the dirt and rock under that.

I lay there, re-centering myself, drinking in solitude until a nearby class let out and the parking lot buzzed with a brief spurt of activity. I let the bustle flow past me, through me, but remained apart. No one out there knew I existed in the van, and I liked it that way.

A familiar foot in a shoe with familiar tread hit the asphalt on the edge of my Sense, quickly followed by a familiar person, and I groaned. My sanctuary was about to be invaded. No way to escape without being seen and pestered with a thousand questions either. I reluctantly sat up and prepared myself.

Robert opened the driver's door and climbed in behind the steering wheel. A little taller and even skinnier than when I had first met him just over a year ago, he had more lines in his face than most people his age could boast. He looked more mature than he acted.

Of course, I was old as dirt, so maybe I was biased.

Hell, the two of us looked almost the same age, but I was ... well, it was hard to tell with Cythymau's manipulations and the time difference between the two Weaves ... Even if I looked young, inside of me lived an ancient crone. Some days I felt as if I had never really been human at all.

Robert frowned as he turned the key in the ignition, and I realized he hadn't seen me sitting in the shadows behind him. It was unfathomable to me how he managed to ignore his Sense like that sometimes, but I cleared my throat anyway. It only seemed fair to let him know he wasn't alone, and I wasn't ready to go back yet anyway.

My lips quirked as he jumped, his Sense springing up and enveloping my own. Outwardly, I just waved a laconic hand, letting it and my Sense do the greeting for me.

"Jesus, Andrea," Robert said, "How did you get back here before me? Class just got out—"

"I needed a place to chill," I shrugged. "I left a little early." I drew my feet up onto the seat and wrapped my arms around my folded legs. "Some girl in there wanted to share my textbook."

"And you ran away," Robert said for me.

I shrugged in acknowledgement.

"You could always have Matt give you a second copy, lug it around with you, and throw it at her next time she tries to get in close to you. Of course knowing you, you'd probably end up braining her with it on accident." He chuckled wryly, and I tried to decide if he was joking or serious.

I grunted a response. Actually, that scenario seemed all too possible. "I'm gonna go now." I started to get up to exit the van.

"Oh hey," Robert said, "Where were you earlier? Amy was about to launch road flares and send out the search parties."

My shoulders twitched defensively as I got down from the van. Couldn't tell Robert I'd been sitting in an abandoned garage studying texts stolen from our evil arch-nemesis, Cythymau. "I went exploring. It helps clear my head," I said instead.

"Well, next time leave a note for us, will ya? Amy was working everyone up."

My eyebrows rose. "I haven't been home yet. Who called off the sirens?"

"Matt convinced her you'd probably just left for classes early. We know you like to get here before anyone else."

I shrugged again.

"But today was super early ..." Robert let his voice trail off, suggesting I fill in the blank for him. Ha. As if I'd do that.

"I'll try not to freak Amy out next time," I said. "Sorry." I slammed the door shut and slouched away from the van as quickly as I could.

Robert rolled down his window to yell after me, "If you're worried about Amy, I can stick around and take you home when you're done. If you want."

I paused, considering. Amy's lecture was likely to get abbreviated if I came back with Robert. "Yeah, that'd be okay."

Even with my Sense up, I almost missed it. Matt's Sense was like a whisper; there and then gone, as quiet and subtle as a whiff of breeze. But the note in my pocket hadn't been there the second before. I closed my eyes, concentrating on the note with my Sense, reading it without ever taking it out of my pocket.

Emergency. Come back asap. Don't delay. Time sensitive.

Robert fished an identical note out of his pocket and gave a low whistle. "Well, never mind. I guess I'm headed back anyway."

I pulled the small piece of paper from my pocket with two fingers, then waved it at Robert. "I got it too. He wants both of us back." Pivoting, I reversed directions back to the van.

Robert shook his head. "Matt doesn't say emergency for just anything. Wonder what got him to hit the panic button."

I immediately thought of two panic-worthy possibilities. Had Cythymau pressed the self-destruct button, ending this Weave like he had his last one? Not that I could ask Robert that. Instead, "What if Cythymau found us already?" I asked Robert. I shivered. Clambering back into the van, I pulled the door shut.

Robert immediately switched the van into gear, before I'd even settled into the seat. I shot him a look.

"I hope we'd know if he found us already. That doesn't rule out any number of other catastrophes though," Robert said, his eyes already on the road.

I considered this. "You're right. Cythymau would already be rubbing our nose in it if he wanted a direct confrontation." I felt marginally relieved.

And hey, on the bright side, I was totally saved. This emergency would keep everyone occupied, and I wouldn't have to answer any awkward questions about my current activities when we arrived. So at least I could feel good about that?

ROBERT and I were the last to arrive. Thad, Matt, Amy, Phineas, and even Francene had already gathered in the small living room by the time we walked through the door.

Thad immediately gestured us to sit. "Alright," he said, "now that we're all here, let's get everyone up to speed. Matt has intercepted what I believe to be credible orders dispatching a large anti-summoner force to the Missoula Grove's main safehouse. The orders include not only the Grove's primary locations, but also a roster of high-value targets. Phineas has sent messages alerting the Missoula Grove to the orders, but I don't think they've taken us seriously. And regardless, they've indicated that even if the orders are legitimate, they need more time to move their people."

Amy snorted. "If it was us, we'd already be de-assing this place with the quickness. Safehouse or headquarters be damned."

"Yes, well, we're pretty easy to uproot," Phineas said reasonably. "We just got here, after all, and there are still only seven of us. The Missoula Grove's been in the same location for generations, and they have the membership, entrenched infrastructure, and internal bureaucracy to match. Not to mention that, from their perspective, our intelligence about a strike against them is highly suspect. They don't know our resident bureaucromancer, after all. To them, the warning is coming from two disgraced former directors that have openly fallen out with the Seattle Grove, and a ragtag band of misfits. So what's easy for us to see and know as a threat isn't nearly as clear to them. They don't have the experience with Cythymau that we have, either."

"You're saying they don't believe us when we say Cythymau will show up and wipe the floor with all of them," I said grimly.

"Correct, at least right now," Thad said. "But that doesn't mean *we* don't need as many allies as we can break loose before the shit hits the fan. And that means going there and convincing them, *before* the attack, so we can smuggle out and hide as many summoners as possible. So we're going to run straight at this hornet's nest and hope to get there first."

Robert let out a low whistle. "Missoula's not a small Grove; smuggling out even a small number of them won't be easy."

"That's why Matt is coming with on this one. He can forge papers for these people on the fly to hide their tracks, so the Feds and Cythymau don't have an obvious mass exodus leading back to us."

"Just from a humanitarian perspective, we need to save anyone willing to leave," Francene spoke up. "There must be children there. Families that will need help."

Thad nodded. "Just so. Our on-the-ground team in Missoula will be me, Matt, Robert and Andrea, as the minimum we need for this to hopefully succeed. Matt because it's his intelligence, he can explain where it came from, and we need his paper skills. Andrea because she knows Cythymau best and may be able make an impression on that rock-hard Montana stubbornness. Me for logistics, and Robert for his raw power potential and ability to improvise. Phineas will stay here and continue to work on diplomatic messages with Missoula leadership. Francene and Amy, please prepare us to receive and hide as many refugees as possible."

Amy and Francene both nodded. Amy looked visibly relieved. She wasn't really very good at improvising or summoning on the fly. She preferred to have the home-field advantage, and this mission was decidedly not that.

"Let's get on the road, people," Thad said. "I want us in and back out with as many as we can evacuate before Cythymau or the military even know we're there."

ROBERT

THERE ARE certain things that hold true for any road trip, whether it's a simple vacation or a desperate rescue mission. One of those standards is the time/bladder continuum—which is to say, the more important it is to stick to a timeline, the more likely it is that *somebody's* bladder will require a stop. The time/bladder continuum, or TBC, is not a standard equation, but rather a multiple-variable thing—the chance of a pit stop is heightened based on the number of people involved in a road trip, and influenced greatly by the time of day at which the road trip began—likely due to the need to ingest copious amounts of coffee for a trip beginning in the early morning.

Which is why, even during our desperate trek towards Missoula, I found myself leaning against the side of the van at the Schrag Rest Area on eastbound I-90, looking awkwardly at Matt as we waited for the Elder Bladder (Nielsen) and Andrea to exit their necessitated pit stop.

The rest area itself had been lovingly groomed and well-watered. It featured a small patch of vibrant, green grass and several large trees to provide shade. The facilities consisted of the obligatory squat brown building with the musty smell of mildew and urinal cakes wafting out of it. Next to that, a smaller building housed several teenagers in maroon-and-gold shirts attempting to sell bad coffee and stale doughnuts to raise meager funds for the Moses Lake High School Jazz Choir.

If they'd been raising funds for the band, I probably would have chipped in. But I wasn't about to help the conspiracy of rest-stop charities to force further rest-stop usage by altering the TBC. Not for a *choir.*

Around us, though, the green grass stood out in a sea of brown as the flat, wide-open, central Washington desert took the sun's pounding like an anvil.

"How bad do you think this is going to get?" I asked Matt quietly.

"The trip or the destination?" he said, answering my question with a question.

"Well ... both, really. Though I hadn't actually considered the trip to be a problem, apart from the occasional, well ... this."

"Trip is starting to be a problem," said Matt. "But there's more concern for the destination. The government is sending a heavy deployment. It's going to happen fast, and it's probably going to take Missoula by surprise. I ... I'm not sure what to do about that. They're not ready ... and in some ways I'm just as glad of that, as sick as it may seem."

"How so?" I asked.

"Ideally," said Matt, "we get there before the Missoula Grove and the military come to blows. We convince them that both of them are dead meat if they don't face the common threat together. We actually manage to pull that off ... and then we counter-ambush Cythymau. That's a perfect world, but it's not the most likely scenario. It's what we can hope for. And the chances of that go far, far down if Missoula actually believes Brandiole's warnings."

"So ... it works in our favor that they don't believe they're about to be killed?"

"I ... yeah," he said, hanging his head a little bit. "I fucking hate it, too, Robert. It feels ... wrong. But a prepared Grove can annihilate the military easily. The government has to strike them when they're *not* prepared to have a chance."

I nodded, understanding. "We show up and there's only one side or the other ... our job gets harder in recruiting allies."

He chuckled a bit, shaking his head. "Well, that's one way of putting it. Another is that the four of us better be enough to tip the scales over what your demonic friend is sending to kill whatever's left over, or we're going down as well. And that doesn't even count the worst-case scenario."

I looked at him, an eyebrow raised in confusion. "Um ... us all dying horribly in a futile gesture is not the worst-case scenario?"

"Nope," Matt said in a faux-cheerful tone. "Worst case is, we warn the Missoula Grove, they believe us, butcher the military, and then Cythymau shows up and *takes credit* for the warning. See what a wise and benevolent leader he is? Missoula—which is a major player in the Great Plains Grove—Missoula now owes Cythymau a great debt. Instead of eliminating both sides, Cythymau eliminates one side *entirely* and makes devoted allies of the other." He paused, thinking for a moment, then added, "And, of course, we still die horribly. So that sort of nets out."

I groaned—the picture Matt had painted began to sink in. "So ... why hasn't Cythymau done exactly that?"

"Well," said Matt. "who knows? He's a demon, so he might not think the same way we do. But regardless of that, he's good at conserving resources. He lets them fight it out, he takes out two. He sends them a warning ... maybe he ends up with allies, maybe he ends up with more effective resistance. It's a coin toss. From his perspective, destruction is probably easier than persuasion ... but he's shown that he'll resort to persuasion if the situation calls for it."

"Mmm," I said, thinking about it for a moment. "So he errs on the side of eliminating everyone, and we have to err on the side of trying to save everyone?"

"Yeah, that about sums it," Matt said. "Not an easy task for us, I know, but there it is."

I took a deep breath, relaxing myself for a moment, before nodding and turning back to him. "All right," I said. "So ... to answer my initial question, unless everything goes perfectly right, this entire expedition has a good chance of sucking?"

"Heh. Well ... would *you* have it any other way?" He asked this with a smile and a nod.

I laughed out loud, good and long, and it took me a moment to recover. "Ok, ok," I said. "You got me. I'm the guy constantly picking fights with things big enough to kill me many times over. You hit the mark, good sir."

Matt chuckled. "Well," he said. "As someone who's actually *on* this particular death-defying mission, I take comfort in that. You've managed to live through those suicidal gestures, after all."

I shook my head at that. "I might have," I said. "Doesn't mean the people next to me did."

This was followed by one of those periods of silence longer and more awkward than it needed to be. Things had gotten weird, there—and I dutifully reached for a change in subject to try to de-weirdify them.

"Um ... you were mentioning travel becoming a bit of a problem?" I asked.

"Right," Matt said. He reached down into his bag and removed a small tablet computer, did some things on it I couldn't see, then spun it around to show me. On it was a map of I-90. And just to the west of Spokane shone a fat, red "X." A quick glance at the key in the corner of the screen indicated a "Checkpoint."

I frowned, looking at it, then looked up at Matt. "So ... what does that mean, exactly?" I asked.

"Eastern Washington and Northern Idaho are fed territory," said Matt. "We, um, we were the last summoners in the area, and Cythymau really isn't showing a lot of interest in areas with no summoners to control. The Feds have moved in and set up checkpoints. They're going to be asking for ID's, that sort of thing."

I laughed a little. "Our papers, please?" I asked in a mocking tone. "I'm guessing our ID's are tight enough to hold through that?"

Matt nodded. "Yeah," he said with a frown. "If it's an ID check, we'll be through without a problem."

"Something has you worried?"

"Nothing I can put my finger on," he said. "It's just that the Feds should know we can easily fake papers, so why—oop!" Matt gestured as first Thad, then Andrea, left the confines of the rest area and we began piling back into the van. Matt fell silent—whether out of concern for Thad or Andrea, I didn't know. Thad got behind the wheel and took the van back out onto the freeway, back on our path towards this checkpoint—and the fight that lay beyond it.

THE WORD "CHECKPOINT" was never associated, in my mind, with something one would find in America.

I'm sorry. I grew up in this country, and I bought into the Eastern-Washington jingoism. America was the Land of the Free, the Home of the Brave, and all that. Greatest country in the world, et cetera. It was a ... well, simple-minded sort of take, but the fact is that most of the American principles *are* things to be proud of.

Which meant that it came as a shock to see something that would have looked more at home in those old photos of checkpoints for the Berlin Wall than it looked here. Concrete barricades, barbed wire, and many, many men with guns diverted traffic into a place that, as I remembered it, used to be a simple truck stop on the hill above Spokane to the west.

It's funny. I mean, I'd been held prisoner by my government—I'd been psychologically *tortured* by my government. But until I really looked at the massive, military complex designed to screen every motorist who passed—I still thought of it as America. Flawed, maybe, and certainly being taken advantage of. But still a country whose *goals* were liberty and equality, if not its *results.*

The complex I saw while Thad turned into the truck-stop-cum-fascist-scanning-zone cleanly stripped that belief from me. Each car, every motorist on the I-90 was stopped—and there were far fewer cars than there used to be, likely as a result. Each was directed into its own zone, far separate from others ... and I didn't know why that was. But as I watched the proceeding, it sunk in on me.

Whatever else had happened as a result of Cythymau's invasion, "America" as it existed in my childhood—as an ideal of freedom, liberty, and equality—that America had already been destroyed by Cythymau. Whether it could ever recover from something like this remained an open question, but in this moment it simply did not exist. And I didn't really realize how much that would affect me—until it did.

"What the—" I heard Matt breathe as we sat in our line. "Dogs?"

Sitting in the back of the van, I didn't have quite Matt's view of the thing, and it took me a little longer to notice ... but there were dogs. Mostly German shepherds, circling each of the vehicles, sniffing at them.

"Bomb-sniffing, maybe?" I asked. "Or blood, perhaps? I could see trying to detect that with—"

"They're sensitive," said Thad in an icy, calm tone. My head whipped over to look at the man. "Animals—some animals, mostly predators—can be trained to feel us using the Sense. I need to be very clear—and this is for you two especially, Lorents, Andrea—do not bring your Sense up."

"Not just paperwork, then," said Matt—though he pulled the appropriate papers from a folder regardless. "That explains a lot."

"Mmm," said Thad with a nod. "Yes—it does. Though it's pretty crude, and once we're aware of it, easily avoided. Funny how people grasp for things to make them feel safe when there's no way to actually *be* safe."

I nodded in understanding. Sense-sniffing dogs ... that was a new one, and I shook my head. How they trained a dog like that I didn't ask—giving a summoner access to the Sense in order to test their abilities seemed chancy—but it was clear these soldiers at lease *believed* that their dogs would do ... something.

"Right," Matt said. "Just ... keep your Senses down, present the paperwork, we'll be fine."

I took a breath and nodded in agreement ... then a thought struck my mind. "Uh," I said. "Andrea? Are you ... "

She looked at me, her mouth compressed in a frown. "I'll be fine," she said in a clipped tone.

I had never Sensed Andrea with her Sense down. Anytime I brought mine up ... hers already was. Now, anytime I brought my Sense up, it was generally a good time for people to have their Sense up, and I knew Andrea could be a bit paranoid ... but I couldn't help but hold her gaze for a bit, here. If anyone in the van was going to tip off those dogs ...

I shook my head, focusing forward. "Good," I said as we pulled into our slot.

I didn't recognize the uniform the men surrounding our van wore. They looked military—helmets, body armor—but there weren't any of the standard military patches. No nametags identified the men. In fact, there wasn't much way to glean any information from the uniform save that they were clearly about a half-second away from shooting everyone who wasn't one of them at any point in time.

The part of me that mourned the loss of America's soul wept a little.

"Papers, please," the man at the driver's window said. His voice came out curt and stern, almost as though he assumed all persons before him to be nefarious unless demonstrated otherwise.

I almost laughed, but held back. That phrase. Being used in that way. It was astonishing to hear it said in all seriousness while standing on the West Plains, overlooking the city I had, for so much of my life, called home. Then I looked to my left, to Andrea sitting on the bench seat next to me.

Her eyes had scrunched up in a look of overexaggerated concentration—I had no idea why. She'd never looked like that, and I frowned ... it didn't make sense. Then I looked out the windows of the van and watched the man with the dog approaching. So did Andrea.

Huh.

The man at the driver's window thumbed through the papers,

reviewing them all and looking at each of us in turn. "Purpose of travel?" he asked.

"Business," responded Thad. Thaddeus Nielsen had many, many flaws—but I'd back him in a competition of bureaucratic stick-up-the-wahoo-ity against anyone the government had to send. Thad's tone wasn't just acidic—it carried that edge of condescension only someone who's used to being important could ever master.

"What *sort* of business?" asked the soldier.

"Sales trip," said Matt helpfully. "We represent a grower's collective from the Moses Lake area, and we've a meeting with the Spokane-Area Grange."

"A meeting," added Thad in his best bureaucro-fu tone, "that we would very much like to be *on time* for."

"Travel restrictions are posted," said the officer. "If you're running late, should've left earlier. We'll just run a sweep of your vehicle, then you'll be free to—"

"To?" asked Thad.

The man didn't respond. Instead, he was looking at the German shepherd whose handler had escorted him up to the side of our vehicle. The German shepherd had sat down on his haunches, staring at the van.

I looked around—every other canine on active duty walked about their car, never stopping to sit.

"Piss and shit," breathed Andrea next to me, and in that instant I realized we were in trouble.

"Sir?" said the officer at the window. "One moment. This is probably nothing, but ... wait here. Do not attempt to exit the vehicle. Do not attempt to leave. Please keep your hands where officers outside the vehicle can see them at all times. Do you understand?"

Thad nodded, clearly afraid. "Is there a problem, officer?" he asked.

"I'm finding out," replied the man. "Sit tight and I will return momentarily."

The officer stepped away from the van. So did everyone else. Unlike all the other vehicle pads in the lot, we had nobody in uniform within thirty feet of our vehicle. Not one person.

"Something's wrong," I said.

Three faces in the van turned to me, all of them exasperated at my stunning ability to state the obvious.

"All right, all right," I said. "My point is ... we might want to take this opportunity to think about plan B. I ... think they're onto us, and I'd prefer not to fight my way out of this if I didn't have to."

"They're not coming back," whispered Andrea.

"What?" asked Thad.

"They. Are. *Not*. Coming. Back," she said again, then tension and volume of her voice growing louder and louder.

"What do you mean, Andrea?" I asked. I turned to her, and risked placing a hand on her shoulder, trying to comfort and steady her.

"I mean," she yelled, "that THEY AREN'T GOING TO COME BACK. They're just going to ... oh Gods."

Thad, Matt and I all looked at each other. We couldn't make out heads nor tails of what Andrea was saying ... but then we heard a loud *clang* and looked back up and out the windows.

Around us—in an octagonal form—walls snapped into place. Big, thick steel walls powered by hydraulics sprung into position, and everyone on the other side of the walls hit the deck.

There's moments in my life that I'll never forget. I don't mean I remember them happening. I mean that I can close my eyes and be there, in that moment. Standing atop a bridge over the Spokane River and summoning an energy drink to piss off an overfed Cornuprocyon. Battling a pack of Lycaon let loose on my high school graduation. Shielding myself desperately from a nuclear blast even as my friend and mentor died in the fiery heart of it. Being tortured—and watching my foster father die with a bullet in his head.

But no moment to this point—none—will have the crystal-clear immediacy in my mind of the moment where we all realized what was about to happen.

"Oh shi—" Thad and I said at once—but we didn't get the chance to finish.

ANDREA

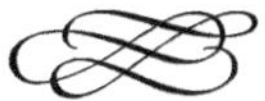

I'VE MADE big strides in the last year with getting used to being around people. The ones in my adopted Grove especially. Road trips, though, are still a kind of hell for me.

They require sitting in one spot for an extended period of time, in an enclosed place, in extreme proximity to others, as a flimsy plastic box on wheels moves at a high rate of speed alongside *other* equally feeble vessels full of strangers. This all—the landscape, the people, the cars, the businesses, everything— cascades through my Sense and into me, like water spewing through a floodgate during a storm. What you can't stop, you can only find a way to cope with and survive. The good news is that since I wasn't driving the van myself, I didn't really need to pay attention to any of it. I could just surf above it, treating it as so much white noise.

That is, until something snagged my attention.

We were pulling off the freeway. All the eastbound lanes had been blockaded, forcing traffic to exit. Flashing signboards with their own external solar panels and battery packs directed our vehicle to proceed through a "reality terrorist" security checkpoint.

I frowned. "Reality terrorist" was the new propagandized term for any summoner. And besides, this type of checkpoint wasn't

Cythymau's style. It cost way too much in terms of effort and resources for far too little return. That meant this was none of his doing. But how did civilian law enforcement expect to screen for summoners, barring the kind of tip-off in advance Cythymau had already gifted them with?

And even assuming they'd found some way to not make the checkpoint totally worthless, what did they expect to do if they did find a summoner, let alone a full car of them? It would be like netting a whole whale pod with a rowboat. Exhilarating maybe, and good job to you, but then what do you do after?

The traffic slowed down to a crawl, rolling forward at the same glacial speed that theoretically meant cars at the front of the line were getting inspected.

I hadn't been at this exit before, and it looked like whoever had set the check point up had thrown up ten-foot cement barriers, twenty-foot-tall chain link fencing, all topped with razor wire, around what had been a pretty standard gas station/truck stop. I supposed the location's advantage was a *very* large parking lot divided into individual pads for inspections. Plus, there weren't many businesses around to gawk at military operations as the cars slowly filed through.

Outside the immediate truck stop, it was mostly wheat fields. The checkpoint itself had been set up a good 200 feet away from the gas pumps and accompanying restaurant/minimart.

My brow creased as I tried to predict how they might detect us. Cythymau had said I was still bound to him somehow. If I believed him, as dangerous as that could be, did that mean he had given my description to –

Matt inhaled through his nose suddenly, his heart rate increasing.

"What the—" I heard him say. "Dogs?" Whatever he was looking at was outside of my Sense radius. I leaned forward, trying to get a better look at what he was seeing.

"Bomb-sniffing, maybe?" Robert said. "Or blood, perhaps? I could see trying to detect that with ... "

"They're sensitive," Thad said. His tone was flat, but his brow beaded with sweat and his pulse picked up, belying that calm façade.

"Animals—some animals, mostly predators—can be trained to feel us using the Sense. I need to be very clear—and this is for you two especially, Lorents—do not bring your Sense up."

Thad's words were directed at Robert, but I could Sense him looking at me. I tried to flatten the sudden bolt of panic that lanced through me. Don't bring my Sense up? But it was just there. It was already active, as it had been for millennia. I tried to remember a time the Sense hadn't been there as another overwhelming and challenging part of my sensory input. I couldn't come up with one. My inner consternation grew. People in the car were still talking, though, and I tried to focus.

"Right," Matt said. "Just ... keep your Senses down, present the paperwork, we'll be fine."

My mouth grew dry. I didn't know how to bring my Sense up. Which meant, I didn't have any *clue* how to take it *down.*

Sure, I'd been aware that the summoners here seemed to be able to extend their Sense or curtail it at will. But the whole process had always seemed a little silly to me. I'd often found it infuriating or amusing, and sometimes downright baffling, how they stumbled around unaware of ninety-nine percent of what was going on in the Weave surrounding them most of the time.

Next to me, Robert took a deep breath, the air rushing in and temporarily bulking up his skinny torso as he squared his shoulders. He exhaled, shooting me a concerned, doubtful look. "Uh," he said. "Andrea? Are you ... "

I shot him a look back. *Damn* him for having me pegged. I felt paralyzed, called out, and powerless to stop anything that was about to happen. The van had crossed the point of no return a long way back. There was nowhere to hide here. Nowhere for any of us to go. We'd all be caught, and it would be all my fault. This was absolutely the worst.

"I'll be fine," I lied, biting off each word. The car kept inching forward toward the front of the line. I frantically focused my attention on my Sense, trying to stuff it down, squeeze it in, roll it up, drag it back, flick it off—any image I could think of that might cause it to go 'down' like they'd talked about.

Robert said only one word in response to my lie. "Good." I bit the inside of my lip, tasting blood.

It can't be that hard, Andrea, I told myself. *Everyone else can do it. Just let it go. Relax. Stop doing it. Whatever "it" is.*

The armed and armored personnel manning the check station crossed into the periphery of my still-active Sense. Red-hot shame filled me. Piss and shit. I should have told Robert's skinny ass to knock me out, instead. But even then, who says I wouldn't unconsciously continue to broadcast my Sense? Then I would be a danger to everyone *and* a useless unconscious lump. I just didn't know enough about how my own Sense worked.

I continued desperately trying to shut-off-and-shut-out the extra information my Sense insisted on feeding me. The Kevlar-riot-suited checkpoint personnel carried radios and assault weapons loaded with real bullets, but no incapacitating weapons, and no tranquilizers. The checkpoint pad under the van had been modified, metal plates embedded at all sides, wires trailing off into the distance from some kind of plastic-filled metal box. Thirty feet ahead of us, a metal plate had been activated to shoot up a spike strip and block the way in case anyone was foolish enough to try to run before they'd been cleared.

Our van rolled onto the checkpoint pad proper, coming to a stop. Matt was talking to the riot-suited soldiers out of the driver's side window now, passing some kind of papers, but I couldn't focus on the vibrations his voice created in the Weave or the words they represented. I had my own fight going on. One of those dogs Thad had just talked about approached dangerously close to the outer edge my Sense.

Get it together Andrea. I yanked on my Sense, pulling it away from the dog—the Sense equivalent of flinging myself backwards and away from the canine. My Sense still refused to totally obey my wishes. It twitched, recoiling into something more egg-shaped than spherical, warping and wobbling. My stomach cramped, flooding with acid, making me nauseous as my temples pounded. I wrenched on my

Sense some more, trying to keep the dog from coming in contact with it.

In desperation, I managed to flatten my Sense into something resembling a disc by thinking of the Weave directly above and below me a massive net, winding and cramming my Sense between crosshatched weft and warp. My Sense ended up punching out of the roof of the van, pancaked into the Weave and twice as long as usual and just barely wider than the vehicle. Sweat broke out on my forehead, and my eyes crinkled in pain and effort. If I could just hold this, I *might* somehow be able to get us through this without blowing our cover.

The German shepherd paced clear up to the edge of the van with its handler, and I held my breath. It paced around the edge of my Sense, never setting its nose or one paw inside. And yet it sat down on its haunches. Staring at the van. At me. Even though it couldn't possibly see me.

"Piss and shit," I breathed, letting out the lung-full of air I'd been holding. We were so screwed.

"Sir?" said the officer at the window. "One moment. This is probably nothing, but ... wait here. Do not attempt to exit the vehicle. Do not attempt to leave. Please keep your hands where officers outside the vehicle can see them at all times. Do you understand?"

Thad nodded, clearly shaken. "Is there a problem, officer?" he asked.

"I'm finding out," replied the man. "Sit tight and I will return momentarily."

Straining to hold my Sense like this was futile now, I decided. Whatever the result, the shit had already hit the fan. Anything I did now would only minimize the spray. Especially since this was my fault. I let my Sense spring back into its normal shape, the pressure in my head letting up slightly.

The officer stepped away from the van, not stopping until he was on the other side of the big metal plates bracketing the pad the van sat on. So did all the other checkpoint soldiers. I examined the big steel structures in the ground around the pads, and the wires trailing from a strange, plastics-filled box. Wires and sensors meant a trap waiting to be trigged, but what? And how to counter it without making it worse?

"Something's wrong," Robert said.

I stared at him and suppressed the urge to make a sarcastic comment. This situation was my fault, after all. I groped for answers, trying to put together the pieces in the puzzle my Sense was showing me. *What do you do when you catch a tiger by its tail, if you aren't prepared to tranquilize it?* I asked myself.

Pfft! Cythymau's voice whispered in my ear. *Foolish plentyn. Powerful creatures that can't be used must be destroyed. Speedily, using the most effective method possible, hmm?*

"My point is ... we might want to take this opportunity to think about plan B. I ... think they're onto us, and I'd prefer not to fight my way out of this if I didn't have to," Robert said next to me.

Realization hit, punching me in the gut.

They were equipped to use lethal force only.

"They're not coming back," I whispered, my mind racing. They had set up measures designed to funnel all summoners exactly right here. Onto a pad, flanked by snipers, bracketed with thick steel plates, sitting on top of wires, sensors, plastic ...

Comprehension hit me like a ton of bricks, knocking the breath out of me. Plastic explosives.

"What?" asked Thad, swiveling to look at me over the back of his seat. Matt stared at me in the rearview mirror, his expression pinched, his face slowly draining color.

"They. Are. *Not.* Coming. Back," I said again, louder, emphasizing each word. We had no time. I didn't even know what to tell them. How to react. All I had was my worthless Sense that had gotten us into this situation in the first place. Even my charm bracelet didn't have any tricks that would be near powerful enough to save us from this one, even assuming I'd had time to dig it out of my bag.

"What do you mean, Andrea?" Robert asked, turning to face me on the bench seat where we sat. He gripped my shoulder, confusion and fear warring on his face.

"I *mean*," I yelled, exasperated— though to be fair, my frustration was aimed at myself, not him. "That THEY AREN'T GOING TO COME BACK. They're just going to ... "

One of the soldiers spoke into the radio he carried. Around us, the hydraulic pistons snapped steel walls up into place. Simultaneously, the soldiers on the other side of the big steel barrier dropped prone, covering their heads.

"Oh Gods." I whispered. My eyes snagged on the three other people in the van— they had put themselves out for me, protected my interests, allowed me to be a royal bitch to them all more than once. They each had their flaws, but so did I.

Time seemed to slow and stretch into eternity.

I rejected a reality where I caused their deaths with a visceral desperation and force of will that welled up unbidden from somewhere deep inside me.

Somewhere outside the range of my Sense, someone pressed the igniter. For a fraction of a second, I Sensed the fuse triggering beneath us. Then the small nucleus of what was about to become a massive, directional explosion. An explosion aimed specifically to obliterate this one van and all its occupants, and leave the rest of the checkpoint intact.

My Sense vibrated against the Weave, against my skin, as if I'd somehow become a tuning fork. I needed to get them out of here. I needed us *all* to be somewhere other than here. My heart thundered in my ears with the heat of my emotions, but I didn't have the time to examine them or unpack them. I just acted.

Electrifying tension danced under my skin, illuminating the scars of my long captivity. Blue rune tattoos, identical to the ones that always decorated Cythymau's body, erupted on my flesh, welting up like hives against my usual paleness. My Sense fused into the runes; energy crackled through me, using my own blood, my body, as the medium.

As the runes activated completely, I could Sense the spot where I was, together with an empty wheat field somewhere outside the van. I frantically latched onto Robert, Thad, and Matt with my Sense, dragging them along with me.

We hit the ground on the perimeter of the wheat field one hundred yards outside the wall of the checkpoint facility with jarring impact, rolling and sending up three small puffs of dust— just as we heard the ear-splitting reverberation of our van being blown up in the distance. All of my focus had been put into transporting us, and none of it had gone into cushioning the landing. The fact that no one, except myself, had time to tuck for impact didn't help. We crashed down and rolled, the three others yelling in what I assumed was pain and disorientation.

But I could feel Robert, Matt, and Thad all in the field with me. I could smell the earth, feel the dirt grinding into my palms, Sense their hearts still pumping next to mine. We all lived.

I sat up and knelt on the ground, feeling wrung out. As if I'd just run a marathon. Black dots swam in my vision for a moment. I blinked, trying to clear them. I glanced over at Robert, Matt, and Thad. They'd stumbled to their feet and were staring toward where we'd come from — at the smoke plume where our van used to be. Their clothes were smeared with dust. They had a few scrapes and skinned elbows, but they looked whole. A breath I hadn't realized I was holding rushed out of me in relief.

"Everyone ok?" I asked, "Nothing's broken? I—" Everyone's heads slowly swung back to look at me. I attempted a smile. It felt wobbly. Now that all of their attention was focused on me, I didn't know how to handle it.

Thad was staring at me as if I'd grown two heads. Matt just looked shellshocked. Robert's eyes took a moment to focus on me, dazed.

The weight of our almost-deaths crashed down on me.

"What just happened? How did you—" Robert started to ask.

"I'm sorry," I blurted to all of them. I took a deep breath and hiccupped. "I am so sorry. I couldn't do it. I couldn't bring my Sense down. I *tried* to hide it, but nothing worked. This is all my fault. I'm so sorry."

The tears burning the backs of my eyes traitorously started leaking down my cheeks.

I nearly killed you all. I couldn't even say the words.

Unconsciously, I held my hands out to them in instant repudiation of the thought. "Forgive me," I said instead. "I didn't realize until much too late. It's my fault. I'm sorry." The tears poured out of me in earnest, and I shivered with power of my regret, feeling my face contort into a grimace as I tried to bring my emotions back under control.

Robert moved first. He took my hand in a surprisingly firm grasp, kneeling down and putting one arm around me, awkwardly patting me on the back.

I heard him clear his throat, Sensed its vibration. "Well, it looks like you saved us too," he said. "So I think this time, you get a pass."

I let my head fall forward and soak his t-shirt with my tears. For such a skinny kid, his embrace felt surprising warm and sturdy. Before this, I never would have imagined I'd grab onto him like this, taking comfort in the human contact, thankful and relieved he was alive.

"Bygones and all that. You know I've done my own share of monumentally stupid stuff," Robert said.

Matt took my other hand, and I could Sense him staring at where it rested on his palm. I knew he was looking at the blue rune tattoos that were still slowly fading, bleeding away with the tension that had filled me and vanishing back to wherever they'd came from.

"I'm with Robert," Matt finally said simply. He patted my hand gently. "I know you did the best you could. I get it. We're good."

"Thad?" Robert asked in his most menacing voice. "Are we good?" A small bubble of amusement pushed back at my tears. Robert, always super protective of my super-ancient ass. This time, if it got chewed, it was my own fault. But I believed I could hold my own.

"Yes, of course," Thad said in his most crisp tone, finally walking over. "Andrea, as Robert says, you extricated us all, so in this instance, I believe all is forgiven. Though perhaps, you can be a little more forthcoming *before* there is a next time. You've obviously been holding on to more secrets than I realized."

"I hate to break this up," Matt said squeezing my hand, "but we need to get moving. They're going to realize sooner or later that there's no bodies in that van. And I have to assume that they've got at least me and probably Thad on their surveillance footage, since we were both sitting in the front. So we can strategize later about how to avoid anything like this ever happening again, but for now ...."

"For now, we need to de-ass this place with the quickness," Robert finished, climbing back to his feet and then helping me up next to him.

Thad quirked an eyebrow at me. "Is there a possibility you can just transport us away from this field like you did the van?" he asked. His question was genuine, but also a test.

I shrugged. "I don't think so? I honestly don't know what I did back there." I spread my fingers and lifted my hands in front of me, looking at the fading blue tattoos on my hands and arms. They were already fading, becoming indistinguishable among the faint web of scars that Cythymau had cut into my skin over many, many excruciating sessions. "I just moved on instinct, and my Sense took over somehow." I hunched a shoulder in a shrug, not wanting to dive into exactly what I remembered and what I could never even hope to explain.

"Kind of like muscle memory?" Robert asked me.

"I dunno," I mumbled. "I did it. I don't know *how* exactly I did. I was just desperate to fix the mess I'd made."

Thad put a hand in his jacket, obviously looking to pull something out, then patted all his pockets, coming up dry. His voice came out a little strangled. "Does anyone else have any personal items like wallet, ID, keys, a Grove book?" he asked in an attempt at a conversational tone.

Robert and Matt patted their pockets, then looked at each other, and then me.

"Uh, that's looking like a no," Robert said.

"Sorry," I said helplessly again. "I don't know. I just grabbed you all and pulled."

Everyone stared at me, their expressions frozen. I assumed how close we'd come to *not* escaping hit them anew.

"I guess we should be glad we still have clothes and shoes then," Robert quipped finally, attempting to look unperturbed, patting me reassuringly on the back. "Very minimalist, but you got your priorities right."

His words were obviously ninety-nine percent bravado, but also meant to comfort me. It was actually kind of cute, and I didn't hate it. As soon as the thought flashed through my mind, my blood shocked me by rushing to my face. My cheeks heated until they felt like they were on fire. Piss and shit, I'd gone round the bend.

Robert paused, his hand faltering mid-pat.

"Everything's fine," Thad said, sounding anything but. "I'll just need to summon a spare Grove book and supplies, I guess. Matt, any ideas where would be best to pick up new transportation from here?"

"I might, but I need a laptop and a little time."

"Well, let's get moving then. I want to find the nearest ditch or shed and get us some supplies, but I don't want to risk someone noticing us popping something out on the edge of this field. I *think* that we're far enough away that they won't notice four people leaving on foot, but let's not test that any longer than we have to."

We moved into a dry drainage ditch at the edge of the field.

Thad found a stick, smoothed out a spot, and began drawing runes into the dirt at his feet. When he'd finished, he squeezed blood from a scrape on his elbow to power it. I winced.

A few seconds later, a Grove book, several vials of blood, a laptop, a pen, and a stack of rune tags popped into existence next to him. Thad handed the laptop to Matt, then began thumbing through the Grove book.

Matt drew and blooded several runes, then snapped the laptop open, pulling up a map. He studied it thoughtfully for a moment.

"If we continue east four miles," Matt said pointing at the screen, "we'll be at the Spokane airport. I can create us new IDs and travel papers. We should be able to rent a car there. I think that's our best bet. But we're going to need to find a better internet connection for me to do that. If it's at the airport, so be it, but ... the sooner we can get there, the better."

"Agreed," Thad said. "And I can't think of anything that will let us leave more quickly and quietly than on our own two feet." He drew out a rune formula and blooded it, creating a spherical web of light reflections around him that shimmered like a mirage and then hid him from sight. "This will work for about a 10-foot radius, so I need you all to pack in here together. Let's get our butts moving, people. It's going to be a very long walk."

～

MY FEET ACHED, my calves throbbed, and my skin felt sticky from heat and lack of water.

But we stood in our invisible bubble on the outer perimeter of the rental car pick-up and drop-off outside the airport.

"Okay, I'm going in," Matt said, "I forged IDs and the papers as we were walking. I'll be right back."

I shifted uncomfortably on my abused feet, trying to find a way of standing that wasn't pure agony as I waited for them to decide who was going to go in. After the truck stop fiasco, it certainly wasn't going to be me.

"But if there's a situation," Robert said, "you're the most likely to get stuck."

I snorted unintentionally, earning a look from both of them. *Not factually true. I hold that particular distinction, thank you.*

"I'm the one least likely to *cause* a situation in the first place." Matt said reasonably. "I made the documents; I know exactly what they say if anyone asks. AND I'm not the kind of person most people pay any attention to," Matt said. "I'll be in and out. Like a boss."

I hoped that was true.

"I don't see that we have any other options, Lorents." Thad said. "Not if we want to have a chance to put any kind of wrench in Cythymau's plans for the Missoula Grove. As long as Matt doesn't take any unnecessary risks, I endorse his plan."

"I won't," said Matt. "And we don't know if they've realized that no one was in the van, or how good their surveillance footage is. If they

68

have any more of those Sense-sniffing dogs in the airport, I don't want you or Andrea anywhere near them. Besides, you face is too well-known in Spokane, Robert."

"I can disguise myself—" Robert said.

"Using your Sense," Matt answered.

"Which the dogs can detect," Robert said, then groaned.

"And we know how well that just went," I said bitterly.

"Bingo." Matt said. He checked for cameras or any other pedestrians, and then quietly slipped out of our invisibility net. He sauntered confidently toward the airport entrance.

My getting us almost killed had already cost us close to three hours. And would cost us more, because now we'd have to use back roads, where check points were unlikely to have been set up. I just hoped Missoula would survive whatever Cythymau had planned long enough for us to still get there.

ROBERT

IT's funny how a couple of hours in a car can make even the most dangerous of experiences feel ... almost pedestrian. We'd already blown our clock, we knew that the checkpoint incident had heightened the problems, and we'd all crammed into the little sub-compact rental Matt had come up with.

Don't get me wrong—I was happy he found *anything*, but the journey over the Bitterroots and deep into Montana would have been a lot more pleasurable had I not spent most of it eating my knees. Next to me, the much-smaller Andrea didn't seem to have as many problems fitting physically, but even I could tell she didn't exactly enjoy being in this close of proximity to ... well, to anyone, really.

I left her to her thoughts, though. Adding to her stress wasn't likely to help things, and so as we ascended Lookout Pass, each of us kept to ourselves, looking out the window and letting our thoughts drift while staring at our surroundings.

When you're growing up in the Spokane Valley, Coeur d'Alene is a common destination. Lakefront beaches are always a popular attraction in the summer, and Coeur d'Alene had some good ones. But I'd never actually gone farther into the big mountains beyond Coeur d'Alene.

Washingtonians like myself know the Cascades, and we know them well. Mountains, on the whole, are not a thing we're unfamiliar with. But the Cascades—and the Olympics, too, now that I mention it —feel like living things when you enter them. They're volcanic mountains, pushed up from below into all manner of patterns, and the water from the coast rains down on them constantly, creating the network of streams, rivers and waterfalls that gives the mountains their name.

The Rockies ... are different. Where the Cascades feel like a living, breathing thing, the Rockies are distinctly a *force of nature itself.* Driven up by continental drift instead of volcanic activity, the Rockies carry with them an implacable sense of inevitability. There are a couple of streams—indeed, Lookout Pass ran next to one—but on the whole they don't dance and play the way the Cascades and Olympics do. Instead, I got the distinct impression that they didn't care for my presence one way or another. They simply *were,* and they would be long after I was gone.

That sort of raw power took my breath away as I looked out the window. Perhaps I felt a bit melancholic. Regardless of that, by the time we pulled into the grassy, high-mountain valley that contained the city of Missoula, my mind couldn't help but ponder whether our current fight was any different than picking a fight with one of those mountains.

Matt drove through the city of Missoula and ended up at a small parking lot. On the left sat a lovely little park, well-manicured. In front of us, the Clark Fork River flowed happily through its valley, blissfully unaware of its surroundings. And to our right, a set of blue-painted steps led up to the footway on a bridge.

"That's Higgins Avenue," said Matt, gesturing at the bridge. "The café should be on the right side of the street after you get over the river. If you hit a gas station, you've gone too far."

The three of us gratefully freed ourselves from the confines of the small vehicle. Matt, for his part, reached under his seat and brought out his laptop. I watched him beginning to do Matt-things with it for a moment, then a stretch attack hit me. I raised my arms above my head with a sound halfway between a yawn and a yell.

"Hush," said Thad. "We've no idea what the situation is, but we need to be—"

"We have an idea," said Matt in a horribly still voice. The three of us bent down to look through the windows at him.

"We're ... late," said Matt, gesturing to his laptop. On it, feeds from what appeared to be body cams had appeared, as well as a couple from what could only be drones circling above us. I instinctively looked up, and after a moment could barely make out the winged, circling things.

Looking back at the screen, I saw Matt's finger indicating one of the other feeds ... and I saw why. The camera was clearly in motion, but when it stopped, I saw a pile of bodies ... and another one tossed on the pile, coming into frame from the top as the soldier wearing the cam tossed it.

The Missoula Grove. Or, rather ... their corpses.

Damn.

"Let's go kill them," said Andrea in the same sort of voice one would use to suggest adjusting the thermostat.

For once, I didn't want to disagree with her. I knew I should, but ... damn, this was ruthless. Whatever had happened, the Feds were clearly no longer bothering with non-lethal measures. And a part of me ... no. Most. Most of me wanted to give them *exactly* the same amount of mercy.

"No," said Thad, and I could hear what it cost *him* in the soft tone in which he said it. "We're here to *save* them."

Thad opened the hatchback, then cracked open a large, plastic foot-locker that hadn't been there a moment ago ... that had been *slick* on his part. When did he blood the runes for it?

He reached into the footlocker and began removing clothes ... clothes that matched the ones I'd seen on Matt's screen. Khakis, tactical vests, the full nine. I blinked as he handed me a set. "They're baggy," he said. "Should fit over your currents."

I nodded to him and accepted them, then began to don them as he handed Andrea another set. Atop those, a Kevlar vest, which I slipped on gratefully. After that, though—and I deeply suspected Thad wasn't storing all of this in a single footlocker, but rather using the footlocker to cover his summoning—he pulled out the weapons. First, a pair of what I guessed were M-4 carbines, then a belt with a pistol already holstered and attached to it.

"Um..." I said as I took them gingerly from him. "Grace never really ... that is ... I've seen these things in *movies*..." Next to me, Andrea nodded in agreement with my words.

Thad took a deep breath, then released it. "Which, Lorents, is why they're unloaded entirely. We're not here to fight *against* the military ... we're here to help them against our enemy. They just killed our friends ... and were there a chance of saving the Missoula Grove, I'd take it. But there isn't. They're dead, Lorents. Soon these Feds will be as well if we do nothing. Now, we have to get close enough to them to talk, which means looking like them. The gun is for appearances ... but we both know you're better off not trying."

I couldn't help but notice that, as he was talking, *Thad* loaded both of his guns and stashed several clips in his tactical vest.

I took a deep breath. "I know," I said. "I get it. It's just ... "

"It's just hard to take that stance when you see the bodies," Thad sighed in agreement. "I know," he said. Then he turned to Andrea. "It'd feel good, too, getting the drop on them the way they got the drop on that Grove. But ... we have to take the long view. If we want to kill every last non-summoner on the planet, we may as well sign up with Cythymau. If not ... then we can't go vengeance-killing normal people." He racked the slide on his carbine, noisily chambering a round for emphasis.

"Much as we might want to," he added.

Matt, from the front seat, passed Thad a small case from inside his laptop bag. "Earbuds," he said. "Let's face it—I'm worthless in a fight, but I'll have eyes on the military and on the sky. At least I can tell you what's coming," he said.

I grinned as I took the earpiece and began slipping it into my ear. "Do I call you Oracle, now?" I asked.

Matt frowned at me in an exaggerated sort of expression. "It's not the gender thing I've got a problem with. It's only that I am not *nearly* as badass as Barbara Gordon—and she's in a wheelchair."

I laughed, at that. "Few are," I said. "But still—this should be helpful." I passed the case around to both Thad and Andrea, each of whom slipped in their own earbud. "And given that we're about to throw ourselves between two different forces—both of which I'd rate a lethal enemy—well, any advantage we can get,"

～

WE CLIMBED the staircase above the parking lot with a sense of trepidation. Halfway up the three flights of stairs, Matt's voice sounded in my earbud.

"All right, they've set up a roadblock on the bridge, just south of where you'll come up," he said. "They haven't sent out patrols, yet—not on this side of the river. Not sure how far those uniforms will get you."

Ahead of me, Thad sighed. "All right, you two," he said over his shoulder. "Let me do the talking. I'm aware that you're the big guns, but when it comes to maneuvering in a bureaucracy..."

I gave Thad a little chuckle, then nodded to him, "Yeah," I said, and I meant it, too.

Talking our way past a group of soldiers was going to take a real anal-retentive jerk with an eye toward meticulous orders filled out in triplicate. In other words, Thaddeus Nielsen could not have been more perfect for the task.

Behind me, Andrea didn't protest, and so the two of us followed him, looking every bit the green recruits we were dressed to be—and letting the man who'd once tried to kill us lead us into what could end up being the hardest fight we'd been in yet.

The first time I'd really expected to die, I'd been standing on a bridge as the Spokane River rushed a hundred feet below, just downstream of Post Falls. In that moment, I learned to lean into the idea. *Assuming* that the worst was going to happen, embracing the idea, and simply moving forward in spite of it.

I'm not sure if that's how everyone who's ever been in a combat situation does it. I can't speak for all the soldiers or warriors of the world—hell, I never really set out to be one. But the fact remained that, as of this point, with the sole possible exception of Cythymau himself, I had more actual combat experience than any other summoner I knew.

And that feeling—that detached, almost euphoric feeling that came with *accepting* one's death before a fight—came easily, now. Before, it took a pair of earbuds blasting music and a couple minutes of simply standing and dealing with the idea. Now I shed my hopes of living through the next hour of my life as easily as I'd step out of a bathrobe heading into the shower.

Funny how constantly fighting for one's life, being tortured, and watching loved ones die does that to a person.

I'm aware, of course, that this sort of reaction isn't entirely healthy. But at the time—walking into the very teeth of the people who'd tortured me—it had a sort of usefulness.

As we crested the stairs, Andrea and I fell in side-by-side, flanking Thad. The roadblock consisted largely of dark-black SUV's and a single, military-style HUM-V, complete with a .50 caliber machinegun mounted atop it—and a rather twitchy-looking soldier manning it. Behind the vehicles, a number of men and women dressed similarly to us stood, assault rifles at the ready ... and all of that weaponry trained on us.

No dogs, though. Apparently these soldiers didn't actually care much whether or not the people walking at them had the Sense. They likely had orders to stop *anyone* from entering, and our uniforms presented the only reason they hadn't already opened fire on us.

Given the lack of dogs, I brought up my Sense and added a second reason. I pulled the smokeless powder out of the first ten cartridges in every soldier's clip ... and the .50's belt of ammo. I transported all that powder directly under the bridge, letting it drift down into the Clark Fork as I waited for Thad to speak. If one of them pulled the trigger, the jig would be up. Then again, if one of them pulled the trigger, the jig was *already* up, and better to rig the odds in our favor.

Thad, for his part, began waving cheerily at the men behind the vehicles. I'm honestly not sure that, before that point, I'd ever even seen Thad smile, but I have to admit ... his thespian skills impressed me.

"Identify!" a man wearing three sergeant's stripes on his sleeve shouted back.

Thad took another couple of steps. "My name is Thaddeus Nielsen," he said calmly. "This is Robert Lorents and Andrea Rothstein. We seek a parley with your commanding officer."

I heard a couple of *clicks* from the barricades, followed by cursing. "Yes," Thad said, nodding calmly in the direction of one of the men who'd just pulled their triggers. "*That* Robert Lorents. But, as you've just discovered, if we wished you harm you'd already be harmed. And if we wanted to approach your commander by force, we could do that, too. We do not wish you harm. In fact, we're here to save you from an ambush. Now, we're headed in that direction ... perhaps you could be so good as to inform your superiors that we're on the way?"

The sergeant didn't exactly blanch. He stood, leaning back, and took a deep breath. "Don't seem as I've much choice in the matter," he said, shaking his head with a wry little chuckle. "Stand down," he said, gesturing to his troops. "Ain't much you can do anyways, and if these folk are willin' to do us the favor of not killin' us, then let's not give 'em a reason to change their damned minds—though I ain't goin' to speak for what happens up the line, you understand."

Thaddeus nodded to the man. "Of course," he replied simply. Then he led Andrea and I through the picket. Heads turned toward us. Some troops kept their useless weapons aimed at us ... some others simply clutched them close to their chests like children clutching comfort blankies. But they allowed us to pass.

I tried smiling softly to one of them in a quiet assurance, but watched him recoil back. It's hard to convey 'quiet assurance' when they think you're the devil.

By the time we'd crossed the bridge over the Clark Fork, a second team had gathered at the far end. I kept my Sense up, readying myself for a fight—but one didn't come. I looked down Higgins Avenue and saw a number of shops lining the street on my right. This included the little diner the leaders of the Missoula Grove had been meeting in—and which was now being cleaned out by khaki-clad goons.

At the second end of the bridge, though, a woman stared at us. I didn't need the insignia on her uniform. The way the other troops moved around her told me they followed her lead. She stood in what I can only describe as a parade-rest posture, an air of professional lethality in the cool, calculating gaze she levelled at us with her brown eyes.

"Stop!" she called out as we approached. "That's close enough, I think."

I inhaled quickly ... she'd stopped us *just* outside my Sense range. I could still do a significant amount of damage should things get nasty ... but those weapons pointed at us *were* loaded. If I were going to summon the bullets, I'd have to do it *after* they fired. Worse, I didn't think her positioning a coincidence. She'd been briefed on me, on where my Sense stopped, and she'd acted accordingly.

I could still take her, I thought—but knowing that she'd prepared this much gave me pause, because I wasn't sure what *else* she might have prepared. Besides, despite what she and these troops had just done—my eyes drifted back to the body bags being pulled from the diner—I wasn't here to take her.

"Very well," said Thad calmly, though he put some volume into it to carry over the distance. "I am Thaddeus Nielsen, former Director of the Spokane Grove of Summoners and representative of the true Seattle Grove. This is Robert Lorents and Andrea Rothstein, also formerly of the Spokane Grove. To whom am I speaking?"

"Captain Sonia Tomas-Padilla," she replied. "Field Commander for the Anti-Summoner Operations Group. And the woman who's about to order you to be shot."

Thad sighed at that, then looked at over his shoulder and said quietly. "If they open fire... can you two keep it off us?"

My eye caught Andrea's for a moment, then we nodded to Thad. "Yeah," I said. I left the "probably" out, though it would have been more truthful. There were a *lot* of guns pointed at us, and summoning at the speed of bullets is a tricky business. Best to let Tomas- Padilla see a sense of confidence, whether or not we meant it.

Thad nodded, then took a deep breath of his own, the first sign of nerves I'd seen from him on this little operation. Then he turned back to look at Captain Tomas-Padilla with a pleasant little smile. "Then order us shot," he said.

Her eyes went wide for a moment, then narrowed in concentration. I braced myself, prepared to pick up any incoming bullet. The bullets never came, though, and instead Captain Tomas-Padilla simply sighed. "I'm dead if I try, aren't I? Dammit ... they didn't tell me Lorents was going to be here for this."

"Not dead, Captain. But your fire would prove ... ineffective. Now, since you're not going to have us shot, and we've no intention of harming you—despite what you've done, here, I might add—let's have a little talk."

"About what?" asked the captain.

"About saving your lives and the lives of all your troops, to begin with," answered Thad.

"You *are* threatening us, then?" she accused, her tan features frowning at Thad. Around her, the troops tensed.

Thad shook his head with a sigh for a moment, then opened his mouth to speak. He didn't manage to get any words out, though.

I didn't see, at first, who'd thrown the summons. Couldn't tell where the enemy forces were. But a massive, four-legged beast with the body of a cat and the green scales and neck-ruffle of a lizard burst onto Higgins Avenue a couple of blocks on the *other* side of the military, and I knew our second deadline had come.

"No," shouted Thad to the captain. "But *that* is," he said.

The captain cursed and watched as the beast slammed into her security force to the south, their fire deflecting in sparks off its scale hide. It mauled one soldier with its claw, then bit another, and I heard the soldiers near us begin cursing.

"Lorents?" said Thad. "You're up. That tattoo—use it."

I blinked. I didn't even know That *knew* about the tattoo I'd had done on my left arm. Brandiole must have told him more than I'd thought. But I nodded to him and began to run forward, drawing my knife and making a shallow cut on the inside of my arm, just above the elbow, then smearing the blood upward to cover the runes there.

The soldiers trained their guns on me, but I ignored them. None fired. I'm not sure if that was by their own choice, or because of some order the captain had given that I didn't see. My Sense was already on its way through the runes ... and for this particular summons, I found it far, far easier to reach through the runes with my Sense than I normally did.

It helps when the thing you're summoning already has a chunk of your Sense in it.

Rick—all thirty feet of him—appeared in the middle of Higgins Avenue, just on the other side of the soldiers. I'd summoned him facing south, but of course the big doof turned and looked at me, first. "The cat-lizard," I shouted, "Stop it! Keep the soldiers safe!"

Rick cocked his head to the side. *Saving* soldiers wasn't his normal *motus operandi* and it took a moment for him to process the idea. But once he did, he leapt into the air with one of his signature *woomph*s and sent himself into an arc to descend atop the other beast.

And I focused on other things. I'd leave Rick to battle their Visitor. I had a demon of my own to fight.

ANDREA

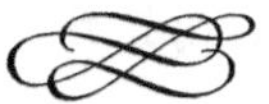

ROBERT HURDLED the barricade a split second *after* the massive lizard-cat-thing sprang into being at the far end of the military's occupied area. He sprinted past the guards, completely leaving his back turned to an armed force who'd just talked about killing him.

It took me another split second to realize he was trusting *me* to keep that fire off him. He'd said nothing. Hadn't even gestured. He'd just *assumed* I'd watch his back while he turned away from an armed squad. As I saw him blood a rune tattoo, I realized he didn't even have his Sense *here;* he sent it through runes. Absolutely defenseless. Except for me.

I'm not saying I wasn't going to help him. But the blind confidence —the complete surety I'd do it—shocked me.

It didn't shock me into *inaction*, though.

I sprinted forward, pushing myself to cross the twenty feet between me and the soldiers' guns before they could take the situation in. Their disbelief and, possibly, the fact that Robert had something of a boogeyman reputation, were the only things that saved him. It made the soldiers hesitate just a second longer than they should have.

I Sensed their fingers beginning to pull the triggers on their guns, and I did the simplest thing I could. I got rid of those triggers. Ten fingers squeezed empty air. Ten soldiers then double-checked their weapons. A ten-person chorus started cursing.

Rick crashed into the cat-lizard down at the far end of the street, with Robert hot on his tail. The soldiers stationed there—those that had survived the initial attack—began to open fire on him as well as the cat-lizard.

"Call off your people," said a calm, sure voice next to me. Stuffy—Thad. Thad still had that cold, bureaucratic tone, even in the middle of the chaos. I paused to listen.

"We've been tasked with neutralizing *all* summoners," said Captain Tomas-Padilla. "That includes you."

Piss and shit. Here we went for real.

"Regardless," said Thad with a dismissive gesture, "*we* will continue to aid you. We'll also try to minimize collateral damage, although—" He pointed down the street.

Rick leveled a force blast at the cat-lizard. The cat-lizard disappeared just before the attack landed, then appeared to the side of Rick. The blast took out a post box, two parked cars, and a rather nice-looking decorative tree.

"—minimize and prevent are, of course, two different concepts when dealing with a conflict of this scale," Thad finished, then added, "*Perhaps* it would be to your tactical advantage to prioritize targeting the people trying to kill you, instead of those trying to save you."

Without waiting for Tomas-Padilla's response, Thad turned to me and simply said, "Shall we?" He gestured down Higgins Avenue, as though inviting me for a pleasant stroll.

I took it to be a rhetorical question.

And so, I took off at a sprint, closing the distance between me and Robert. I didn't like our odds. I despised the people we were trying to rescue. But if they perished, then the Missoula Grove had died for nothing. *Something* had to come of this.

As I cleared the barricade myself, I saw Tomas-Padilla bringing a radio to her lips. "All units engage *all* summoners," she said. "Repeat: engage *all summoners*. You are cleared to fire at will."

Piss ass.

I Sensed the fear in the soldiers, the racing hearts, the quickened breathing, the elevated cortisol, the pumping adrenaline, and their skin slickening with cold sweat. Three of them had the wherewithal to draw their pistols from their holsters and fire at me as I ran down Higgins.

I didn't disable their pistols—they might need *something* later—but I did put the bullets on a trajectory to enter the Clark Fork.

Thad stayed behind, somewhere. I'd run past the point where I could Sense him—he'd take care of himself.

The bulky Kevlar armor made running more difficult. My rune tags crinkled beneath the vest where I'd stuffed them. The only real familiarity I had came from the charms on my compound-rune bracelet against my wrist.

Higgins Avenue had been splattered in blood even before this battle. The body bags in the street reminded me what these *bastards* I was saving had just done. I bit my lower lip as I streaked toward the fight.

In front of me, Rick spun, trying to face the cat-lizard. *Lacerfelis,* a small memory in my head offered. I grimaced as that bit of knowledge surfaced from Cythymau's repository within me. *Lacerfelis demon. Strong, clawed, agile, short-distance teleportation.*

The Lacerfelis blinked away from the more lumbering Cornuprocyon, appearing at Rick's back. But Rick, our good boy, had set a trap for his opponent. His club of a tail took the giant feline in the side, sending it crashing into a small minimart.

"Heads up that there are still people in these stores," came Robert's voice over my earpiece. I looked to the side, to the plate-glass windows, and saw the forms huddling low. Piss, why hadn't they evacuated when the army hit?

"Acknowledged," said Matt over the radio. "Be advised that you have what appear to be hostiles on side-streets flanking the gas station. Four groups of five. They look to be starting some runework. One moment."

From high in the sky, a pair of missiles jetted down into the side street. Moments later, I heard the blast as they impacted. "Correction," said Matt. "Three groups."

"There are *people in the stores, Matt*," said Robert desperately. "Easy with the explosives!"

"Targeted mid-street," said Matt. "Shouldn't have been too terrible in the buildings, if they were taking cover."

There was tense silence over the radio. In my mind I could almost *see* Robert's nervous expression.

At the far barrier, the soldiers crouched down, as though avoiding fire. Robert stood there, assessing the situation. Looking for a way to help Rick, no doubt, as he checked anxiously down the side streets for the summoners Matt had warned us about.

He didn't seem concerned with cover at all, but that made sense. That barricade wouldn't do anything against a Rick-sized attack, and we both knew it. The soldiers had either decided not to harm Robert or concluded their fire was useless. Regardless, I took up a position down the line from him, covering the opposite side streets should our enemies show themselves.

I Sensed the summons before I saw anything. I couldn't tell *what* the hostile summoners were bringing in, but I knew they were summoning it in directly above us. I didn't have time to think. I remembered being in the van, on the pad, the explosives underneath. I remembered how I felt then. I remembered *what I could do*.

My tattoos began to come alight in their whorl patterns, and I fractured my Sense. I used it to grab five of the soldiers near me. Then like the Lacerfelis, like before with my colleagues in the van, blinked us backward.

As I did, I felt my grip falter. Five had been too many. I lost the farthest one from me. I felt him slip from my grasp as I moved. My head pounded and spots swam before my eyes as I tried desperately to cling to him, but to no avail.

I saved four. I did *not* save five.

Four weapons clattered to the ground where the soldiers had stood.

The fifth turned toward me at the sound, startled. I saw his face then; young. Scared. In another life, perhaps I'd have said handsome. He'd grown a bit of peach fuzz, in an attempt at a beard. I couldn't see his hair for the helmet, but he had these light green eyes that stared about him in bewilderment.

I'll never forget that face. I was looking straight in his eyes when a wave of flaming napalm doused him and the position I'd just vacated.

"Piss and *shit!*" I ran towards him as he burned and screamed, using my Sense to move the flaming gel out of my path. Once I Sensed him, I did the same for him, removing all the napalm from his charred skin.

What remained lived. I wondered if he wanted to.

I pulled one of the tags from under my vest. *Blood* was actually not difficult to find, and I swiped some across the rune and quickly summoned in my nursing-class bag from home. I fished out gauze, then looked to the four soldiers I'd saved.

"I'm a little busy," I said. "Wrap him, and get him the hell out of here. Keep his wounds as clean as you can." I paused after handing it off, looking at the still screaming man, then shook my head. I could do more elsewhere.

I grabbed a second to look up and down the line. At the far end, where Robert had been, no napalm had landed at all. Instead, it had all been piled neatly, forty feet down a side alley. Slick—sometimes I envied Robert that extra twenty feet of Sense range.

At the center of the line sat a pair of pillars topped by a concrete roof that reminded me of a wide, squat Stonehenge. A pool of napalm merrily burned on its roof. Crowded underneath stood Thad and another group of soldiers.

But three others had been caught without a shelter. Their screams had stopped, but their charred corpses continued to blaze.

Out of the side streets, flanked by her summoners, stepped a woman I recognized. The small, bird-like figure of Analisa Miller surveyed the damage she'd done—or failed to do—with that napalm attack and shook her head. She and each of her summoners had a magnetic rune-board strapped to one arm—the sort of board I'd only seen Robert's mentor, Grace, using before this. Behind her, Rick and the Lacerfelis continued to duel—she ignored them.

"Ms. Miller," said Thad in that calm voice of his. "As you can see, these soldiers are under our protection. I suggest that you call this one a loss and retreat."

Miller placed her hands on her hips, staring at Thad with a haughty, aloof expression. She had the tidy, reserved appearance you'd expect from a Grove Historian— it contrasted so heavily with the burning smell of flesh and gasoline, the screams of the injured, and the great battle of monsters behind her that I had to give a humorous little laugh.

"Your presence here," she said to Thad in a condescending voice, "will only slow the military's inevitable defeat. Are you sure you want to take up arms against your own kind?"

"*Own kind?*" yelled Robert, echoing her. "Any group that can back Cythymau with this sort of attack isn't *my kind.*"

"Oh?" asked Miller. "Interesting. I seem to remember you doing just that in Airway Heights last fall. Regardless."

"Where is he?" I asked, raising my voice just loud enough to be heard over the crashing contest between Rick and the cat-demon behind Miller.

"Cythymau?" asked Miller. "What makes you think he'd be needed for something like *this?* No, he's got bigger things on his mind. Saving the world for summoners, that sort of thing. We needn't fight, though. The federal forces are clearly our common enemy."

The soldiers looked to us. We'd saved them, but they *did* have orders to engage us, too, and we all knew it.

"Fuck you," said Robert.

"Just like your mentor," said Analisa. "She had problems toeing the line, too. We never should have let her apprentice you."

Robert scoffed and pointed at the magnetic boards. "Seems like you've learned *something* from her yourself," he said.

Just then, a mighty *woomph* sounded from Rick. He'd managed to catch the Lacerfelis in one of his blasts, and the cat-lizard sailed upward in an arc, over us. A second later, a second *woomph* sounded, and Rick leapt to follow, one Visitor pursuing another in a smooth sweep over our heads.

Lacerfelis, unlike the cats they resemble, apparently *do not* always land on their feet. This one struck Higgins Avenue behind our position, bounced, rolled, and then came skidding to a stop. Everyone turned. *Everyone* stared at this spectacle.

Except, apparently, one person.

In that silence between the Lacerfelis crashing to the ground and Rick pouncing on top, six gunshots rang out. I turned toward the sound. Rick's *woomph* ringing in my ears from behind me, I saw Thad, carbine raised to the firing position, pointing at the hostile summoners. He'd taken advantage of the distraction Rick provided.

Miller herself now stood behind a stone pillar with a single bullet-hole in it. Miller's summoners all fell, hit by Thad's warded bullets.

"Lorents," said Thad calmly. "I leave Ms. Miller to you. I will deal with the other summoners. Andrea, you take defense. Protect these soldiers."

Robert and I both nodded, and Thad launched himself into a side street. On the radio, Matt began to chatter in our ears, guiding Thad to his position. Robert slowly strode towards his intended victim, bringing Miller into range of that massive Sense.

I turned my attention to the soldiers. "All right—I need you all to back the hell up. Grab your wounded and fall back. Go down Higgins to the Missoula Grove HQ."

I glanced at the battle between Rick and the Lacerfelis—Rick had landed atop the cat-lizard. The big Cornuprocyon began launching *woomph* after *woomph* against his foe, battering it into the ground. Good—that bit looked just about wrapped up.

I paid Robert no attention—one-on-one, it was hard to imagine *any* summoner getting the better of that massive strength of his. Instead, I shepherded these troops that I hated to safety, clearing them away from the barricades. From an alley to the west, the final group of summoners emerged and began to make some adjustments on their boards.

Piss. Piss and shit.

"Down!" I shouted at the soldiers.

"Covering fire!" one of them responded, and they sent a wave of bullets down the alley. Two of the summoners stopped fiddling with their boards and looked up. They must have Sense-deflected the bullets, because none hit, but the remainder each managed to pull a single RPG out of thin air. They pointed them at me and fired.

I didn't try to deflect them—these weapons had to be warded. Instead, I raised both my hands, runes on my bracelet already blooded. I forced a chunk of the pavement in between the rockets and me up, summoning it into the path of the explosive projectiles.

The resulting blast looked almost pretty. I could Sense the eyes of the soldiers around me widen, fixing on me, but I had no time. Using my Sense, I snagged two of their standard-issue knives. Then I focused toward the new group of summoners. My tattoo whorls began to glow, and I blinked myself forward.

Right into the middle of them.

Guns, I don't know how to use. A knife, though, is a simple tool. It would be no use summoning against these people; they had five Senses to counter my one. If it was something they expected.

But when I suddenly appeared in their midst and physically buried those knives into first one's chest, then another ... the odds cleared up a bit. I remembered the Lacerfelis dodging Rick, and blinked out of the way just as the third raised her gun at me. Now behind her, I casually sunk my knife into her neck, then used her body as a shield as the other two opened fire with their own pistols.

I freed my knife from the corpse's neck, then hurled both blades at my final two opponents.

Let me be clear here. I can *stab* someone with a knife just fine. *Throwing* a knife, especially one not built for throwing, is a whole different skill. I had slim hope of doing any damage with those knives —but my enemies didn't know that.

So they used their Senses to deflect the blades. Which left a momentary gap in their defense against my Sense—a gap I was counting on. In an instant, I wrenched their hearts out onto the sidewalk, and they collapsed to the ground like puppets whose strings had been cut.

I didn't bother to retrieve the knives, just calmly walked back to the assembled soldiers, my own military uniform coated in blood. Their mouths hung agog. I bit my lip, looking aside—the weariness of using my Sense, of summoning so much so quickly, had begun to set in behind my temples, and I couldn't take the pressure of their attention.

Over by the River, Rick continued to pummel the Lacerfelis with blast after blast. I suspected that the giant cat-lizard had long since expired, but that didn't stop Rick from worrying at it like a dog with a dead squirrel.

Down Higgins Avenue, Thad emerged from his own side-street, looking much calmer than me and with pristinely clean clothes to boot. Show off.

As for Robert, I really can't say how that duel went, except that when I emerged from the alley, Analisa Miller— the one surviving opponent we had— knelt on the ground. She had her hands behind her head, fingers interlaced, but still glared up at Robert with that haughty stare of hers.

"I surrender," she said icily.

Robert hesitated. I'd killed in cold blood, before, but he hadn't. Hot blood, sure. Robert was about as hot-blooded as they come. But never like this. Never after someone surrendered, already helpless. He stepped forward to help her up. She grinned.

Her hand flashed under her jacket, but she never got farther than that.

A single shot barked. The bullet made a small wound entering one side of Miller's head, and a much more dramatic one blowing out the side of her skull on the other. Her form crumpled to the ground, and a knife skidded across the pavement.

A knife coated in whorl-like symbols.

Robert stared at Thad.

Thad shrugged. "No prisoners," he said. "Got nowhere to put them, and no way to neutralize them when we need to move."

Robert continued to gawk at him, stunned.

I stepped over to the ancient stone knife and quietly collected it as those two engaged in their umpteenth testosterone-measuring contest. If this was what I thought it was, no reason to share it with anyone. Not yet.

The scars etched into my skin throbbed. We didn't need any more of Cythymau's tools out in the world.

Not until I knew more myself.

ROBERT

I'D KILLED BEFORE.

They say it's an experience that changes you, and they're almost right. Taking a life in the heat of battle is a terrifying and exhilarating thing. I'd had nightmares, in the months following, of the absolute carnage I'd wrought during my escape attempt from Airway Heights. I'd watched myself killing men who'd tortured me, and wondered if there wasn't a better, more peaceful way for me to have done it.

I still think about the raw fury of that moment ... and the disgust and despair that followed it. Not because it changed me; because I realized something that had always been in me. In all of us, if I had to guess. That wild bit of us that, left unchecked, would happily club Urug to death for hunting territory. I don't think killing someone changed me—I think it gave me a view on the deepest, darkest layer of what I always was. It's on me if I don't like what I see there.

Even after, when I'd committed to fighting Cythymau, I'd known that this primal rage would have to be tapped once more. It's the only part of us that allows us to take the life of another—or so I thought.

Watching Thad kill Analisa Miller, on the other hand, changed me. Because he *did not care.* There was no dark fury, no emotional drive. No buildup to the moment. He'd executed her in an offhand manner that suggested he'd performed nothing more than a simple chore—and I *did not comprehend* the mental state one had to be in to do that.

And I remembered the moment where he'd tried to do the same to me.

I ... didn't complain. Didn't even object. All of these things blurred through my mind in a split second. It took me only a moment to recover my composure and nod to Thad. He'd done what was necessary ... which is all he ever tried to do. I revised my estimate of how dangerous—and how useful—Thaddeus Nielsen truly was.

"Um," said Andrea, next to me.

Thad and I turned to see Captain Sonia Tomas-Padilla approaching us with a contingent of her men, guns raised. Once again, they stopped shy of the forty-foot mark—keeping themselves out of my Sense-range.

This time, however, things went a *bit* differently. Because Andrea, Thad, and I were accompanied by a recently-triumphant Cornuprocyon, who landed with one of his trademark *whoomphs* directly *behind* the good Captain.

Captain Tomas-Padilla and her men were well-trained. They *had* to feel fear, but they spun with viperish speed and immediately began unloading their clips into Rick.

Rick ... just looked to me. He cocked his head to the side like a confused dog, his expression clearly telling everyone that he simply didn't understand what was happening. The bullets ... those had about as much effect on his armored hide as they'd always had. Rick had survived onslaughts of *much* heavier fire than this—a certain incident involving Grace and a mounted GAU-8 Avenger Cannon sprung to mind—and all the fury of this elite company of soldiers came across as a mild irritant at best.

Once the clips had run dry, I simply said "Down, boy," which prompted Rick to sit down on his haunches, tongue lolled out to the side and tail wagging. Granted, his tail crashed loudly into a small Hyundai and sent it rolling across the street, but without harming anyone.

I winced as the Hyundai shattered the plate glass window of the store front across the street and ended up upside-down in the middle of a small boutique. As I've said, an *excited* Corunprocyon is only slightly less dangerous than an *enraged* one. Still, nobody was getting hurt, and the property damage paled in comparison to what we'd already wreaked on the streets of Missoula.

The captain turned to look at me with a shocked expression on her face. "He's the one from the mall," she said. "And the freeway, with the soldiers ....you summoned him? We always pegged that to Moore. We figured she'd sent him to rescue you from the jail in Spokane, as well."

I shook my head. "It's more complicated than that," I said. "Much, much more complicated. Neither Grace nor I summoned him back in the beginning—but I'd love to tell you the full story."

"I'd love that too," said the captain in all her militant formalism. "I take it you're surrendering, then? Getting you into an interrogation room—again—would be quite the coup for me."

"Not surrendering," said Thad, stepping in front of me. I let him —Thad was far better positioned than I to negotiate, and likely more skilled at it. "But ... well, there's a nice little café over there, and we appear not to have destroyed it yet. How about we all put down our weapons and go get a cup of coffee together, have a little chat?"

Captain Tomas-Padilla snorted in derision. "You don't seem to understand," she said. "You're covered. There's us, yes, but you don't think we rolled into this with just our small arms, do you? I could call down the fire on you any time I wanted to."

"Heh," sounded Matt's voice in my earbud.

Before Thad, Andrea, or I could respond to that—before Captain Tomas-Padilla could make whatever futile demand she wanted to from us—one MQ-9 Reaper Drone crashed into the Clark Fork River. Matt managed to fly the thing so it dipped a wingtip into the water just downstream of the bridge, sending it cartwheeling down the straight-open stretch of river in an impressive display.

The captain wheeled around, watching sixty-four million taxpayer dollars destroy themselves with her jaw hanging. Her reaction fortunately caused her to look away from the three of *us,* which allowed *our* jaws to recover their normal places before she turned to look back.

"So," Thad asked in a nonchalant voice that I couldn't help but respect after the sheer destructiveness of that display. "Coffee?"

THE MILITARY HAD ALREADY CLEARED the inside of the small café that had, as of dawn this morning, been the headquarters of the Missoula Grove. I tried not to think of it as betraying those summoners while Andrea and I slipped behind the counter to prepare fresh coffee for the people that had murdered them. Outside, medics scurried about, collecting and treating the wounded.

The place did have an espresso machine—a massive device with all kinds of knobs and buttons and turny bits. I'm pretty sure that, prior to being murdered by our new potential allies, the summoners who'd been here could make delicious caffeinated beverages with the monstrosity.

Andrea and I stared at it for half a second, then turned back to look at the massive stainless-steel urn coffee maker instead. *That* seemed a lot more manageable.

We didn't talk. Andrea filled the thing with water, I found the filters and the grounds and got that bit assembled, then we stood at the counter and watched as Captain Sonia Tomas-Padilla and Assistant Director Thaddeus Nielsen sat on opposite sides of a small table.

Neither of these leaders saw fit to begin speaking. They simply stared at each other. The only sounds that punctuated the silent tension in the room came from outside, where Tomas-Padilla's unit had begun the cleanup, and the rather loud percolations of the massive urn. To kill time, I scrounged through the kitchen and discovered a small stockpile of some recently-baked Danishes, which I immediately found some small plates for. When I returned, Andrea had begun pulling mugs of deep, black coffee out of the urn.

Andrea set one mug and a plate before Nielsen, and I did the same before Tomas-Padilla. Then the two of us retreated back behind the counter, as though that were our proper place, and let the two leaders deal with each other.

"All right," said the captain, raising her coffee to her lips and taking a sip without bothering about either cream or sugar. "Talk, then."

"Before I begin," said Thad, "I feel the need to tell you a couple of things. This isn't a stall tactic on our part—we've no help coming, and if we wanted you dead, we would simply attack. It isn't a stall tactic on *your* part either—or at least it isn't going to be a successful one. As far as the world outside Missoula is concerned, for the moment, you've had a very successful mission. Yes, I'm aware of your transmissions for help—I'm also aware that they never reached their recipients. We are both on our own, for the moment. There's no sense pretending otherwise."

"Impossible," said Tomas-Padilla. "Our communication system is unhackable."

"As," said Thad with a little grin, "unhackable as the control links for an MQ-9 Reaper, I believe. Though 'hack' is word that implies a purely technical angle. We have certain advantages that you simply do not."

"Magic," said the captain in a venom-filled voice.

"Yes," said Thad politely. "Magic. Now, as I was saying—it's just us, here. Just me and you. So let me get something else on the table. We —especially young Robert over there—have killed your fellow soldiers in the past. You may have even known some of the people who've died fighting us. Not summoners in general—us. In particular."

The captain's face set into stone as Thad said this, and her eyes looked like they could drill right through the man.

Thad had that way with people, sometimes.

"Ah," he said in a soft tone. "I see that you did. I'm not going to apologize for doing what I believe was necessary—and I don't believe Mr. Lorents will, either. However—I will say this. I had two cousins in the Missoula Grove. I had friends in the Missoula Grove. This morning—just before we arrived, in fact—you and your soldiers killed a great many people that I've known personally on some level or another. You killed my friends. You killed my family."

Thad paused to let that sink in—and the commander's eyes widened slightly.

"If I were to act on how I felt about that," said Thad in an icy voice, "you and everyone here wearing that uniform of yours would die a very slow and torturous death." He punctuated that statement by taking a long sip of his own black coffee.

The soldiers at the far end of the café began to raise their weapons. I, in response, brought my Sense back up. Beside me I felt Andrea tensing. Outside, Rick uttered a low growl as he felt the emotions rippling off both of us.

Thad raised a warning hand to me and, after a moment, Tomas-Padilla did the same to her troops.

"I don't propose forgiveness," said Thad. "I don't think either of us is in a place where it'd be genuine even if I did. What I propose, however, is a mutual acknowledgement that *both* of our issues with one another were caused by a third party. And dealing with *him* is far, far more important than turning on each other. That is why we are not attacking you, despite all you've done to our people. It is why we came here today—to save you from the attack you just witnessed."

Tomas-Padilla heard all of this with that same stony look on her face.

"Talk," she said calmly. "I can't tell you I believe you. I can't even tell you that I *want* to believe you. But tell me about this threat you believe exists. The information you give me will make it into my report— assuming we all walk away from this."

"That," said Thad, "is our goal."

I'LL ADMIT IT. I thought the whole idea of the coffee a bit frivolous when Thad suggested it. I'd gone along with it because of how shockingly nonchalant it made us seem. It had driven the idea home that we were on nothing more important than a leisurely morning jaunt. Serving coffee seemed, to me, to be something of an exclamation point on the power we had over the military.

I've been accused of several things over the years. *Subtlety* isn't one of them. Watching Thad and Tomas-Padilla talk, though, a second reason for the little impromptu brunch began to dawn on me.

It is impossible to partake of refreshment with another human being and not, on some level, feel at least some basic connection. In the old Urug-and-Urog days, I supposed, anyone you were willing to actually share your bit of mammoth with *had* to be someone you liked. Part of your tribe. Through the years, that evolved into a complicated set of rules—all really intense nerds like myself knew about the old laws surrounding hospitality and breaking bread under a roof.

The same instincts that caused mankind to make those rules in the first place kicked in as Thad explained what we knew of Cythymau. He began with all of Grace's reports concerning her initial trip to Spokane and went right on through—even acknowledging the point at which he'd tried to kill me. And as he did, he and Captain Tomas-Padilla continued to work their way into their coffee cups. Eventually, they began eating their Danishes together. By the time the Battle of Airway Heights came up, we'd refilled their cups, and the captain had asked some follow-up questions, clearly engaging with the subject matter.

I won't say that the two of them exited the conversation as *friends*. That'd be pushing it far beyond what happened. But Thad's level of transparency, his willingness to admit his own shortcomings (and, in several places, provide a rather pointed reference to my own), and the act of breaking bread had Captain Tomas-Padilla at least interested.

"So," she said at the end, "you summoners are in the midst of a civil war. One group of you wants things to be as they always have— operating in the shadows, keeping things quiet. The other wants to use your magics to assert dominance over the rest of us, and are led by a demon from another dimension who may or may not be simply trying to end life as we know it."

"That," said Thad, "is as succinct a summation of the issue as I've heard. Though I'd add that this demon is using you, and your troops, to provoke summoners to his side—and to kill the ones that won't join. Summoners like, for instance, the ones that called this little café home."

"And you're proposing ... what, exactly? What did you hope to gain from this little tête-à-tête?" asked the captain.

"Allies," said Thad succinctly. "Failing that, neutrality on the part of normal citizens. But seeing as Cythymau's stated goal is your enslavement, I really think it's in your best interest to work with us."

"Won't work," said Tomas-Padilla. "Can't work. Can't go back to the way things were. There's a war on, and you're looking to be allies. But you're asking the official government of the United States to throw in with criminals."

"Yes," said Thad. "I am. Of course, as there won't *be* a United States if it doesn't, perhaps that government can be persuaded to accept the lesser of what it considers two evils."

"I—" said the captain, shaking her head. "I don't know. And it's a decision far, far above my pay grade. All I'm going to do is put all this in a report and let one of the paper-pushers make the call."

"And what," said Thad in that same, pleasant, nonchalant tone I'd come to identify as being very dangerous, coming from him, "do you think the chances are that any of those paper-pushers takes that report terribly seriously?"

Tomas-Padilla barked a little laugh of someone caught out, and leaned back in her chair. "Honestly?" she said. "I think it's more likely that I get demoted, or at least transferred. Then somebody takes my report and puts it under the nearest carpet. What you're talking about —the kind of change in thinking it would take—bureaucracies don't work like that anymore."

Thad drained the last dregs of his cup and looked at me, giving the thing a little shaking motion. Arrogant bastard—but I didn't have much choice. I filled a fresh cup, went to the table, swapping out his empty mug, and gave an inquisitive look at the captain, who simply put a hand over hers in the time-honored gesture of diner customers who do not wish a warmer. I nodded and began to walk back to the counter—which is why my back was toward Thad when he said, "Then I guess we'll need something a bit more substantial to get their attention."

Once again, the air in this little café—this memoriam to the violence spawned between mundane and magic—began to hum with the tension between the two forces. Was Thad planning on throwing down after all? I stood on the knife's-edge, ready to take my battle-weary self to the final conclusion at last.

"Which is why I'd better go with you," Thad said.

From behind the counter, I heard the crash of Andrea's mug falling and hitting the floor. For myself, I could only turn and stare aghast at Thad's suggestion. And over my earbuds, I heard Matt's spluttering voice asking, "Did ... did he just ...."

"Nielsen," I said. I tried to imitate his calm nonchalance, but I'm pretty sure I failed in achieving Thad's flair. "What are you talking about?"

"It's simple, Robert. There are people who need to be convinced. I should go convince them. The good captain here can make introductions and assure people that she is only alive because of what we did—that should at least buy me a little goodwill."

"Thad," I said. "You don't know. What it's like, in their hands. The torture ... "

"Would be very stupid on their part," he said. "I don't think the captain here would be so inclined. Despite her bluster, I'm pretty sure she takes a life-debt sort of seriously. I've no doubt she realizes how bad things would have gone for her, absent us. Her superiors may have other opinions, though—but it's the only chance we have, in the long run."

"Thad?" said Andrea from behind the counter in a forlorn little voice. "Stuffy?"

"Don't fight this—either of you," Thad said in his most imperious voice. A miscalculation; nothing made me want to fight him *more* than him giving me a direct order, but I stuffed all that down.

"You're surrendering, then?" asked Captain Sonia Tomas-Padilla.

"No," said Thad. "I am accompanying you. I won't be bound. I won't be drugged. Try it, and you'll probably end up killing me, but a lot of other people will die first. In return, I give you my pledge that I shall work no ill upon you or yours so long as no harm is intended towards me or mine."

"And how do I know that this isn't some ploy to infiltrate us and assassinate people up the food chain from me?"

"Because," said Thad calmly, "assassination is frightfully easy where you mundanes are concerned. I assure you, all we'd have to do to assassinate anyone we chose to would be to simply locate their mug of coffee and summon a little cyanide into it, problem solved."

Tomas-Padilla looked down at her mug in shock.

"No," said Thad. "You're fine. My point is simply this—we don't need to get close to assassinate. This would be a stupid and cumbersome way of doing it. That's how you know."

"Ah," said the captain. "Well then. Mount up, Mr. Nielsen. I'm not sure about much here, but I am sure about this: there are *definitely* people who will want to talk to you. I just can't guarantee they'll be gentle."

"That," said Thad, "would be rather a mistake on their part. But lead on, good captain. A brave new world awaits."

ANDREA

THE MORNING after we made it back home, I flopped onto the couch in the Shelton headquarters' small living room. Staring up at the ceiling, I folded my hands behind my head and pondered the current situation.

The return to Shelton had been rather anticlimactic, after Thad's bold decision to stay behind. I still couldn't "take down" my Sense, whatever that really meant. We'd had to use back roads, taking less-travelled, windy, twisty, narrow roads that bypassed any possible check points.

The preparations Amy and Francene had made for refugees remained unused—we'd returned with one less person and the prospect of a ceasefire instead of refugees.

Phineas and Robert clattered down the stairs together, and I shook myself out of my thoughts. No doubt they had been getting the latest update on the situation from Matt.

"I'll be back," Phineas said. "Try to lay low, okay, Lorents? I keep expecting to see a new BOLO with your or Andrea's face on it."

"BOLO, hell," Matt said, striding into the room with a laptop open in his hands. "Take a look at this." He turned the TV on, then fiddled with something until a blown-up picture of the front page of a newspaper appeared.

Robert whistled, and my mouth dropped open.

The headline blared, **SUMMONERS TO THE RESCUE?** And underneath that sat a massive black and white photo. A photo that immediately made my stomach sink down into my knees.

It depicted a few soldiers in the foreground, a girl in military gear standing with her back to them, hands raised, and a jagged wall of what obviously had recently been roadway risen in front of her, fire exploding outward around its edges.

Matt grinned at me. "Turns out that brick building right after the bridge was a newspaper office." He fiddled with his laptop again and a newscast popped up next.

"Breaking news," the anchor said, "a military operation in Missoula, Montana, close to the University of Montana campus, apparently went south on Tuesday." In the background, they started cycling through images of the destruction on Higgins. The newscaster continued, "It appears a simple strike against known reality terrorists turned into a full-out sorcerous battle that raged for blocks and destroyed much of Missoula's Higgins Ave. Our reporter on scene has more."

"That's right, Tim," the reporter said. "As you can see behind me, the damage to the bridge leading into Missoula is quite extensive. We haven't managed to gain access to the area where we believe the attack was centered—the military still has that scene under wraps. A bigger surprise came after talking with witnesses who had to shelter in place inside their businesses during the whole pitched battle. According to those eyewitnesses, the military would have been defeated— possibly annihilated—had they not received some very unexpected assistance. We were able to obtain some examples from the Missoulian, whose staff were also sheltering in place on scene during the incident. I believe you should be able to see those on screen now."

A full-color slide show of images started scrolling past. Rick shoulder-blocking the cat-lizard away from soldiers, Rick and the

Lacerfelis wrestling, a group of soldiers standing under the fat, Stonehenge structure Thad had built, napalm still burning on top.

Then the one that made me cringe again. This time in color. Black smoke and orange-yellow flame billowing out from the torn edge of the pavement, echoing the copper of my hair and the black Kevlar. My hands raised in stark contrast against all the chaos. The soldiers even more discernable in the foreground.

Robert gave a low whistle.

It was, no doubt, a prize-winning photo. Whoever had taken it captured the moment perfectly. That asshole.

Back at the news desk, the anchor said, "What exactly are these pictures showing us according to the—"

I groaned and jumped up, pushing past Matt to turn off the TV.

"No more," I told him. "I can't."

"How does it feel to be famous?" Matt asked, smirking.

"Horrible," I answered. "I don't need any of this."

"Really?" Matt said, "Because this is amazing." He chuckled at the face of distaste that I made, then continued. "Do you know what an opportunity this is? I've got to keep monitoring it, but with this, we have a real possibility of getting our own spin out there and making it go viral."

Phineas stared at Matt, an arrested expression on his face that I couldn't quite read. "Yes. Keep tabs on that situation, Matt. Try to push it in the right direction if you can. Do you have anything else you can send them to help with that?" Phineas asked.

"Hell yes, I've got drone footage and body cams," Matt said. "I'm sure I can find a good selection to send out anonymously to various news sources. Let me get on that." He closed his laptop and headed back up the stairs.

Phineas nodded and rubbed his chin thoughtfully. "This could actually be very good. It does give me some other matters to attend to now, though. You two stay here and stay safe. We don't need to kick up any more dust right now."

Phineas waved at me and Robert and headed out the front door.

Speaking of safety, for myself and everyone around me, I still had an eye I needed to be able to shut. "Hey Robert," I said, sitting up and looking at him over the back of the couch. "What does it feel like to drop your Sense? How do you do it?" I asked.

Robert glanced in my direction, then paused. "Uh," he said, his voice uncertain, "I have to focus to bring it up in the first place, so I just stop focusing and it drops on its own. Yours doesn't work like that?" he asked.

I nodded. "I've been trying to remember if I've ever had my Sense down, and what it felt like. But as far as I can remember, it's just always there. An extra ... well, you know ... sense."

"Doesn't that get sort of overwhelming?" Robert asked curiously.

I considered this. It was an honest question, and so I answered it just as honestly. "Of course," I said. "There's times it can be maddening as hell. But when you're tied down to a slab in a room that never changes, that doesn't matter so much."

I sighed, pulling my hair out of my face. "Out here, trying to function like a normal human, there is always so much going on all at once." I could feel frustration creep into my tone as I told him. "Of course it gets overwhelming. And I'm pissed as hell that I'm a walking danger to you, everyone, and everything else we try to do, with those Sense-sniffing dogs. But until I figure this out, there's nothing I can do about any of that."

"What happened at the checkpoint is already done and gone," Robert said, "You should really—"

I held up a hand to stop him. "The point is," I said, deliberately deflecting whatever he'd been about to say about the massacre of the Missoula Grove. "I don't focus to bring it up, and when I tried to manipulate it, roll it up, or stuff it back down—whatever I could to get rid of it—it didn't work."

I looked up at him and met his eyes, the words stuck in my throat for a moment. "I could only change its shape, not its volume. Just doing that got pretty painful, to be honest."

Just speaking about it made me feel more vulnerable, I cleared my throat. Robert waited for me silently, out of patience or shock I really didn't know.

I'd tried so many times not to think about what Cythymau had used me for, but I'd been puzzling at this myself since I'd realized it was a problem. I needed help.

And I could finally admit that now.

I tried to put how I felt into words. "You know how your Sense is like another muscle, an extension of yourself? You can feel where it goes, what it does, know whether you've accomplished what you meant to?"

"Yeah," Robert said. "I do."

"When Cythymau was using it, manipulating it and controlling me, I could still feel that, still Sense everything. I just didn't have command of what that demon did with it. But I *know* what he did. What he accomplished using me, what he said, who he killed."

"That's hella fucked up." Robert said.

I laughed humorlessly. "You're telling me. Cythymau even told me why it was all justified with that twisted logic of his. All that blood, death, and agony, even that logic, is steeped into me." I sighed, feeling exhausted, helpless. "I don't even know if having my Sense constantly active is normal, or just a kind of hyper-vigilance on my part, or something that I've just plain forgotten how to undo."

I looked at my hands, holding them in front of my face with a grimace. Blood-soaked hands. "I did all those things. I didn't choose to, but I did. And though I hate to admit it, killing still comes easier to me than it should."

"Hey," Robert said, "I was there when we freed you, and you sure as hell did not want to be there. You wanted to be freed from Cythymau."

"Yeah, so I could try to kill him. And give him back just some of what he'd made me do. Which is kind of my point. Even *that* I failed at, spectacularly," I said flatly.

"Stop being so hard on yourself," Robert said. "It's not like you're the only one in this room who's made some questionable decisions. It's easy to get down on yourself in hindsight." He paused, appearing to think over everything I'd just said. "So this issue with your Sense, was it like this before Cythymau captured you?"

I shrugged. "To be honest, I don't remember the time before he captured me all that well. In what I can remember, I couldn't tell you if it was up or down, or if I even realized then. I know it sounds ridiculous, but I just don't *know*." I blew out an explosive breath of frustration and flailed my hands at Robert for emphasis. "Apparently everyone else can turn off this hyperawareness of everything and everyone around them at will, but I can't. I'm already defective and I don't want everyone in more danger than we're already in. If we run across another checkpoint ... or more of these Sense-sniffing dogs ... I suppose I could split off by myself. That would—"

"Absolutely not be ok." Robert said firmly. "Your Sense is pretty big isn't it? About half mine?"

"I suppose so," I said. "It's about twenty feet or so?"

"For me, and most summoners, they must concentrate to see the oneness of everything that makes up our reality. Maybe what you should try instead, Andrea, is to focus on the part of the Weave that's just you. Narrow yourself down to the boundaries of your own body, and try to shut out anything that's not you."

I closed my eyes and turned my Sense inward. I could feel the blood flowing through my veins, my heart pumping, the rush of the air in my lungs.

The couch I sat on, the TV across from me, and Robert all became more distant, but they didn't go away.

I still knew exactly where they were. If anything, focusing my Sense inward like this just reminded me of being strapped to the slab with nothing to distract me from Cythymau's cruelty except my own heartbeat and breathing.

With that thought, I started hyperventilating, breaking into a cold sweat . Panicking, I tried to stop Sensing anything, to close my Sense like slamming a door. A spike of pain tore through my head, and my vocal cords vibrated with a groan.

Robert came closer, reaching out to grab at my shoulder. "Andrea! Andrea, we'll just have to take our chances with any dogs or checkpoints. It not like we can't plan around them. This isn't worth it. Stop hurting yourself."

I shrugged it away with a shooing gesture that I was okay.

"Sorry," I mumbled, rubbing at my throbbing temples. "It didn't work. And I thought about Cythymau instead. Maybe next time, if I don't—"

"I think that was enough of an experiment for tonight," Robert said. "I'll ask the others and see if anyone's ever heard of similar problems. Or you can ask them."

"No, I'd appreciate the help," I said, surprising myself by meaning it. Just talking about it with him was difficult enough.

"If I find anything useful, I'll let you know." Robert paused, his face thoughtful. I gave him a weak smile. At least my ringing headache gave me something new to concentrate on as I pretended I didn't want to cry.

"So what do we do now?" I asked him. "What if we find ourselves in another situation like Missoula again?"

"Honestly?" Robert said, "We probably do it again, and hope we get better results with everything we've learned. Or we don't. But either way, right now we wait."

~

AND WAIT WE DID. For months.

The days in Shelton steadied into placid sameness, the true backwater eddy of a small town. The war between the two factions of summoners and the military raged on around us, but didn't really impact our daily lives that much. Sure, Matt and Phineas pored over every piece of intelligence they could get their hands on, and Thad sent regular updates. A kind of proof of life, I guessed, but I wasn't really part of that.

I attended classes at the college with Robert and tried to avoid people. Most days I more or less succeeded. I did attend one college party that the still-overly-friendly Miranda Klein badgered me into. That's where I discovered that cheap beer, horny twenty-somethings, and an ever-active Sense don't mix. I now knew a sickening amount about several of my classmates and their erotic prowess or lack thereof. Not shockingly, I left early.

But I tried to be more social. And I thought maybe I was getting better at it, ever so slowly.

As the days stacked up waiting for news, I also played force ball with Rick. Much as hated to admit it, the rambunctious racoon spirit was growing on me, much as he had Robert. So I played with the Visitor and stole time whenever I could to study the scrolls and artifacts I'd hidden away from Cythymau's Weave. It made me feel like I'd turned into a paranoid hoarder, careful not to expose any of the items outside of my wards.

I can't say Robert or I *missed* having Thad around, with his arrogant attitude. I certainly didn't miss his constant pestering for clues about Cythymau. I'd absolutely dreaded the interrogation that loomed about my tattoos after returning from Missoula. But instead, he'd made himself the government's hostage. I had to credit Thad where it was due—he'd proven more than once that he took protecting our small Grove very seriously.

But the fact that he'd voluntarily given himself over to the killers of the Missoula Grove just didn't sit well with me.

I'd originally given myself over to Cythymau thinking I was protecting people precious to me, too.

Turning himself over to the Feds didn't exactly carry the same type of risks as accepting a contract with a powerful demon ... but still.

I understood what he had attempted to do, but all my hard-won instincts screamed that he'd just walked into a trap that would be difficult to escape. I could never step into that kind of situation with eyes wide open like he had.

While we waited, I ended up finishing out my first year at the community college. Then the hot summer months passed in a sticky haze, until we headed back into the fall. Leaves began to change colors and the weather turned to rain and cold blustery days that smelled of wood smoke and wind through pines. My second year as a student started, but Thad still did not return.

I kicked off my shoes as I came back through the door after attending classes. Despite my attempts to fly under the radar, I was gaining a reputation at the college for being the loner. The girl who almost never went out to parties or social events, and slunk out of class as soon as it ended. I sighed.

Matt stuck his head out from the dining room, checking who had come home. "Andrea, now that you're back, I need to talk to everyone," he said.

I walked over and quirked an eyebrow, surveying the room. Francene and Amy sat at the dining table, Robert reclined in an armchair, Matt walked over to the foot of the table facing the three of them, and Phineas pulled up another chair at the table. I trundled past in my stocking feet and took the other armchair. It was as far as I could get from most of the people while still remaining part of whatever discussion was about to be inflicted on me. Whatever necessitated this, I doubted it'd be anything good.

Matt cleared his throat. "As you all know, Director Nielsen has been sending me regular dispatches since he's been with the Feds."

I nodded, waiting.

Matt fidgeted a bit and then took a deep breath and continued, "His communications suddenly stopped last week, and there's been no response to any of the checks I've sent him *this* week either."

"So we haven't heard from him for two weeks?" Amy asked, her lips pulling down in a frown. "Why are you just telling us this now?"

Matt nodded in the affirmative. "I've had gaps in communication before, but none that have gone on this long. I'm starting to get concerned."

"If it was anyone else," Phineas said, "I'd suspect some kind of foul play, possibly to draw us out, but Director Nielsen is a formidable summoner that voluntarily went into this situation. I'm sure he thought through just about everything they could possibly do to him before he set foot inside that door. I think it's unlikely that the Feds have the ability to completely stop him from warning us if his plan went totally south."

I raised my brows skeptically. I wasn't sure if I believed that. Thad was highly trained, and lethal when the situation required, but it wasn't like he was some all-powerful god of summoning. Robert, if he could ever get over his clumsiness with runes, was much closer to that. And Robert had been—

"I've been in fed holding cells before, and I've participated in plans that went south both with and without Thad in the mix," Robert said. "If they dosed him up on those hallucinogens or other anti-summoning drugs without his knowledge, I'm not so sure what might happen. Thad is one tough bastard; I absolutely agree on your assessment about that. But he could still be in big trouble."

"Let's think this through," Phineas said. "If his negotiations fell apart and the Feds have used interrogation drugs on him—which I think almost certainly they would have, or they wouldn't be able to verify his version of events—they probably already know everything about us and this place."

Amy raised a hand, waving it to get everyone's attention. "If that's true, shouldn't we be working to evacuate this place as soon as possible? Aren't we just a bunch of sitting ducks here? And, I mean, even if the director is in trouble, it'd take storming a military installation to get him out. I think it's more likely that any rescue turns into a suicide mission. After Robert's jailbreak last time, and everything they've learned from Nielsen, they'll be even more prepared for anything we can throw at them."

Francene spoke up. "I, at least, am absolutely against anyone trying to 'storm' a military installation. Especially not my son. We have already seen how that turns out. There have *already* been too many sacrifices made, and I can't believe any good would come of it. I think Mr. Nielsen, were he here, would agree with that."

Matt spoke up, cutting off more conversation in this vein. "The good news—if there is good news in this situation—is that nothing in the military communications I've intercepted so far suggests military resources moving in our direction. We should still get some warning if they split a summoner strike force off to engage us. I just haven't been able to pinpoint the Director's current whereabouts with any accuracy."

"So let's continue to monitor things, and have an evacuation plan in place in case the situation changes suddenly." Phineas said. "Matt, keep trying to find the director. Once we get more reliable intelligence about his current whereabouts, we'll make a decision about moving. Sound good enough?"

There were reluctant nods around the table, and the meeting adjourned, people dispersing to other tasks. No one seemed to notice I did not nod.

I latched onto Robert's elbow and pulled him through the side door into the backyard, so it was just the two of us.

"Are you really okay with this?" I asked Robert. "I mean, Thad's a bit of an obnoxious, nosy, prude sometimes. But if we're going to leave him captive and in trouble, then I don't know—"

"I don't like the guy; he gets under my skin like no one else. But no, I'm not okay with it. Phineas is right; storming a Fed installation is no joke, and we don't even know where he is right now."

I thought about this.

"So," I said slowly, watching Robert for his reaction, "we set a deadline, and we prepare until we get to that date. If we hear from him before then, and he doesn't need a rescue, great."

"I'm following so far," Robert said.

"But if Thad really needs help, I'm not okay leaving him alone. He may have walked in there on his own two feet, but I struck a similar bargain too, once upon a time. We all know how that turned out."

"And we all know what we paid to get you out from there. And what we lost to the Feds to get me out last time. Are you sure saving him is worth it?" Robert asked me, sounding unconvinced.

I glared at him. "Are you trying to say saving me was too expensive? Or that saving Francene wasn't worth it? Or me saving you? None of it had value?"

"No, I wouldn't go that far—"

"Well, I would. It's all stupid risky and too expensive. But I'd still want someone to do it. And I can't believe I'm the one saying this, but we've already paid the price more than thrice over. I hate to admit it, but I'd rescue you again," I said somberly.

Robert barked a laugh at that.

"I'm serious. Maybe even faster this time, since you all insist on including me in your piss-ass-crazy club, despite all the things about me that could be walking time bombs. So what's one more time with our lives on the line, really, for someone willing to step between this Weave and Cythymau's war? To me, it's a rescue worth trying. But going alone really is a suicide mission. So I'm asking, what are your thoughts? Is Thad worth it to you?"

Robert squeezed his eyes shut, groaning. "Fuck no, he's not worth it," he said.

I pressed my lips together, disappointed, angry.

"But we're going to do it anyway. 'Cause that's what we do in this 'piss-ass-crazy club' after all," Robert finished. "November 30th. That's two weeks from now, and almost a full month from when Matt says he lost contact. If we don't hear from Thad by then, we get the best intelligence we can from Matt on his probable location. We go in, hope we survive, and come out with one stick-in-the-mud."

"Deal!" I said, sticking out my hand.

Robert placed his hand in mine, grinning at me. "If we do this, you know he's not going to be grateful, right?"

"Yeah, probably not."

IT BECAME a daily ritual for me the next two weeks. I would get up, get ready for class, then anxiously eat cereal until I or Robert could catch Matt's eye as he wondered through in search of coffee, being more of a night owl.

"Any news?" Robert asked. Matt didn't have to ask *what* news. Like a code, we all knew that "news" only meant contact from Thad. The war still raged, Cythymau still launched his all-out offensive against the military and any moderate summoners, but that was "the situation." Not news.

Then Robert and I would head off to class, where I would pretend to be a normal young adult, not an old crone whose nerves were being wracked to the breaking point while we waited. After classes, I would rush home. And repeat the same questions.

Everyone's expressions got more harried, more pinched, the longer the silence went. We'd never gotten updates from Thad every day, but this had gone beyond concerning to a full blown crisis.

After what felt like much longer than two weeks, we finally approached the promised one-month deadline. Tomorrow, we would take matters into our own hands, since Thad had remained dead silent.

I winced. Poor choice of words.

"Have we heard from Thad yet?" I demanded of Matt for what must have been the fourteenth time that day.

"No, nothing yet." He said simply, and headed back up the stairs. "Nothing has changed from the last time you asked. We know where he was when he went radio-silent, and that's it. Sorry, Andrea."

Robert and I nodded at each other. Okay. We were doing this.

AT DAWN ON NOVEMBER 30TH, I pulled the battle fatigues out of my closet, strapped the Kevlar vest on, and stuffed a rolled sheaf of runetags into the pocket within easy reach of my right hand. I coiled the runed rope I'd created over one shoulder, and clasped my rune bracelet onto my left wrist. I grabbed the duffel of summoning aids and supplies from under my bed and slung it over my other arm.

I met Robert in the living room. He wore similar fatigues with his own duffel slung over one arm, runed silver bracers clapped on each wrist, and an acorn ring I'd never seen before slid over his pinkie finger.

"You ready?" I asked him.

"No, but we're going to do it anyway," he said, giving me a lopsided grin. "After you."

I jerked the door open, and then froze. Thad stood on the stoop, reaching for the doorknob. I stared at him, my mouth dropping open. Robert jostled me from behind, unprepared for my sudden stop. Thad lifted his outstretched hand in a wave, then raised his eyebrows as he took in Robert's and my outfits.

"What are you two doing?" Thad asked suspiciously. "Surely you two aren't idiotic enough to go blow up all my carefully laid groundwork. Is there some terrifying emergency about to engulf us all that I don't know about?"

Robert put one hand on his hip, lowering his other arm to point at Thad dramatically.

"Well, how would you know?" Robert asked, "I mean, you don't call, and you don't write. You just left your mother and I here to wonder whether you were even dead or alive. I mean, what were we supposed to think?"

I turned and punched Robert in the shoulder, then jerked a thumb in his direction. "What he said, but without the parental analogy. Explain yourself, oh, eminently responsible one." I crossed my arms over my chest and glowered at Thad disapprovingly.

"I think you two have been hanging out too much together," Thad said. "And while I am both touched and dismayed that you two would apparently rush headlong to rescue me, what I've been doing while I was out of touch, is getting us a foot in the backdoor with the government. I'm going to need a public place with conference rooms, preferably somewhere that isn't here, for our two delegations to meet and discuss."

"How do you feel about the beach?" Robert asked.

ROBERT

I'D ONLY EVER BEEN to the sea once before.

It's a funny thing, the ocean. I mean, it's just water, right? Same stuff we drink, shower in, flush our waste with. One of the most plentiful substances on the planet. It composes the majority of our own bodies.

And yet somehow, when you put a *lot* of it in the same place, the result can be spectacular.

When I stepped out of the driver's door of what Matt was calling Van 3.0, into the parking lot of a second-rate vacation hotel in Ocean Shores, it all hit me. Past the hotel, the sound of the breakers as they crashed and receded. That clean, salty smell that wafts in off the sea—before you get close enough for the rotting seaweed to take over. All of it hit bits of memory I hadn't even realized were in my brain and took me back to a simpler time.

A time when I knew nothing of magic or demons. A time when I had simply been a child in the tow of two loving, biological parents. And a time when the sea had seemed to me to be the most amazing thing in the world. Building sandcastles with my mother. Playfully helping her bury my father. I must have been ... six? Maybe seven? I couldn't quite tell, and the flood of memories that smell resurrected didn't carry my age back with them.

"Robert?" asked Andrea tentatively from next to me. She'd gotten out of the van after me, as well as Phineas, Matt, and Amy.

"Hmm?" I said, and looked at the blurry outline of Andrea. Quickly, I rubbed away the water that had begun to build in my eye—purely as a reaction from the sea air, of course.

"You all right?" she asked.

"Um…yeah," I lied.

She just stared at me. Damn that Sense of hers. She could probably tell my blood pressure and heartbeat were up or something, and that made lying to her about my emotional state futile. But after a moment —a long enough moment to convey that she *knew* I was full of it and had simply chosen to give me a pass—she looked away.

"I'm ... going to head down to the beach," I said. "Be with you in a second."

And without waiting for a response from any of them, I took off on foot to go look at the ocean up close and personal.

WHEN LAST I'D been here—here, on this very beach—it had been summer. Summertime, on any proper beach, is a time of staking one's claim to a bit of sand. It's a time for vacationers to enjoy their share of hot sun and cool water. The beach is something of a living thing, in the summer, with children running in and out to challenge the waves and adults wading in the wash, watching them warily.

The beach in mid-December is a much different prospect.

For starters, I wore boots, jeans, and a decent sweater. A cold wind whipped in off the sea and brought goosebumps to my flesh anyway. Up and down the length of the beach, I only saw a couple of others standing on the sand, looking out at the frigid water. In mid-December, the ocean was less a living thing and more of a stark, primal force of nature, beating ceaselessly against the shore.

I couldn't help it. I brought up my Sense.

Power.

Gods.

A summoner is only capable of moving things around. We don't create matter or force—that's not within our magic. Certain beings could—Rick being one of them—but for the most part, the magic of humanity involves moving things around. Usually that involves complicated rune sets—for me, it had usually just been moving things around that existed within forty feet of me.

I had *never* had access to this much kinetic force before. The waves beating against the shore carried such mass, such inertia, that even limiting it to the range of my Sense gave me access to virtually a bottomless well of kinetic force. The sheer amount of it staggered me, and I had nothing to use that much power *on*, so I simply sat there, Sensing the waves, and in awe of the raw majesty that nature had provided me.

Which isn't to say that I missed Sonia Tomas-Padilla approaching me from behind.

I didn't turn around—with my Sense up, I didn't have to. I could feel her—feel everything about her. She was, in that moment, a part of me. Had she presented a threat—and she was armed with a pistol mounted in a shoulder-holster—I could have killed her in a split-second. As it was, though, she approached within range of my Sense—and if she had hostile intent, she'd never have done that.

"Hello, captain," I said, not even bothering to turn toward her.

"Jesus," she said. "Thought I had the drop on you."

"Did you?" I asked. That was an interesting piece of information—she knew me to be lethal inside forty feet, but she hadn't figured out *why*. Good to know.

She stood for a moment, then chuckled and shook her head. "Should have known better that to try sneaking up on a warlock."

"Warlock?" I asked. "I ... no. I'm a summoner."

"Same thing?"

"Tell me," I said casually. "You're Latina, right? Are there other words that mean the same thing, but whose connotations would provoke a different reaction from you?"

She laughed a little. "I ... hadn't thought about it like that," she said. "Right, then. Summoner. I suppose I should get used to being polite, at least for today."

I chuckled and let my Sense drop, then turned to face her. "So," I said, "why come down to the beach one-on-one? I'm ... not the one who's going to be speaking for us, after all."

"Ha!" she said. "Maybe not—but you're like me, aren't you? You don't do the talking—but when the conversation stops, it's you and I that get sent out to extend diplomacy by other means, as von Clausewitz would say."

"That's an interesting way of putting it," I said. "Apt, though. And yes ... I'm one of the heavy hitters."

"So," she said, "if I'm being honest, I came down here because my orders are to account for you. Make sure you're not about to, you know, storm the meeting at the head of a legion of demons or something. But I came this close to you because I was hoping we could talk."

"Why?" I asked her, genuinely curious.

"Because," she said, looking me in the eye. "Know your enemy and know yourself."

"Ha! Any teenage nerd who's played enough tabletop war games knows Sun Tzu," I said. "So ... am I your enemy?"

"Not my decision," she said calmly. She shrugged one shoulder and shook her head. "At this moment? No. Tomorrow? Who knows? That's for the big-wigs to decide."

"Mmmm," I said. "So, what do you want to know?"

She looked at me, startled. I sort of shrugged. Despite myself—despite all she'd done—I couldn't help but like Captain Tomas-Padilla. She reminded me a lot of Carlenos, the Spokane cop who'd been my friend on the force back in the day.

"You're just ... going to tell me?" she asked.

"Within reason," I said. "I mean, if you ask me what my greatest weakness is, I'm going to tell you it's kryptonite and try to keep a straight face while doing it. But other than that ... yeah. If we're actually going to be allies, then this little talk might very well figure into the 'know yourself' side of the equation."

She stared at me, open-mouthed. "I'd ... never thought of it that way," she admitted. "God, I've been fighting summoners so long it's hard to think of you as anything *but* the enemy."

"I'm not, you know." I said quietly.

She looked at me with a raised eyebrow.

"I thought summoners were evil once, too. You saw that footage from the security cameras at the Valley Mall, right? Well ... I'd never really met a summoner before that. I didn't summon Rick—and neither did Grace. Grace was trying to save me and everyone else from him. And even after all of that, she still had a rather long way to go to convince me that summoning wasn't endangering my soul."

"How would you know it's not?" she asked.

"Because ... I'm still me, I guess," I said. "I still get up in the morning and put my pants on one leg at a time. I still like a good piece of pizza. I still can't stop my stupid hormones from making me attracted to every girl I meet. I still love my foster mother. And I still care enough about the world to want to save it. I spend most of my life trying to save it. If summoning were corrupting me ... I'm not sure that would be the result."

"You could be lying to me right now," she said.

I laughed. "Maybe. What you don't know about me is that I'm a terrible liar. Ask the Spokane cops about that sometime."

"The ones who did the lying for you?" she asked pointedly.

"Fair," I said. "But did you ever stop and consider *why* they did that? It's because we—Grace and I—saved their lives. Repeatedly. They knew that, knew we were the good guys ... so they helped us."

"All right," she said. "So, here's the ninety-million-dollar question: where *is* Moore? Woman's been in hiding since she blew up your school gym with a dirty bomb."

"Dead," I said quietly. Even now, the thought of Grace's sacrifice made my heart heavy, and the steady roar of the tide wasn't helping my melancholic mood. "And it wasn't a dirty bomb. Not the way you think of it. It was a full-blown atomic explosion. Critical-mass uranium stuff. It just happened in another world. What hit the gym came through the portal, just a small fraction of the blast. That's why you didn't find the body—her body was ... at the epicenter. In the other world."

"Whoa," she said. "You mean you could actually ... "

"Me?" I said. "No. That ... was one of the most complicated summonings I think anyone has ever performed. Grace had a knack for that sort of thing—the truly complex stuff. I'm ... more of a brute-force weapon."

"A nuke isn't brute force?"

"It's more a question of how one gets the nuke than the eventual result. Tell you what, if our respective big-wigs can agree that you and I are working together, I'll give you a full briefing. If they decide that we should be killing one another, though, I'd prefer to keep you guessing on some things. No offense."

She snorted a bit at that. "None taken," she said. "Smart, actually."

She paused, not pushing things. We both looked out at the ocean— without my Sense up, it had gone back to being gorgeous and not insanely powerful. "You know," she said after a bit of time had gone by, "your friend Nielsen was right. We've each killed each other's friends. Part of me ... hates you for that. And acknowledges you must hate me."

I turned my eyes away from the sea to look at her. "A part of me," I conceded. "But you called Thad my friend ... when he and I once tried to kill each other as well."

She whipped her head toward me in surprise. "Really?" she asked.

"Oh yeah," I said. "Groves don't like me *at all.* Figured everything I did brought too much heat down on them. Which is fair ... but most of it was necessary to fight Cythymau. *He's* the guy everyone needs to be pissed at. If I wanted to kill you ... if that was my truest, deepest desire ... you'd be dead right now. A couple of times over, in point of fact."

"I'm tougher than I look, kid," she said with military bravado.

I sighed. "Not about tough," I said. Then I brought up my Sense. Instantly, I felt that raw power of the waves ... I didn't need all of it. Channeling that much power into someone would get lethal really fast. I just needed some. I judged the amount—tricky, but I'd been getting good at this—and applied it directly under Captain Sonia Tomas-Padilla, accelerating her straight upward. Fast.

I'm actually not sure how high the captain went, but she cleared the forty-foot radius of my Sense with momentum to spare. There was a slight breeze coming in from the ocean, so I took a couple of steps back to line myself up with her descent. I gradually pulled momentum away from her as she fell, reducing her speed and dissipating the energy harmlessly away, allowing her to softly settle on the sand. Of course she landed on her posterior, and not her feet—but she landed gently.

She stared at me for a moment, eyes wide, and then burst out laughing. "That ... " she said, "was *fun. Dios mio,* Lorents, if this war does settle down, you could make a pretty good living as an amusement park ride."

"Ha!" I said, joining her in the laughter. "An exciting career track, no doubt." I let my Sense drop and offered her my hand. She looked at me for a moment ... and I should have recognized the mischievous twinkle in her eye as she grabbed it.

She pulled with her hand, and at the same time scissored her legs around mine. One of them caught me at the ankle; the other hooked around behind me and took me in the back of the knee. I went face-first into the sand next to her—and not nearly as gently as I'd put her down, either.

"Payback's a bitch, buddy," she said.

I rolled over, my face crusted with sand and sputtered a bit. "So it is," I said with a little laugh. "And that's fair. Still—I don't *want* to kill you. I—the only time I really, really *wanted* to kill mundanes, I was in the midst of being held and tortured by them. The guy responsible for all those deaths, ultimately, is Cythymau. He's the one we need to be killing—and I hope to God that the people up in that hotel right now realize that. I know my people do."

As we lay in the sand next to one another, she said "You're not how I pictured you."

"No?" I said. "How did you picture me?"

"You're ... Lorents. You consort with evil and summon demons.

You helped your wicked master dirty-bomb your school gym. You launched a terrorist attack on your graduation, committed mass murder in a mall, rode down the Spokane cops and killed a bunch of them, then when you were finally taken into custody, you ended up killing half the people there and starting a war to boot. So I don't know ... a little more mustache-twirly."

"You know only that last bit—about what happened when I was locked up—is accurate, right? The rest was me fighting *against* the thing attacking."

"I know you're saying it. And after talking with you ... I think I actually believe you. But that's a hard, hard pill to swallow."

"Oh?" I asked. "Is it so important that I cackle maniacally and tie damsels to railroad tracks?"

She gave me a look and shook her head. "No," she said. "But if *you're* not the ultimate expression of evil ... then who was I killing in Missoula?"

"Innocent citizens, for the most part," I said quietly.

"A hard pill," she said. "Because if you aren't twirling your mustache ... starts to feel like maybe I need to make an appointment at the salon to get my lip waxed."

"Nah," I said, trying to keep things light. "At best, you're the henchman in that melodrama. And they *never* get the cool mustaches."

She frowned at me. "Not actually the point," she said, no hint of levity in her voice.

"I know," I said.

I'm not sure how long we lay there, listening to the ocean. There's something truly relaxing about that sound, though, and I think both of us took the peace of the moment as the blessing it was. I knew I should get back, and she likely thought the same, but in that moment, it felt like we did more for the peace process by laying there and remembering what it felt like to be at ease.

After ... I'm honestly not sure how long, I rose to my feet and dusted sand off my clothes—a futile act, but compulsory. I offered her my hand again. "There's only one guy twirling a mustache in all of this. And he wants nothing more than for you to shoot at me, and me to use my power against you. All those deaths ... I lay them at his feet. You should, too."

"Not up to me," she said again, taking my hand and coming to her feet. "Up to them." She jerked her thumb back at the hotel, where undoubtedly Phineas and Amy were trying to deliver the same message to a number of people wearing nice suits.

"Yeah," I said. "I suppose so."

~

"NICE of you to join us at last, Lorents," said Phineas, sitting in the little rolling office chair in the hotel suite.

"Had a talk with a lady," I said, looking around the room. Andrea fixed me with a glare that seemed a little much for simple tardiness. Thad had his eyebrow raised, but said nothing. Amy got a smirky little smile on her face. Phineas, on the other hand, simply snorted.

"Well," said the former Director of the Seattle Grove, "I'm glad for you, I suppose. But we did come here for something a bit more important than flirting, you know."

I coughed a bit. "That wasn't—" I said, then shook my head. "Never mind. Sorry."

Phineas looked at me for a moment. "Regardless, the government has proposed a three-month cease fire, during which we plan for a summit meeting. High-security all around, but their people will meet with whatever Grove heads are willing to come. We've assured each other safe passage, and agreed to limit our forces accordingly."

I blinked. "That ... seems like good news," I said.

"It's news," Phineas replied. "But it could be a trap. Or *they* could be thinking it's a trap, and do something to counter us. It's all very tenuous right now, but the fact that we managed to have this meeting without killing each other was a good first step. Or ... second step, really, after the groundwork Thaddeus has been doing."

I nodded, at that. "What now?"

"Well, Thaddeus is going to return with the bigwigs to D.C. He'll continue his work there, as our liaison. In the meantime, we'll be joined by one Deborah Crenshaw from the Department of Justice as well as a Captain Tomas-Padilla, whom I believe you met in Missoula. Their purpose will be to help us speak to the other Groves ... and also as something like hostages for good faith, much as Thaddeus will be."

"So," I said, "all we have to do is gather the heads of every Grove we think might be willing to join us, then convince them to all show up at the same spot—a spot that we absolutely know the government is going to know about—thus presenting the most tempting military target ever?"

"Yeah," said Phineas. "And all while keeping in mind that Cythymau's going to see it as an even *more* tempting target—and doesn't care a wink for either of our hostages."

"So ... how do we do this?" I asked.

"That's the big question," said Phineas. "And I'm not entirely sure we can cash the checks we've written here. Still—it's worth trying."

I thought about my conversation with Captain Sonia Tomas-Padilla, and lying there on the beach in peace next to her. "Yeah," I said. "It is."

ANDREA

I POURED myself a new cup of coffee from the urn in the corner of the room and glowered at the new "members" of our little delegation. We hadn't taken anyone home to Grove headquarters proper. Phineas preferred to use the conference rooms at the hotel to set up preliminary contact with the Grove leaders we were going to try to bring over to our side.

Deborah Crenshaw, or Debbie as she preferred to be called, stood next to Phineas, a politician's brilliant smile pasted on her face. Phineas smiled back at her just as professionally and just as opaquely. I knew after we were done here, he'd have another round of private calls and meetings in his room, as the Groves met with him a little more privately.

These initial video calls with everyone present were all show and posturing, and it set my teeth on edge. I didn't know why I had to be here for any of it, except that Phineas liked to point me out as our "inside woman," figuring out what Cythymau had planned next, as if I had some kind of Machiavellian master grasp of Cythymau that went beyond the scope of mere humans. I snorted at the thought. It might look good in a soundbite. But if that were true, I wouldn't have spent an eternity manipulated, locked up, and tortured.

I supposed there was also the added bonus that news stations wouldn't stop showing that darn picture of me. Phineas liked to trot me out as the newest pro-summoner propaganda tool.

The whole thing was grinding along very ponderously. I wondered if three months really was going to be sufficient to pull together such a big, distrustful mess of people.

Robert and Matt had gone ahead to make other arrangements, leaving me, Naggy—err Amy, and Phineas to start reaching out to the Groves that weren't firmly allied with Cythymau already. There were six regional Groves that Cythymau hadn't managed to bring under total control yet, though he was slowly eroding city councils away from all of them. His power was growing. If we didn't do something soon, the window of opportunity might very well disappear.

The one exception where Cythymau might actually be losing ground was the Prince Rupert region. Since they weren't even in the states, I wasn't sure how much interest they'd have in whatever the US government had to say. Even if they were up to their necks with the rest of us in this summoner war.

Regardless, they were a heavy hitter in the anti-Cythymau faction, so we were going to court them for this summit. If nothing else, they'd be at least one more warm body to cover up that our Grove was an underdog comprised of ousted directors, reject summoners, and one demon's ancient-ass ex-magical-battery.

Phineas and Crenshaw stood in front of the screen waiting for the conference software to load.

Captain Sofia Tomas-Padilla walked over and stood at the back of the room a few feet away from me, where she'd be able to see the screen better. Amy lowered the lights in the room, so that the parties actually participating in the call would be able see the screen and each other better.

In the gloom, I found myself staring at the captain's profile as she stood at rest, watching the screen. Her stance oozed self-assurance and training. I supposed she would be considered elite, as she'd been commanding the strike force that took out the Missoula Grove. I frowned. Her thudding heart and elevated cortisol belied that a bit. In my Sense, she appeared just as nervous as the rest.

Just standing there, she didn't look like much. Not that tall, not that muscled, not that lethal even.

I raised my chin a notch, focusing my attention back on the screen. But.

Robert had looked awfully at ease with her down on the beach.

Not that I was that concerned, really. It was just irritating that he'd lied. After telling me he needed time alone, he'd hung out with *her* instead, looking ridiculously content.

Showing off stupid antics with his Sense even. He hadn't even noticed that I'd come to check on him when he didn't come back, the dolt.

I turned my head and frowned at the good captain again. She irritated me.

"Can I help you?" the captain asked me in a low tone without taking her eyes off the screen or changing her posture. Just underlining that she'd noticed my interest.

I jerked my gaze back around to whoever Phineas was talking to on the screen. I had no clue at this point. I hadn't really been paying it proper attention.

"No. Sorry. I was just thinking," I told her.

"You saved a lot of my people from getting injured or worse in Montana," the captain said.

I shrugged uncomfortably. "Mmhmm," I said.

"As their commander, I appreciated that. Truly. Depending how these talks go, we may still end up on opposite sides, but for that day, thank you."

I turned my head, squinting my eyes at her. "You killed an awful lot of other people that I'd also hoped to rescue that day. Sorry, but I can't thank you back."

She seemed a bit taken aback by my reply, but dammit, I wasn't the diplomat. And she'd started this piss-poor conversation.

"Just following orders," she said. "I'm a soldier. Those in command make the decisions, and I do what they tell me."

"I know." I said shortly. "Been there. Done something like that. In the end, I think it's highly over-rated and stu—"

"Andrea!" Amy came up next to me, her hands fluttering nervously. "What are you and the good captain talking about?"

I bared my teeth at Amy in what I hoped would pass for a smile. "The chain of command and gratitude. Not necessarily in that order."

"Oh my!" Amy tittered. I resisted the urge to facepalm. Naggy dogpiling onto this conversation was the last thing I needed right now. She placed a hand on my shoulder and gave it a squeeze that I knew was supposed to be a warning.

"You'll have to forgive Andrea," Amy said to the captain. "She can be a bit brusque, but she's got a good heart, really." There Naggy went again, talking about me like I was a backwards toddler. I shook her hand off. Amy shot me a repressive look anyway.

Then she continued, "Andrea just has a little trouble expressing it sometimes. If we get to be allies it'll be easier to explain all the circumstances—"

"No, it won't." I said, cutting Amy off. Captain Tomas-Padilla's eyebrows rose.

"I'm older and grumpier than I look." I said, daring Amy to contradict me. It wasn't like it was untrue. "You can take my grumblings to be those of the resident octogenarian. We need all the allies we can get against Cythymau, so either way, I'll welcome you as an ally, if not a friend. But don't worry. I don't have many friends anyway." I pushed myself away from wall and extricated myself from the situation.

Amy hadn't needed to intervene; I wasn't going to blow anything up. Not on purpose anyway.

I'd play nice with the good captain for the next three months, but I didn't have to like her.

FOR THE ONE-ON-ONE, in-person meetings after the initial video conferences, Matt and Phineas had chosen to move our delegation to a small conference hotel next to the Portland Airport.

If we were going to have people travel covertly, we needed a big enough airport their arrivals and departures wouldn't incite comment from anyone. With SeaTac being right in the heart of Cythymau's controlled territory, that left Portland as the closest, and the safest. They had staggered out the delegates' arrivals and departures such that only one was in town at a time; their itineraries did not overlap.

I sat in the small hotel suite, sprawled over the arm of the couch, one leg dangling over its edge as I munched on a cheese Danish while drinking a mug of the hotel coffee. One thing I did enjoy with all these travels is that someone always seemed to have fresh-brewed coffee on tap.

"I don't know why you're insisting I be included in all these in-person diplomatic meetings," I grumbled to Phineas.

"Because I need every possible piece of information I can get my hands on," Phineas answered. "Besides, I need to unify a bunch of angry people, and the Maiden of Missoula has already become a symbol to both sides."

"It's not like I'm good a schmoozing people or chatting them up," I pointed out, gesturing with my Danish.

"No you aren't, but with your Sense up, you can catch on prettily easily if someone is lying, and pick up a hundred other side conversations, whether you mean to or not. That all makes you a great spy. You can leave schmoozing to me or Amy anyway."

"Hey," Amy said. "I'm just friendly."

Phineas smiled. "Yes, you are, and we're going to use both of you to our advantage. I'll do my best to lay the groundwork for any negotiations that might happen. The two of you are going to be the friendly face and the listening walls in this little endeavor. One noticed and one mostly unnoticed."

Phineas rubbed his chin thoughtfully, then continued. "I'm sure you both know that a great deal of our position relies on promises to the government that are largely bluff until we can get more summoners on our side. But we absolutely must come through on them. The Feds have no idea how understrength our Grove is compared to others. *They* see Lorents, Nielsen, and Andrea. It appears to them like we've got all the big guns in our little delegation. Now *we* know that's not the whole picture, but they don't. So we're actually trying to accomplish two things here by performing a bit of sleight of hand. We can't let the federal delegation know how tenuous our position with the other Groves is, but we also can't throw our weight around so much that the Groves feel like we're trying to exert pressure and demand action they know we can't back up. We have to appear to be the perfect mediator to both sides for the sake of a working partnership."

Phineas wiped sweat off his forehead before continuing, "We don't have to get everyone to agree to everything yet, either. We just have to provide sufficient incentive to get everyone to agree to show up at the table. We can worry about the seating arrangements and how exactly to set it later."

"So, come again. Precisely how do I help you with that?" I asked.

"Andrea, I want you to lurk, much like you usually do. I know you can do it extremely well. But if you find out anything interesting from either side, bring that to me. I don't care if you piff a note into my pocket, or use an earbud from Matt. Whatever is more comfortable for you. I'll use the information to our advantage as best we're able. And no doubt the others will be trying to get just as much information from us covertly. So I need both of you to be as careful as possible."

"You just need me to chat with people, right? That's all I'm doing?" Amy asked.

"Yes, but in your case, I'd like them to be chats aimed around several specific, helpful topics. Namely, I want you to find out attitudes toward summoner-controlled states, and if they're keeping any political heavy-hitters in reserve that we should talk to before the summit is held. For example ...."

～

I HUGGED the back wall of the tiny conference room, my now-habitual cup of coffee in hand. I tried to remember if this was my third or fourth cup today. From the small fire taking up residence in my stomach and the fine tension running through my head, I guessed fourth. No doubt I'd have a fifth before the meeting ended.

The Director of the Prince Rupert Regional Grove, Martin Tremblay, ended up being a tall, solidly-built older gentleman who looked like he'd spent his entire life outside on construction sites, or possibly working some kind of forestry job. His eyes also crinkled into crow's feet at the corners when he smiled. I didn't mistake the crinkle for simple jolliness, because behind all that Canadian civility and cheerful mask, I could Sense he was constantly thinking— the synapses in his brain firing fast, taking in everything around him.

I might not be able to read minds, but I could tell he was a man who thought on his feet very, very quickly. No one who had risen to the level he had should be trifled with. I decided instantly that the best thing I could do would be stay out of the way and keep my mouth shut unless Phineas asked me a direct question or signaled that he needed my input.

I pulled a seat into the back corner of the room where I could watch the entry, positioning myself so the door, Director Tremblay, and Phineas were in range of my Sense. Captain Tomas-Padilla scanned the room and then entered, with Debbie Crenshaw right behind her. They were last to arrive, and the two exchanged a few words before Debbie went over to greet Phineas and Director Tremblay. Tomas-Padilla signaled the diplomat that the coast appeared clear, but urged her to stay away from the doors and windows. Standard protocol and old hat, no news there.

There were no surprises on Tomas-Padilla's person either, just her standard equipment, though that did include one small pistol that I considered laughable.

It was ridiculously easy to unload it without her knowledge, and in fact I had played that game several times over in these meetings when I was bored out of my mind. So far she'd never caught one of my small thefts before I returned it to its original state. Childish of me? A bit dangerous? Maybe. But I hadn't been able to resist doing it anyway. These meetings were long.

"Thank you for coming all this way to meet with us, Director Tremblay," Phineas said.

"Well, it's not every day that someone like me would get a chance to meet a delegate of the US government—where that meeting wouldn't immediately be followed by a death threat or imprisonment. Shall we say it was too unique to pass up?" He turned to Debbie Crenshaw. "A pleasure to meet you, Ms. Crenshaw." He extended a hand to the lady.

"The pleasure is all mine, Director." Her hand was engulfed by his much larger one. As soon has he was holding onto her hand, his Sense sprung up, overlapping slightly with mine. It wasn't small, but it wasn't that large either. Maybe only a five-foot radius total.

"Now I must ask, though. Is this all a trap?" He held her gaze intently, his eyes deadly serious. He monitored her reaction to his words like a police officer reading a polygraph machine.

"There is no trap waiting to be sprung here, Director," Debbie answered, her tone calm and measured. "We come to assure that this offer for talks is being made in good faith."

"You understand my skepticism, I hope," he said. "The current US government has done its utmost to escalate tensions between summoners, the public, and authorities at every level. Your government's actions in detaining and exterminating my kind are the worst in the world currently. That makes this kind of backdoor gesture very hard to take at face value. What keeps you from taking what you learn here and using it against us as soon as we return home?"

"As with all negotiations of this nature, there is always risk," Debbie said, not trying to reclaim her hand, letting it rest peacefully in his like she had not a care in the world. Though I knew, and Director Tremblay would too, that she was very carefully controlling her breathing, choosing her words before releasing them into the room. Debbie Crenshaw excelled at high pressure situations, which was probably why she'd been sent into this one in the first place. She had pluck.

"I can give you my guarantee that my government is not waiting to inform yours about anything learned in this room, nor will they after you leave. I am here solely to aid in setting up talks. In an attempt to put an end to the deaths on all sides. You have my word on that."

Director Tremblay gave her one more assessing look before releasing her hand. "Assuming that to be true, I still have grave security concerns about a proposed summit between all the parties involved. While I agree that the current situation is untenable, and talks would hopefully be advantageous— though I don't think anyone can guarantee they won't end at this point—how are you prepared to guarantee the safety of anyone who promises to attend?"

Phineas stepped in to answer this. "We are taking the security of these talks very seriously. The delegates will all be flown in at separate times, and taken to the venue by different routes. The venue itself will be wired up with both mundane and magical surveillance, as well as warded, so that no one can directly summon anything or anyone directly in or out of the building. Each delegate will also be given their own set of personal wards that will reinforce their clothing into armor and generate a personal force field against attacks. Each delegate at the summit will be damn difficult to take out separately, even if they are not a summoner themselves. Even more so if they are. We have our best summoners crafting all the necessary wards as we speak."

"And if someone decides it's the perfect time to assassinate us all, say with something more ordinary like a mundane sniper rifle or bomb?"

"The venue's location and security will be of utmost importance," Phineas said "We will be using conference rooms not unlike this one, in a venue that is public enough to be neutral, with civilians as well as military and summoners on premises. We will have air surveillance of the surrounding areas via drones and summoned wards. The premises will be thoroughly inspected before, during, and after the event to ensure the safety of all involved."

"The government contingent will also be bringing plain clothes security, bomb sniffing dogs, and a tactical unit if needed, though these are just precautions." Debbie said.

"And what happens if, after all these preparations, Cythymau or the government or some other wacko still shows up at this 'summit' with an assassination squad?"

"If all these security measures and precautions fail, which I don't believe they will," Phineas said, "then we deal with any attacks with extreme force using preset and staged offensive spells, while making sure that all the delegates to the summit remain unharmed. And then we make sure that any attackers don't have the ability to report back and/or circle around to try it again. You have my word as a Brandiole on that."

I had never heard Phineas sound that serious or that lethal. But I believed him. And after a moment, Director Tremblay nodded.

"I still have concerns that, no matter what security measures you put in place, it will be too good a prize not to attack for anyone who wishes an escalation of the current situation."

Phineas started to speak again, but Tremblay waved him off.

"I have some suggestions to add to yours on the security and secrecy side of these talks, but you have my tentative agreement to attend," Tremblay said.

ROBERT

THE LITTLE MISSOULA café certainly looked a lot cleaner this time than the last time I'd been in it. Easier to get to, as well.

But no less strange to walk into. Especially alongside Tomas-Padilla and Crenshaw.

Let's be clear: I believe in ghosts. Or rather, I *have actual proof* that spirits exist post-mortem. I've talked to a couple. I've even summoned two of them, in my time—including Grace, though I'll admit she wasn't very happy about it. There is some piece of us that continues to exist after we're dead.

I also knew that our spiritual energy transferred to another realm upon death. So I knew, not as a matter of faith but as a matter of tested and proven fact, that the former headquarters of the slaughtered Missoula Grove contained no spirits at all.

Which did *not* make it feel less haunted to me.

Ryan Wilson sat at one of the little tables. I expected ... more people with him. By all accounts—including some rants I'd heard from Grace about the man—he tended toward the pompous. Yet here he sat, in a small coffee shop, entirely alone. No staff, no waiters, just ... starkly, distinctly alone.

"Cunning bastard," Phineas said under his breath, and that's when it clicked. He *meant* the large, empty room with just the one man in it to be a dramatic display. It's why he'd brought us here.

Tomas-Padilla, for her part, did not look Wilson in the eye. A couple of months travelling with us and speaking with our kind, and the good captain showed nothing but shame upon walking back through these doors. What she'd done here had been, by any definition, monstrous. Now she knew it. Wrestling with that is not the sort of thing that makes for a light heart.

Crenshaw, on the other hand, looked unmoved. She hadn't been here during the Battle of Missoula, and while she was *academically* aware of it, she hadn't the first-hand knowledge that Tomas-Padilla and I shared.

Phineas approached Wilson and made introductions, first of the mundane representatives, then Amy, then me.

"The famous Lorents," Wilson said as he reached to shake my hand. "I've wanted to meet you for quite some time."

"Have you?" I asked, then paused for a moment, simply looking at him. " ... Why?"

"Curiosity, mostly," he said in a nonchalant voice. "I mean, you're the guy, right? The reason everything's gone to hell? The reason all of this happened? We wanted you killed off years ago—I even sent Thaddeus to do it. And yet somehow, here you are, the harbinger of doom for us all."

"I'm not the reason," I said quietly. "Just the first target."

He waved his hand dismissively at that. "Maybe," he said, but his tone sounded laced with doubt. "Even were that the case, you and Ms. Moore badly handled the situation. You gave a demon a giant powerbase and sent him after everyone. If you really thought him dangerous, you should have stopped it sooner."

Phineas stepped in front of me, cutting me off by waving his arm abruptly.

"They tried," he said in icy tones. "I seem to remember you humiliating Ms. Moore at a Vegas buffet while she was trying. So badly she threw a drink in your face, if I recall."

"Yes, well," said Wilson, his polite, pleasant tone unchanged despite

Phineas's clear anger. "I can hardly be blamed for not taking someone seriously who'd resort to such juvenilism. Perhaps if you'd sent a *professional* instead of a loose cannon to Spokane, your own Grove wouldn't have risen up against you, Phineas."

Wilson turned to Crenshaw, dressed in her Brooks Brothers pantsuit, and asked, "Did you know that, about him? When he started trying to put all of this together? This man isn't even qualified to lead his own Grove, let alone all of ours, and yet he comes to you and pretends to speak for all summoners?"

Deborah Crenshaw, ever the professional herself, simply responded, "The internal politics of your criminal conspiracies hardly matter to me," she said. "I am here simply to ask if you wish to meet with members of my government to discuss the possibility of legitimizing your organizations and practices and allying against this … Cythymau."

"Ahhhh," said Ryan Wilson. "*Now* you want to talk to us. Madam Crenshaw," he said. "Do you know where we are, right now?"

"Yes," said Crenshaw. "I do. I've been thoroughly briefed on the Battle of Missoula."

"Battle," Wilson scoffed. "Missoula didn't do much *battle*, here. I believe the appropriate term, where the Missoula Grove is concerned, is *massacre*."

My eyes flicked over to look at Captain Tomas-Padilla. She stared at the floor and winced slightly as the barb hit home.

"Ambush tactics are generally one of the few methods effective against summoners," said Crenshaw, keeping that level tone. "I believe Captain Tomas-Padilla used an appropriate level of force to carry out her orders. We are at war, sir, and I am offering peace talks."

"No," said Wilson. "You're not. *He* is," he said, pointing back at Phineas. "*He* came to you with those peace talks. And he did so after sending *this one*," at this, he gestured at me, "and his massive demon to save the life of your precious captain over there. And they arrived conveniently just after all *my people had been killed*. But they arrived before I could send any reinforcements of my own. Which makes me wonder—when did you send yours, all the way from wherever the hell you are now?"

He stood from his chair and walked at Phineas, his voice now raised in accusation, his finger pointing. "You sent notice to us in advance," he said. "You *told* us it was happening. You had plenty of time to send reinforcements. You could have saved *all of these people.* But for *some convenient reason,* you show up in time to save only the military? Only the Feds? I can't help but notice how sacrificing *my people's lives* has put you in a convenient bargaining position, Brandiole. And now, here we are, in the home of a dead Grove, and you offer *peace?* Seems like they already have peace—but it's not the kind I favor."

Phineas drained of color, whether from anger or guilt I still didn't know. Wilson was an absolute dickhead, sure, but ... he was spot-on about this. We *had* let his people die. Not by intent, as he seemed to think, but ... it had happened. I looked around the empty coffee house and sighed.

"We thought we could save everyone," I said softly. All eyes whipped to me. "Thought we'd get here in time to stop Tomas-Padilla. We ran into a checkpoint west of Spokane and got slowed down ... and didn't make it. That wasn't on Phineas—that's on me. And Nielsen, I suppose."

"Yessss," said Wilson, and a glimmer in his eye told me I'd just walked into his trap. "Yes, it was. You and Nielsen. The Director of the Spokane Grove and his apprentice. The Spokane Grove is at fault for this failure. The Spokane Grove has cost the Great Plains one city's Grove. Therefore—I claim recompense."

He leaned back in his chair and looked to Phineas. "Spokane—and let's throw in Boise, as they're half-ours anyways—shall become part of the Great Plains territory. The line between Pacific Northwest and Great Plains territories shall be drawn at the Columbia, south to the Oregon Border, then east to the Idaho Border. Great Plains assumes jurisdiction over all of Idaho as well as Eastern Washington. We put *proper* management in place in those Groves, and we make sure they are run correctly so that this sort of thing does not happen again. That is my price for attending these talks."

"For *attending?*" asked Phineas. "You'd add a state and a half to your territory simply for agreeing to come and listen." Phineas's jaw clenched in anger, and a bit of malice made its way into his tone.

"I'm the one who was forced to sacrifice a city's Grove of my people so you could set the talks up," retorted Wilson. "If it's Great Plains blood that pays for the talks, then I want something more than talks. So, yes—that's my price."

He paused for a bit, taking a long sip from his coffee. Only once he placed the mug back on the table with a firm *clack* that echoed through the empty café did he then add, "Obviously, I can't hold you to this deal unless and until you get reinstalled as head of the Pacific Northwest, so it will be in my interest to support you in the talks."

Phineas let out a deep sigh. "You ... have a point," he said, then he looked at me. "As the senior representative of the Spokane Grove, do you concur?"

And this was why he'd asked for me. Why he'd held the meeting here. Grace had been right; this wasn't an emotional play from him. Ryan Wilson was exactly as much of a viper as she'd made him out to be. If I agreed to this, I'd be placing my hometown under his control. I wouldn't be able to return to Spokane after this—the man had already tried to have me killed once. I'd no doubt he'd do it again.

Cythymau had forced me out of my home city. Ryan Wilson would keep me in exile.

But if we didn't have these talks, Cythymau would end all of us, and he knew that, too. We were all speeding toward a cliff, and Wilson had just demonstrated he was willing to go over if I didn't stop first.

Chicken is a stupid, stupid game to play, but a part of me wanted to. Wanted to simply flip this asshole the bird and walk out of his little coffee shop. Really see if he was willing to drive over a cliff. But ... I think he'd have done it.

I swallowed my pride, then nodded. "The Spokane Grove ... concurs," I said. "Such is the price for our actions."

"Done, then," said Phineas.

"And done," said Wilson calmly, with only a small curl at the corner of his mouth. "So ... where and when are we having this little shindig?"

~

SPRING, in the middle of the Olympic rain forest, is a wet time.

All right, all right—that's probably obvious. You'd think the words "rain forest" would sort of clue someone in to the downpour that was the beginning of March. We'd hit the Lion part of the month, and with the summit approaching quickly, any day that offered even a bit of sunshine was a day I needed to go play with Rick.

I mean, you know what happens when you leave an overly attached dog alone in a house for a day or two? Poor thing gets anxiety and just starts shredding stuff. Kiss your upholstery goodbye. Now, imagine that, but instead of the word "upholstery" use the word "buildings" or "municipalities" or "greater urban area" instead. Rick needed the attention, and I enjoyed giving it to him—but there's reasons that it ranked so high on my list of priorities.

Which is how, even in the midst of all this turmoil, I found myself following the link out to an old, abandoned building and a large field behind it, wherein lay my good friend/pet/Visitor. His head lifted off the ground as I approached and that massive, armored club of a tail began to wag back and forth in the tall grass.

"Hey, buddy," I said as I approached him. "What's up?"

He grinned at me, then let loose with a *woomph* of force. I'd been expecting this, of course—playing catch with freight-train-sized balls of kinetic force was how Rick liked to get his exercise. So I whipped the ball around me with my Sense and sent it hurtling back towards him, only to have it countered by a second *woomph* from him.

So far, so standard. At least Rick didn't long for *creativity.* I could wish that his playtime didn't violate *quite* so many OSHA regulations, but proper care and feeding of a Cornuprocyon simply involved an elevated level of risk.

We played back and forth, forgetting the rest of the world for a moment. I'll say this, for the activity—there's a reason my Sense-based summoning in a fight had gotten so sharp. Once you've played catch with Rick a couple of times, fending off a platoon's worth of small arms fire really seems sort of second-rate.

And that's when I noticed her.

Down by the garage, Andrea was kneeling, looking at something on the ground. I paused, staring at her, wondering what she could possibly be doing all the way out here ... and Rick immediately jumped in between me and her.

"Buddy?" I asked.

The big Cornuprocyon stepped forward a couple of times, then nudged me with his snout. Figuring this to be his signal that playtime had evolved into scritchum-time, I dutifully took my hand and gave him a couple of scratches alongside his muzzle before saying, "Let's go see what Andrea's up to. Maybe you can cadge pets off her, too."

I tried to walk around his massive body ... and he *shifted,* putting himself directly between Andrea and me.

"Boy?" I asked.

In response, he lowered his muzzle and pushed—a little more forcefully this time, shoving me back and *away* from Andrea.

"Rick?" I asked, confused at the Cornuprocyon's actions. "What are you doing? Andrea's right down there."

He *woomphed* at me.

It wasn't a full-strength blast. Not even close. Which was good, because this time, I *wasn't* ready for it. It came with none of his usual playfulness. No bouncing, no wag of the tail, just a comparatively gentle blast of force, aimed straight at my torso.

The key word there is *comparatively.*

It still knocked me tail-over-teakettle. Rick's ambush sent me sprawling backwards, rolling through the grass. I rolled once, twice, then thrice before sliding, face down, to a stop, and then lifting my head.

"What the *fuck,* buddy?" I asked in an angry tone.

Rick tilted his head down and angled his eyes up in the classic hangdog look of a pet who knew he was in trouble.

"What was that for?" I asked, as though I could possibly get an answer. Rick's intelligence impressed me most of the time, but it was still the intelligence of a well-trained dog, not someone who'd answer back. He just stood there, looking ashamed, and I shook my head and began to walk toward Andrea again.

And he moved again, to block me.

"Wait ... " I said. "Did Andrea ... did she tell you to get in my way?"

Rick continued to give me that hangdog look.

"Buddy ... " I said. "What's it going to take to get you to move?"

Rick chuffed a big sigh, then dug his claws into the ground and shook his head at me. So.

"I don't want to do this," I said. "I don't think you do, either."

He leaned forward and licked me. A big, face-bathing lick, coating the side of my face with his rough tongue.

"Yeah," I said. "I love you too. So please, let me by."

Another chuffed sigh. Another shake of the head.

She must have used the link. I knew a bit of Cythymau's old link still lingered between Andrea and Rick—she'd used it in an aborted attempt to rescue me at one point, back in Spokane. I had a chunk of the same link, but I hated to use it to *compel* Rick. He'd spent so long being whipped that way by Cythymau ... and so had Andrea. How could she do this to him? And why?

"Buddy ... I'm going down there," I said as I brought my Sense back up. "I need to straighten this out with Andrea. How far are you going to go to stop me?"

He cut loose with another blast—this one a bit more forceful ... but with my Sense up I easily caught it ... and applied it underneath me, sending me up in the air.

Rick growled a bit as I began arcing overhead, and I watched that great club of a tail begin to swing my way.

There'd been a time when Rick had been the subject of my nightmares. Going toe-to-toe with the big Cornuprocyon had absolutely terrified me. I'd seen him—under the same sort of compulsion Andrea had him under—kill more people than I could conveniently count, and he'd come damn close to nailing me, as well.

Since then, though, I'd learned him. "Playing with" Rick and "fighting" Rick differed only in ultimate intent, really, and when I saw his tail coming up, I stole the force directly from it and used it to adjust my trajectory. His tail sailed by me on the right, and I used my Sense to slow my fall, coming to rest behind him and facing away.

I heard the next *woomph* and felt the force-ball coming in. *This* one had intent. It was a full-strength, building-levelling blast, and my good friend had aimed it directly at me. But just because *I'd* learned *his* moves while we were playing didn't mean I'd shown him all of mine. I'd trained against him for hundreds of hours, and I had this.

I took his force ball and shaved it in two. Three-quarters I kept flowing around me in a circle ... the other bit I sent back at him, from his right. One of Rick's weak points is this—it takes him a couple of seconds in between projections of force. And he always, *always* blocked my response ball by negating it with a second one.

Which is what he did, here. Only my throw back to him didn't have nearly the strength he'd anticipated.

A great swathe of the Olympic Rain Forest tore itself up by the roots as Rick's blast overwhelmed my feint and carried through, a full-strength ball of force blocked by one only a quarter as powerful. I'd aimed it so his counter-blast hit nothing *but* forest, but my friendly pet still managed to rip apart several hundred yards of timber.

And leave himself entirely defenseless when I used the rest of the force I'd saved.

I hit him in the head with it. I'd killed Cornuprocyon with that move before, but I'd sharpened the force to a small point. This time, I was going for a concussive effect, so I kept it broad and spread throughout. I hit him from beneath, right in the jaw, and he flipped end-over-end onto his back and lay there for a moment—but the rise and fall of his chest told me he was still breathing.

I let out a sigh of relief. Trying to use *nonlethal* force to stop Rick once he's committed is a tricky business. But I only needed to stall him for a moment. I took off sprinting toward Andrea, hoping the compulsion she'd forced onto my friend would fade once I made it to her.

And found out what the *fuck* she had been thinking.

ANDREA

My nightmares are made of cruelty, imprisonment, blood, gore, pain, and death. I was about to add one more thing to that list—though I didn't realize it.

I heard a series of *whoomphs* and then crashing as Rick tore up a bunch of trees somewhere nearby. I supposed he'd gotten bored with waiting for me to be done before we could play.

I looked up from the rune sigil I was trying to decipher and was surprised to see Robert sprinting through the trees toward me. Using my Sense, I hastily relocated the sigil below ground, along with the rest of my scattered reading for that day. I quickly scanned the area for any missed scrolls or artifacts outside Sense range.

Seeing none, I stumbled to my feet and strode over to meet him, but not fast enough. He got to me first, and as soon as he hit the edge of my Sense, I knew something was off. His heart was pounding, his adrenaline through the roof. A simple game of force ball with Rick wouldn't cause this. Speaking of which, Rick should have kept their game well away from here in the first place.

"What happened?" I asked.

"What happened? What do you mean what happened? What the fuck, Andrea?" Robert said. He pointed back toward the woods he'd come out of. "Rick just tried to take me out in order to keep me away from you, and whatever you're doing here. That's what happened. What the fuck were you thinking laying a compulsion on him like that?"

"I—no. That's not what I did—"

"Really? Because I had to knock Rick out in order to get this close." He strode past me, bringing his Sense up and flinging his arms wide. "And what are you doing out here that's so bloody secret—"

He froze, staring at me as he stood on top of my secret stash of Cythymau's knowledge and artifacts. His Sense punched down below the rock and earth that hid my trove, as I'd always known it would if he ever stood here. And the anger and fear in his eyes—no, not fear, revulsion—were like a punch to the gut.

He let his breath out in a long angry hiss. "Why. Is. This. Here?" Each word might as well have been an expletive.

My stomach dropped into the soles of my feet. "I can explain," I said weakly.

"Explain what, Andrea? How you laid a geas on Rick? How you took away his volition? How you justified it because you've hoarded a shit-ton of that maniacal demon's stuff? How you've been out here alone trying to do—I don't even know what. Or how you lied to everyone, including me, to do it? Which of those are you going to 'explain,' Andrea?"

I punched back, "All of it! Any of it! Starting with I never laid a geas on Rick!"

"So what did you do?" Robert asked, his tone no less hostile.

"I asked him to keep people away from here, because the artifacts are dangerous in the wrong hands," I said.

"And how exactly did you ask him?" Robert demanded.

"I talked with him," I said defensively.

"And he understood you because why?" Robert said, his voice scathing.

"Because through the link he can!"

"Through the link," Robert repeated.

"Yes."

"Cythymau's link." Robert said.

"Yes!" I said.

"And you didn't strongly want Rick to do this thing? Have a strong desire for him to fulfill your request?" Robert crossed him arms over his chest, glowering at me.

"I asked. I didn't compel him," I said.

"Yes, you did." He voice left no room for question.

"I didn't, but even if I did, I didn't mean to," I said hotly.

Rick slunk up next to us, his quills flat against his back, his belly touching the earth. He looked worriedly back and forth between the two of us.

"You didn't mean to? How does that make anything better?" Robert closed his eyes, but I knew he was looking around my storeroom with his Sense. "This stockpile is deliberate, Andrea. Hiding it from me, from everyone else, was a choice. Setting Rick here to guard it was a premeditated plan."

"Stop acting like you don't understand me," I said. "You know there's no one I could trust with these things. They're too powerful."

"Except yourself!" he retorted angrily. "You still brought everything here, even knowing the danger it represents."

"My body is already steeped in the secrets that vault contains. Our escape at the checkpoint proves that, if nothing else. And for good or ill, *you* brought me here!"

"Oh, so this is actually all my fault for rescuing you in the first place."

"That's not what I said." I practically screamed the words in his face, my hands balled into fists at my sides.

Robert made a scornful gesture, like he was shoving my words away from him. "Really, 'cause that's what it sounded like from over here. Have some fucking responsibility for yourself, Andrea." He pointed at Rick. "Take a good look at the link, and undo whatever you did. RIGHT. NOW."

"I didn't do anything," I yelled, but I turned to Rick anyway, probing our link, testing how it usually felt. I could feel the Cornuprocyon's anxiety at our fight, his shame and confusion at having to attack Robert, his pain at struggling with our conflicting commands.

And there it was: a command. Like a misty cobweb, wound around and through our connection, subtle but strong, and ultimately binding.

No. I hadn't done this. Had I?

I carefully peeled the command away from the connection I had with Rick, discarding it until it became nothing. And the connection was clear once more.

Rick whined, licking Robert and then me with a rough tongue, and I could feel his desire through the bond that we not fight, and then he scuttled off into the woods, intent on getting away from our argument.

"I didn't try to do that," I mumbled, my stomach sour and queasy. I had stripped away Rick's will just as Cythymau once had. I felt like a monster.

I'd been desperate, but ... why? What had I expected Robert to do? Run off with Cythymau's stuff? Thad might do that. Phineas might do that. But Robert? Why *had* I hidden it from Robert? What exactly was I afraid of?

"You said earlier that you didn't want this knowledge to fall into the wrong hands. That assumes that *yours* are the right ones," Robert said, his words biting. "Hypocrite. Liar. Manipulator. Tell me how you're not all three of those things, just like Cythymau, Andrea. Right now I feel like I don't even *know* you."

I had no answer to any of those accusations. They hit me straight in the heart, truth at their cores.

I hadn't wanted him to know I'd gone back. I hadn't wanted him to realize, while Cythymau lived, I might not be as free as I thought. Or that the apprentice might resemble the teacher more and more. I'd bound Rick twice over now.

"Who do you think you are?" Robert asked. "No matter how I look at it, how could you do something this stupid, reckless, and wrong?"

I snorted. "Like you're one to talk," I said to Robert, lashing out with my own hurt feelings. "Jerk. Cheater. Pretender."

"I don't even know what you're talking about."

"Murderer." I said, bracing my arms over my chest.

"Right back at you, bitch."

"Ha! You wouldn't call *Captain Tomas-Padilla* a murderer or a bitch," I said. "Even though she and her men outright massacred the Missoula Grove. Good riddance to the two of you, then."

"What's *she* even got to do with any of this?" Robert said, sounding confused, flinging his hands wide.

"I saw the two of you getting to know each other down at the beach; you were too busy flirting with her to do anything else."

"She's a potential ally or enemy. I was getting to know her. There's nothing wrong with that."

"Yeah, that was some real alone time you had there," I told him.

"What? What's even your point?"

"My point is: I don't know you either." He'd ditched me, not allowed me to share his pain, then hung out on the beach with the good captain anyway. I hated it, and I didn't understand why. Which just pissed me off even more.

I continued accusingly, "You said you wanted to be alone, and then went off to be with her. You're a hypocrite too."

"Fine! So what?" Robert asked in an explosive tone.

"So get out! Go away!" I yelled. "If I'm such a horrible, murdering, manipulative bitch who can't be trusted, get the fuck away from me already!"

"I'm already gone." Robert said. He turned and strode off, not looking back at me once.

He vanished into the trees, and I sat down hard on the gravel drive in front of the garage. Tears started leaking out of my eyes. Wrapping my arms around my knees, I rocked myself, trying to make the horribleness of it all go away.

I had taken away Rick's will. I had almost killed everyone at the checkpoint. I had carried them to safety without knowing how I did it. I would have killed the military strike force in Missoula without a second thought if Thad hadn't intervened.

Robert was right.

I *was* a manipulative bitch who didn't even know how to control her own emotions or magic. If my "wanting" Rick to guard something had compelled him, what else had I done without realizing, and to whom?

I couldn't trust anyone, least of all myself. I put my head down on my knees and wept in giant, wracking sobs.

~

SOMETIME LATER, I picked myself up off the gravel drive, my muscles stiff, my head feeling like it was stuffed full of cotton, my eyes scratchy and itchy from crying. I'm sure my face was a red, tear-streaked, blotchy mess. Redheads don't cry well, no matter how ancient they might be.

Neither Robert nor Rick had come back. Not that I expected them to.

I took a deep breath and realized I didn't know what to do with myself.

On some level, I had taken Robert's support for granted. Assumed he would always see himself as my rescuer and support my decisions in this new world, no matter what I did or didn't do.

Now that he had stripped that away from me, I felt very small. Alone. All the times I thought I'd been completely on my own in this new Weave turned into a lie.

Now, I had no home. And no idea where to go next. Even if Robert hadn't gone straight back to the Grove to tell everyone what a lying, conniving snake I was, I couldn't go back. If I was accidently using magics I didn't understand, I couldn't stay by any one of them. But I also couldn't afford to destroy the only things that might teach me what I needed to know about myself, about what Cythymau had done to me.

I shook my head. I wasn't a required attendee for the summit Thad was putting together. Even if Phineas would be put out by the sudden disappearance of the Maid of Missoula. It might even be safer without me there. I'd need to relocate my stash of artifacts and myself, and then decide what to do next.

I forced myself to take one step, then another, until I was running, cutting through the woods toward town. If I was going to leave, then I needed to do it now, and I needed wheels. I'd figure out how to deal with any roadblocks or checkpoints I might come across on my own later. Right now, getting away and finding a new location for my library was most imperative.

An owl hooted over my shoulder off to my left, then another in front of me on my right. I paused, my steps faltering.

My Sense gave me a good feel for what usually lived in these woods. And there weren't that many owls in general that called this part of the forest home.

It wasn't dark, not even close to dusk in fact, so the idea that not one but two owls were out of their usual hunting grounds and active during the day, struck me as odd.

I scanned the trees and dense underbrush around me, looking with my eyes and my Sense for anything that didn't belong.

Off the periphery of my vision, I saw a flash of something metallic, not animal or foliage, or anything else natural to these woods. I flung myself to the side, but it just managed to graze my arm, leaving a burning path of pain in its wake. I landed heavily.

Scrambling back up onto one knee, I turned and looked for the projectile that had stung me. Behind me, buried in forest floor up to its green flagging was a dart of some kind. I hadn't Sensed its trajectory or felt its presence at all. I still couldn't. My eyes told me it was there. My Sense did not.

Warded. I scrambled behind a tree for cover, putting the trunk between me and the hidden attacker.

I didn't think Robert had been holding something like this in reserve, and even if he had been, I doubted there had been time for him to go home and return with it.

Plus, it didn't really suit his usual style. For Robert, there were much more direct ways to subdue me if he really wanted to. We'd fought with words. But if he'd really wanted to throw down with me over my recent actions, he could have just done so.

Why wait?

Thad absolutely had the skills to make something like this—there was a reason why he'd gained a reputation as a Grove enforcer before he was a director—but he was off with the Feds.

So, either Thad and the Feds had come up with some kind of unholy alliance none of us had been expecting, or this was something entirely different.

The attacker started toward me through the undergrowth, perhaps thinking their dart had hit truer than it had. I felt frozen, my head stuffed full of cotton, and my hands shook.

Crap. Get it together, Andrea. No time to *think* right now. I glanced around the tree, and there were five of them, fully warded. Only one of me.

Five-on-one in a summoner battle is never a good thing, and I had no idea what their capabilities might be, other than some kickass wards.

If I hadn't just fought with Robert, I would have called him and Rick through the link. Now I didn't know if I could do that without compelling them to come.

Had they ever really helped me just because they wanted to?

A branch snapped a lot closer to me than I expected, and I startled.

Piss and shit. I'd gotten lost in thoughts again. I didn't have *time* for this right now.

I gathered myself and ran for the creek bed up ahead.

Vaulting over the side of the creek, I sailed over the slippery rock.

I splashed down, lost my balance, and let myself sit in the rushing water for just a second. The creek was running high, storm-fueled and full of rainwater.

And frigidly cold.

It helped clear my head.

Since this appeared to be some kind of sniper attack, the creek bank might at least give me a minute or two to get my bearings before the next attempt.

Or you could have just put yourself in a situation where they can snipe at you like shooting fish in a barrel, the cynical side of me said.

Given the way my day had gone so far, I was afraid I'd just done the latter.

Piss, I'd gotten lost in thoughts again. I shook my head, not feeling like myself.

Then I scrambled to my feet, slipping and splashing as I used my Sense to help me sprint down the creek toward the trees, silently swearing the whole way.

ROBERT

I COULD BARELY BREATHE AS I trudged back up the road from Andrea's little stash-house.

I knew, of course, that Andrea liked to remain aloof. Liked to keep to herself. Didn't like to share. And one had only to look at the tattoos coating her in strange, whirly symbols that apparently had a similar function to runework to realize that she had some secrets.

But this went beyond the pale.

I believed her when she said she'd put the compulsion on Rick by accident. But she'd managed to lay a *compulsion* on *Rick* by *accident*. Her power had apparently been running out of control for a while now, and she'd come to none of us for help. Instead, she'd gone *back* to Cythymau's world, all alone, and started delving into the magics of an insane demon on her own.

Endangering all of us.

And ... what was with bringing up Captain Tomas-Padilla, of all people? How in the hell did that figure at all into Andrea's thinking?

"God," I muttered to myself, "she keeps this up, she'll be as insane as Cythymau."

"Whuft!" said a voice from directly behind me—a voice that sent absolute shivers down my spine. "But I am not insane, yes?

Inscrutable, maybe, by your standards, but insane, no. I know what I do, why, and how."

I whipped around, bringing my Sense up, though I needed neither my eyes nor my Sense to know who stood behind me.

"Now, Lorents," said Cythymau. "You and I have fought before, yes? Tell me, when have you won? You've escaped, yes—though once through sacrifice. But you've never triumphed. I propose a trade—you surrender quietly, be a good little *plentyn,* so I do not have to apply force and hurt you or your loved ones."

Shit. This ... was bad. A one-on-one with Cythymau couldn't go well for me, in the end. I knew it, and he knew it. How he'd found me, how he'd gotten on my tail, isolated, I didn't know. But once here ...

I'd knew I could never fight him head-on and win. Not a chance.

Of course, I reminded myself, *I've had a lot of practice since the last time I tried.*

"Fuck you," I said offhandedly. Because ... honestly, did he really think I was going to go down without a—

I felt a *slight* disturbance in the air rocketing towards me. Not a lot ... and even with my Sense it was hard to notice.

If Thad and I hadn't trained for detecting warded projectiles, I'd have been tagged, right there and then. As it was, I took a small bit of force from the light breeze around us and condensed it into a tiny blast in the path of the disturbed air ... and whatever was disturbing it. The warded object zipped inches behind me and make a little *tink* sound as it collided with a rock on the far side of the road.

I looked over and saw the small dart, its tip now bent, and looked up at Cythymau. "Snipers with tranquilizers?" I asked. "Didn't figure that you'd ..." What? *Stoop that low?* That wasn't right. "... use backup," I finished lamely.

"Whuft! This is war, yes?" asked Cythymau. "In war, a fair fight signifies poor planning. You and yours talk of peace with the sovereigns of this nation. I wish ... an invitation."

"Not peace," I said. "Alliance."

"It is much the same for my purposes, yes?" Cythymau said dismissively, then gestured at our surroundings. "Now, Seattle Grove summoners surround you. Not as powerful as you, individually, but still difficult for you to challenge alone. Then me." He quirked an eyebrow at me, his eyes twinkling merrily as he grinned. "What use is there in fighting, hmm? Come peacefully, and no one need be harmed."

"I'd just become one of the power-batteries feeding you, is that it?" I said, skeptically, trying to buy myself time to escape somehow.

"Whuft! You'd join your power to me. That's true, yes," said the demon. "Though I cannot guarantee it to be *mine alone,* in fairness to the bargain, yes?" He gave a hooting laugh, as though this amused him.

What the hell did *that* mean? Who else would ... no. Not the time to think about that. "I'll take death." I told him firmly.

"T'would not be death," said Cythymau. "Nor is that one of the choices I offer you. There will be pain, no matter which route you choose." He fixed me with a lethal stare. "I will not kill you, but I have no such compunction regarding those around you. I remind you, the ultimate results will be the same, either way. Acquiescing quietly will be best for all involved, yes? I have always offered you a favorable bargain, Robert Lorents. We've opposed each other so often, now. I think it's time for this game to close. I wish no harm to you. But I need you, and you must come, even if I must force your pact through threat of harm. I offer you this one last chance to come to agreeable terms."

I knew, in that moment, that I was screwed. The demon had planned this. He knew everything I was capable of, and he'd meticulously thought this little attack out. I had no chance, here. None. And I knew it.

So why did it matter so much to me?

I remembered back to some line from some play—it might have been a Shakespeare thing—from English class. *When the fall's all that's left, it matters a great deal.* Or, as my old friend Jake once put it, *if they're gonna eat you anyways, least you can do is make 'em fucking choke on it.*

So, I didn't do the smart thing. Instead, I took a bladed stance towards Cythymau, kept my Sense up, and said, "Like I said. Fuck. You."

The old demon didn't bring up a Sense, or anything like it. He simply held his hands before him and formed a spear of ice that he sent my way. As opening gambits go, it seemed a bit direct—he knew what I'd do with it as much as I did. I reached out with my Sense and

...

And found myself wrestling for control of my Sense.

Time slowed, and for a moment I was back in Cythymau's little cave, with Andrea slapped on the table and the little demon facing me down. Once again, we struggled for control over my Sense, with him trying to claim my own magic from me, and me pulling it away from him.

This time, I was ready for it.

I'd replayed that moment in my mind, again and again. Because in that moment, I lost that fight. Rick had saved me by bursting in on the scene. But had he not, I'm pretty sure I'd have ended up on a slab right next to Andrea. Cythymau's grip on my Sense had been tight, and trying to pull it back from him had proven impossible.

This time, I simply lowered it, then leapt to the side, rolling. The icy lance sped by where I'd been only a moment ago, and I brought my Sense back up.

And I felt no pull from Cythymau on it, leaving me free to summon as I could, at least for the moment.

It had to be quick. I pulled the boulder from the side of the road—the same one the dart had deflected off—thirty feet above Cythymau and dropped it before I felt him trying to get a grip on my Sense again.

This time, the demon had to dodge. He tucked and rolled back and away from the boulder, and let his attempt to grip my Sense fade as he did.

"The child learns!" he said with a grin. "Whuft! Robert of Lorents, very impressive, yes?" Another hooting laugh escaped him. "I wish you for my work more than ever. So nimble! So potent! Your energy could be used for many great things, yes? Be controlled by those who could use it best! Not wasted on petty revenges like making friends sick, yes?"

"That was a long time ago," I said. "And you know it. Nowadays, I do use my power to help people. Help defend them from you."

"Ah," said Cythymau. "But am I who you should defend from? I came here as a savior only, yes? But liberating even the smallest thing takes so much power, and I find your Weave wastes so much. Summoning illegal, *bah!* What is this? The—what word do you use? *Mundanes?* Holding dominion over those with the Sense as though they know best? They do not even comprehend the powers they seek to suppress."

"No," I said quietly, "They don't. But that doesn't mean you can enslave them."

"These mundanes do not seem to hold your qualms against enslavement and extermination, Robert Lorents! If they wish to peddle war, those with Power must put an end to this foolishness before all is lost. All that represents a handicap must be removed. The sooner you learn the right way, the better, yes?"

"Cythymau," I said with a bit of steel in my voice. "Did you come here to fight me, or to jabber at me?"

"Neither, child." he said. "I came here because I need you. This is not even the first time I've told you. Yet you never believe me. If I cannot find a bargain to strike with you, I have the means to take you prisoner. Either way, Robert Lorents, we leave here together, yes? But you determine the cost to you and others."

I felt a little twinge in my Sense, a familiar feeling, and smiled a little bit. I reached down to the gravel road and picked up a small pebble. "Oh?" I asked. I summoned the boulder back into the air, letting it fall ... and generating a significant amount of kinetic force as it did. Force that I stole, and shaped, and put behind the little piece of gravel as I threw it at Cythymau.

It left my hand like a bullet from a gun, maybe faster, and tore through the checked button-down, but exploded into dust when it contacted Cythymau's flesh. He gave it a little brushing motion.

"Your mentor, Grace," Cythymau said, "could not kill me using a nuclear blast. It injured me, yes, but did not kill. What did you think such a small pebble would do?" he asked.

"Distract you," I said with a smile ... and then from the forest a *woomph* sounded, followed almost immediately by one business-dressed demon flying ass-over-antlers backwards as a freight-train-sized ball of force hit him square on.

~

RICK'S ASSAULT wouldn't last. *Escape or pile on?*

Before I had a chance to decide, five more warded objects—I assumed more darts—hurtled towards me.

Damn.

I summoned a couple of boulders from the side of the road to hide behind, giving me cover against that volley, but as I did, I felt the five Senses coming into contact with mine.

None of my new opponents had more than a five-foot Sense. I couldn't see beneath their Senses, though, as all five were actively warding inside—within their little bubbles, these Summoners had more control than I did. Now that was a damned shame; I couldn't summon their weapons, nor their internal organs.

And small radius didn't necessarily mean weak.

Still, it meant that the same pebble trick I'd used on Cythymau might fare better against them. Smaller Senses were much harder to use *defensively*, because reaction time with forty feet to spare and reaction time with five feet to spare were very different things. And since their Sense represented a perfect sphere, well, I was pretty sure aiming for the center of that sphere would yield results.

So my boulders rose, then fell, and five little gravel-bullets sped on their way.

They didn't summon against me. The bastards. They'd been watching, studying—hell, these ones had probably read through a lot of the action reports concerning my favorite moves, and the drop-the-heavy-to-shoot-the-light thing rated as an all-time classic, from me.

They just dodged to the side and kept closing as soon as my

boulders slowed in their fall. My little pieces of gravel went right by them—no hits.

And if this had been me a couple of years ago, that would be the end of that little exchange. But not now.

I Sensed them moving even as I applied the power to those little pieces of granite ... and the funny thing about kinetic force is, it's still there. I'd redirected bullets mid-flight before—it took next to no effort to surround one of those spheres with all five pieces of gravel, with all their mid-flight power behind them, pointed right smack-dab to the center of the sphere.

The sphere of Sense flickered and dropped. And under it, a young man not much older than myself fell to the ground with his abdomen pulverized by entrance and exit wounds and his face registering nothing but pure shock.

Damn. Why'd I think it'd be someone older? Why'd it have to be someone so much like ... me? Someone who, born in a different place, at a different time ... could *be* me? I'd killed young men before—by the dozens, in a blind rage during my escape attempt—but this one struck a nerve for some reason. He was just so ... surprised. Likely his first time in combat. Likely did *not* realize the stakes we were playing for.

"Stop it," I said audibly. "Jesus, stop it. Don't make me do that to more of you. I don't want to hurt anyone. Just ... stop."

"Cythymau says you have to come in," said a young, female voice, and I winced as I pictured the girl I was fighting based solely off those hesitant words in that rich alto timbre. "It's ... for the best."

"It's not," I said. "Not the best for *me,* anyway."

"For all of us," the voice said.

"For none," I replied. "I don't know what he's told you, or what you believe, but you can't trust Cythymau. He's ... if you'd seen what I'd seen, what he does, what he wants, you'd know. He'll use you up and throw you away. And that's if you live through this little stunt—and sending you up against me means he really doesn't care if you do."

She didn't answer that. Four darts left four Sense-spheres and hurtled toward me, only to get blocked by four boulders. But as I was doing that, the four Senses broke into a run, trying to close the gap between us.

I summoned a trench in front of them, opening a ten-foot-deep gash in the road and dropping the earth and gravel in front of me as a permanent fortification against those damnable warded darts. Two fell in—one of whom landed softly, presumably using his/her Sense to pad the fall. One ... did not, I felt her Sense flicker out and reveal her as she sat in the bottom of the trench, clutching a broken ankle and completely vulnerable to my magic.

I reached out with my Sense to kill her. A simple, split-second summons to rip a vital organ—heart, brain, etc. from her body and leave it next to her. I'd done it before, as had Andrea—most efficient way to kill someone within range of your Sense.

But I ... didn't.

She'd shattered her ankle in the fall, and clutched it in pain. She wasn't going to present a threat to me. And I gagged a little bit as I realized how close my combat-honed instincts had brought me to simply murdering a helpless human being, drawing my Sense in at the last split-second to stop myself from going over that line.

And that's how he got me.

One second of hesitation. That's all it took. One second, in combat, where I pulled back. The remaining two Sense-spheres climbed my little pile of dirt and gravel and my Sense ... flickered out. Not for long ... just long enough for two little darts to embed themselves in my shoulder.

Tranquilizer darts, I thought. *Damn.*

Tranq darts, by the way, don't work like they do in the movies. You get hit with a tranq, you're going to go down—but there's a lag time as the drugs work their way into your system. If I were a trained medical summoner, I might have been able to separate the ketamine from the other myriad of chemicals that run through our bodies and remove it —as it was, I had no clue how to do that without entirely killing myself.

Which left killing others.

I could have done it. I had enough fight left in me to take all of them on, still. They were young. Amateurs. Maybe Rick would beat Cythymau. Maybe the commotion would draw Brandiole out here. Maybe, maybe, maybe. The deep, dark part of my mind screamed at me to go down fighting. To tear apart these bastards who'd done this to me. I had enough consciousness left, enough time. I could kill each and every one of them.

But it wouldn't matter.

I took a knee and lowered my Sense, lifting my hands to the air. My foes—my *captors,* now—stepped towards me slowly as the drugs began to take hold in truth.

They call ketamine a tranquilizer. It's not, really—not in the classic sense. You still retain some semblance of consciousness—you just aren't really in control of your actions. A K-hole is very much like simply being a camera on the world around you. You can perceive it. You can even think, a little. But you're not going anywhere.

Which is why I was able to see Cythymau as he approached, looming over me, and said, "Whuft! So *violent.* So wasteful. No intent behind it at all. Why did you have to hurt them so, hmm? You are still *mine,* Robert of Lorents. As I said, the outcome is the same. But now? One more, dead by your hand. Needless. Be grateful I do not vent my disappointment on your companions here and now."

He slipped a syringe of something else out from his little business suit pocket, now covered with dust from his scrap with Rick. As he injected me with ... I'm not sure what, I felt even the limited consciousness left to me by the ketamine starting to slip.

And the last thing I remembered was the demon's voice saying, "It is time someone put a restraint on you. Sleep, child."

ANDREA

I AWOKE with my back against an eerily familiar surface. Even before my consciousness fully returned, my Sense told me I lay surrounded by runes carved into a stone table beneath me.

My breath hitched, and my heart caught in my throat as adrenaline-fueled alarm rushed through me. My eyes flew open in an attempt to deny what my Sense had already told me.

The room beyond the stone slab was unfamiliar, but the stone itself appeared almost identical to the one I had lay upon for centuries in Cythymau's old cave. I wanted to believe everything was just another one of my recurring nightmares. But no, the collar of my t-shirt cut painfully across my neck, pulled to the side from the way I was laying. The stone was cold and rough under my fingers, and the rune carvings dug painfully into my shoulders and butt.

Another person lay crumpled against one of the walls of the room, unconscious, and I recognized him, too. Robert.

Panic surged through me anew as my consciousness told me no, this was real, we'd both been captured. Again. I sat bolt upright, scanning for signs of Cythymau.

Other than the slumped form of Robert, the room around me was empty. Silence welled around us, and I couldn't feel anything out of place with my Sense. Just an empty room, a rune table, and us. I stayed sitting for a moment, shocked to realize I could still move. I had not been bound. Nothing held me like a pinned bug this time.

At least, not yet.

I wore the same clothes. I had not been stripped bare, either.

Air swished in and out of Robert's lungs, his heart pumped steadily, but his mind was passive, sluggish. If he was injured, I couldn't Sense it. Cythymau was nowhere within the range of my Sense, though I didn't believe for a second he'd really left us alone. Not when he finally managed to get control of both of us.

I swung my legs over the side of the table, and for a second the room swung crazily around me, my stomach heaving. My feet hit the floor and my legs almost went out from under me. Fumbling, I used the table for support until my shaking knees and calves stabilized enough to hold my weight. I wasn't sure if it was a reaction to finding myself where I was, or a consequence of whatever drug had knocked me out. Possibly both. Carefully I pulled myself upright, feeling like a spring coiled too tight.

I walked up next to Robert, trying to see if there were any wards hidden from my Sense that I needed to physically peel away from him, but found none.

Everything about this screamed that Cythymau had set up a test or a trap for me, to see what I would do. But no matter what that demon hoped for, I really only had one option. I had to get Robert out—I owed it to him. To Grace.

That said, Cythymau was not stupid. Manipulative, cruel, ruthless, and calculating, sure. But never stupid. Which meant he'd placed us here, exactly like this, for a purpose.

He was looking to find something else from me. But what? If I knew the answer to that, though, I never would've signed a pact with him in the first place.

I didn't feel evil or manipulative. But did anyone ever, really? That demon certainly didn't seem to feel anything like guilt or remorse toward me or anyone else I'd ever seen him interact with over our long partnership. As soon as *that* thought hit me, I shuddered.

Get it together Andrea. Cythymau was not your partner. And yet, after my fight with Robert, where I'd had to confront everything I'd hidden from him, the thought stuck and rankled.

"Robert," I said tentatively, nudging his shoulder with my sneakered foot. No response.

I knelt and put a hand to his neck. It was warm but he didn't feel fevered, and his chest rose steadily with breath. I tried again. "Robert, wake up," I said. "We have to figure out how to get out of here. Now."

How had Cythymau been able to take Robert without Rick interfering? What had happened to the Cornuprocyon? Had Cythymau killed him? I couldn't feel the Cornuprocyon's presence at all, and that sent a sick shiver of fear all the way down to my toes. If I couldn't feel Rick, he couldn't feel us, and no spiky rescue would be busting down the walls this time.

I bit my lip and then froze as a familiar presence crossed the perimeter of my Sense, pausing at the room's threshold.

"Whuft, child," the demon's voice chided, sounding warm, congenial. As it always had. "He won't be alert for some time yet. That one is quite troublesome and disruptive when he wakes, yes? I am risking no mishaps this time. I find my time and patience are not truly infinite."

I looked over my shoulder at the creature who had spoken, though I already knew who would be standing there. Cythymau, the supposed savior of my youth, my tormenter, the first and only Visitor I'd ever made a pact with, stood just inside the doorway.

Blue swirling rune patterns covered his skin from head-to-toe like usual. But he wore a cable-knit sweater with the sleeves pushed up above his elbows, showing off the rune tattoos covering his crossed arms. The modern clothes looked out of place against his ancient skin. It was not how I was used to seeing him. In his own Weave, he'd favored the hardened leather armor of his far past. His feet, emerging out the bottom of a pair of black slacks, were still bare, their soles observably scarred by age and hard use.

"It would be best for you not to take my patience for granted either," the demon said to me, his gaze sharp, calculating.

Those words woke me up from whatever overload had kept me fixed, mutely staring at him. My fury swelled up, visceral and immediate. It exploded at my core, bursting outward, scalding my throat with a screeching wail. My heart pounded like a jackhammer in my ears, and my skin felt electrified. I launched myself at Cythymau, intending to rip his heart from his chest with my Sense and tear it to pieces.

"Such a lack of control, of gratitude," the demon said, stepping easily aside as if my attack had been clumsy and poorly aimed. It had been neither.

Cythymau stripped my Sense away from my control as easily as if he twitched a piece of paper out of my fingers. He redirected it, driving a ringing blow into Robert's chin that jolted his body and moved it several inches farther away. I stumbled and knelt on the floor, my chest heaving. Blood dribbled from a new cut on Robert's mouth, and he moaned, the skin where the blow had landed already reddening.

"Let me go. Let Robert go," I said, gritting the words out between clenched teeth. My hands curled into fists, nails digging painfully into my palms. I inched back toward Robert, putting my body between him and that demon, even as I knew how futile the gesture was likely to prove. I still had to get him out. Somehow.

"Tsk, tsk. What have you learned all this time?" Cythymau asked, shaking his head, his eyes glinting with the humor that I hated. "You still throw your words, your purpose, around like a very blunt instrument indeed. Surely, I have taught you better than this, if you but reflected for a moment." He chuckled quietly to himself, at what joke I had no idea. Ever since our first meeting ages ago he'd always laughed, as if even his most horrific acts were somehow amusing. It was just one more thing I couldn't understand and doubted I ever would.

"I am not your student. You have never taught me anything." My voice came out strained, scratchy, each word an effort of will forced past my frozen lips. "I am nothing more than a convenient, captive tool you picked up."

"Ah, but you misstate that," the demon said with his easy smile that fooled so many. "We made a pact, a contract, an agreement, you and I."

He walked farther into the room, his footsteps making very little sound despite the mostly empty space. He trailed a finger along the edge of the table where I had lain earlier. "Decided and sealed with your own blood—by your own hand—long before this Lorents boy was ever a glimmer of unnamed potential in the universe." Cythymau leaned over the table, his hands splayed to support his weight, his suddenly sharp gaze boring holes through my skull. "You promised your freedom and your life as a price, a compensation for what you asked of me. A price you willingly agreed to pay."

"You tricked me into paying," I retorted hotly, taking another step back toward Robert.

"*You* summoned me," Cythymau said. "*You* begged to me for my help, not the other way around. As I remember, we discussed our bargain at some length, you and I. You thought it fair enough at the time." The demon spoke in a placid tone, as if we discussed whether to have tea or scones. A part of me wondered at his gall even as my brain frantically tried to come up with some way to distract him and escape.

"I even warned you the road you walked was dangerous and would likely not end up where you expected," Cythymau said.

"I didn't know what that meant. You took advantage of that." I spat the words out like foul-tasting poison.

The demon stood up, dusting off his hands, and then shrugged noncommittally. "I am not at fault for your ignorance, then or now," he said. "The rage you feel is but a symptom."

A disbelieving laugh escaped me. "A symptom of what?" I said, though I should have known better than to ever ask this demon a question.

"A symptom of your self-hatred, since you cannot accept you made this choice of your own free will *long* ago. That you did not investigate this deal as thoroughly as you think you should have actually has very little to do with me."

I crouched on the floor by Robert, my breath coming in great gasps. Hate filled me to the brim, and I waited, my head hanging, my gaze fixed on the cold floor, pinned by his logic.

Cythymau came around the stone table and knelt in front of me. I could see the blue tattoos decorating the pale skin of his bare foot, and I held myself motionless, wanting the perfect moment to strike, my eyes still fixed on the floor.

Cythymau tapped a finger against my forehead. "Andrea. Andrea. What you know, I know. This is not new. You and I are linked, as we have been since the day we struck our bargain. A pact is not so easily broken or frayed as you hope. You asked for access to power, and I have given that to you. I have *done* as I said in the beginning." And his voice actually held a thread of anger, as if *I* had somehow disappointed *him*. I scoffed at the thought.

I grabbed at the big stone slab that stood next to us with my Sense, trying to summon it on top of the two of us. He swatted it away and sent it tumbling the other direction. It crashed into the wall, narrowly missing Robert. A reminder that next time, Cythymau would crush him instead.

I jabbed a frantic elbow upward, trying to smash it into Cythymau's trachea while he was distracted. He caught my attack easily, then wrenched me down with an armlock, my chin banging painfully into the cold floor. Tears of frustration and pain leaked down my cheeks—I was powerless to stop them too.

Still twisting my arm behind me, Cythymau planted a knee in the middle my back. I struggled to breathe under his weight. Black crowded the edges of my consciousness. Whether from the impact with the floor or a lack of oxygen, I wasn't sure.

"I am older and more skilled than you still. If you do not start heeding me, I will visit everything you try to do to me upon the Lorents boy instead. Tenfold worse."

Fear clutched at my heart and squeezed. I knew this wasn't an idle threat. Any further displeasure I caused, he would vent on Robert. The fight drained out of me, and I sagged like a deflated balloon, wanting to just roll up in a ball and cry.

Cythymau shook the arm he held, causing the muscles in my

shoulder and back to cramp painfully. "Quell your temper tantrums. Your dissatisfaction with your deal is your own problem, not mine. But since you insist on having something to do with your rage, I will give you something of use to do for me."

Black despair crowded in at me, and I tried to blink it away. In the end, no matter what I did, I found myself controlled by this demon, subject to a bad bargain I would never get rid of.

"I trust I have your attention at last," Cythymau said.

The pressure of his knee left my back. I sat up dazed. Cythymau walked over to Robert's slumped form and grabbed the neck of his t-shirt, using it to drag Robert unceremoniously behind him.

"Come," Cythymau said. I tried to tell myself that if the demon hadn't been hauling Robert out of the room like a sack of potatoes on the way to the dicer, I wouldn't have gone. But either way, I followed him, my sneakers squeaking noisily as we walked down the long, dank hallway.

Cythymau finally stopped next to a large stone slab in a cavernous room filled with row upon row of stone slabs. I tried not to vomit, though my stomach roiled. He had a job for me *here*?

He hefted Robert's slack form onto a slab several rows away from where a workbench with assorted pigments had been set up. Next to the workbench, a woman lay with several unfinished tattoos traced out on her shoulders. Her mind was quiet, her eyes shut, her breathing even, as if she were simply in a deep sleep.

There were at least ten rows of four stone slabs each in this room, and eighteen of them already had tattooed occupants strapped in. I could feel their magical energy, their Senses, getting added to the resources the demon had at his disposal, their power humming along the tattoos covering Cythymau's body.

"So which of these is to be my pyre?" I asked, not bothering to hide how bitterly fatalistic the words felt.

"Do you wish one of them to be yours?" Cythymau asked, one of his eyebrows quirking.

"No."

"Have you thought about why you are here?" Cythymau said.

"You brought me here," I said.

"On your own two feet, I led you here," the demon said.

"Okay, but you kidnapped me before that." I said, feeling defensive that it even had to be pointed out.

"I retrieved a deserter, and proposed consequences for further derelictions of duty. Lorents is a most suitable prod in some situations, as it turns out."

"You've made your point with me, so if that's his purpose, let Robert go," I said, grabbing onto that like a life preserver.

"Whuft, child! You know I never give something without receiving. What would you give me for the Lorents boy to go free? Remembering that I have unfinished business with him—what do you offer?"

I narrowed my eyes at him, frowning. "I will strike no further bargains with you. The one is bad enough."

"Pity. You quite had my hopes up. Putting that aside for now, then, here is what you must do." He gestured at the workbench. "Come." He pointed to the floor, indicating the spot next to him at the bench. Rage pulsed through me, but I still needed to create an opening to get Robert away.

I forced a neutral expression onto my face and walked over to where he wanted. By the very nature of standing next to each other, our Senses already overlapped.

My skin itched, crawling with sensation at his proximity. I thought it was in my head, a manifestation of the intense hatred I felt anytime I saw him.

Then I realized it was from the power crackling through him from everyone batterized in the room. The Weave around him practically vibrated with the stolen, concentrated potential he held.

"You just said I'm not to be a battery," I muttered, staring down at the pigment and implements laid out, so I wouldn't have to look directly at him.

Which meant I was totally unprepared when he grabbed my wrist, my reaction time much too slow. Several things happened at once, and I felt dissociated, as if I watched myself from a great distance.

The demon reached out through our link, wresting control of my Sense, raising the blue tattoos hidden in my own skin to glowing blue flame. I felt when he deliberately triggered one like a jarring in my bones, and suddenly other Senses, untethered from their owners, flowed through me.

"Your punishment for running away is not to rest, but to tattoo and prepare others for what's needed. As any good student should start by laying out the basics for their instructor."

That demon curled his own fist around mine, using my hand to mix blue pigment with a dark, viscous blood. Then under his command we loaded the resulting pigment into an archaic-looking silver implement that appeared like a cross between a dagger, a syringe, and a ball point pen.

"The ratio of blood to the pigment must be 2:1, or the runes lose potency in the host." He said, as if he instructed me in some mundane recipe.

He showed me how to test the implement, making sure the blue dye flowed out the tip easily.

Cythymau loomed above us both. The summoner lay quietly, her skin defiled by the half-finished tattoos. My hand shook as I held the tattooing artifact.

"This isn't something I wish to learn," I said. Horror choked me as I remembered when I'd been bound and tattooed myself. "I couldn't steal away others' lives and magic in this way."

"These lives are not stolen; they have been freely given for a greater cause."

"Robert's isn't," I said.

"Ah, well." The demon gave me a knowing look that I couldn't quite interpret. He gloated over knowing something I didn't. But then I guess, what else was new?

"His is a special exception," Cythymau said. "He has not agreed, but he kept interfering. I allowed you to stay close to him for a time; you appeared to enjoy yourself well enough."

He was saying I wouldn't get far enough, fast enough. He knew everything I had done, would do. I was weak. Powerless. Chattel to be used and depleted. My only value to him lay in my usefulness to his plans.

He laid his hand over mine and brought it to the woman's skin, carefully pricking and coloring in the rune laid there. To my surprise, the runes appeared red and bloody, not blue. The pigment vanished into the skin as if it never was.

The silver tool carefully pricked over and over again, causing the blood to bloom under the woman's skin, slowly making a map for the demon's magic, a battery that he could use at will, just as he could use me. Another captive.

Cythymau had lied. Again. Rage did not help with this task. Rage would cause even more harm to someone who'd done nothing more than believe a demon's deceptive words of hope. Just like me.

I found myself concentrating on the lines of the traced runes, the contents of silver tool, the calmness needed to keep my hand from causing even more harm.

I squinted. I had previously assumed it was the act of cutting that had created the link between me and Cythymau or between me and Rick. A true blood-bond. But we weren't cutting into this summoner. These were tattoos, with ink sunk below the surface of the skin, like a permanent rune tag, written in invisible marker. In that case, how did it work? Blood was the conduit used for runes, but it still needed a path, a roadway for the Sense. And that usually required an exchange, creating a two-lane road. But these runes lay dormant until …. When?

"What kind of pigment did you mix with the blood? What kind of blood is this?" I asked.

"Ah, she speaks." Cythymau said. "What type of pigment and blood do you think I used?"

"I don't know. That's why I'm asking." I retorted.

"You complain that I do not explain my techniques, and then when I attempt to have conversation with you, your rage prevents you from comprehending the most important details. You need to fully Sense what is happening if you are to learn it, and yet you force yourself to ignore it."

I could have come up with a hundred excuses that sounded like truth. Told him it was because this chamber was too like my own personal hell, or because he had kidnapped another hostage so I would not flee, abandoning Robert here.

Instead, I tried to see what he might be "showing" me.

The runes that Cythymau had brought to life on my skin were blindingly obvious, but in addition to those, now that I could look for the tell-tale pigment under my own skin, I could see I was just as marked as the demon himself. I might not know exactly how it worked, but now that I knew what I was looking for ... My body was a maze of unseen runes. Was I Cythymau's biggest trap? Just how many summons were resting in my body?

At this moment, how many summoners was Cythymau using to power his runes?

How many was *I* using?

I looked down and realized that, at some point, Cythymau had taken his hands away. I was still tracing the runes laid out on this poor woman's body with the tattooer, etching his control into her skin. I took a deep breath and tried to curb my roiling stomach. I paused, lifting my hands away from her skin, unable to continue a firm line.

Cythymau took the tattooer from my hands, making a tutting sound. "Why do you always focus on the most undesirable part of any action?" he asked me.

Robert groaned and shifted on his slab, rolling to one side and feeling his jaw.

"It seems your friend is about to make an appearance," the demon said. He cocked his head to one side, looking at me consideringly. "I believe you and I have come to an understanding, yes? If so, I will let you check on him. Remember, if you do anything reckless, I will return him to you in a way you will hate to see. Go now."

I stared at him blankly for the space of two breaths. Then nodded jerkily.

I knew this demon too well.

Opportunities squandered would not come again. This would be the only chance I had to do something.

I had to try to save Robert now, or give up on it completely. My hands felt numb, and yet somehow also freezing cold.

Consequences be damned.

I walked shakily over to where Robert lay, trying to keep my head empty. Not to think. Not to feel. I needed to just exist and ride above this moment. I had done it before. I could do it again.

I couldn't let Cythymau see into me. To see my thoughts. My plans. I wouldn't stay just another extension of the demon.

Finally close enough to Robert's prone form that he was a part of my Sense, a part of me, I paused.

Throwing all my strength, all my will into it, I pried at my Sense. Attempted to wrench it away from Cythymau's control.

The demon hooted with laughter. "Did you think I did not see this coming, foolish *plentyn?*" he asked me. "You are a millennium too early yet to fool me. Though you value the well-being of Robert Lorents less than I expected, to risk him so."

He yanked back and his tattoos crackled into incandescence, swirling under his skin. Straining against our contest of wills, I saw double, edged with stars.

Moving instinctually, I fed power into my own tattoos, tearing against Cythymau's grasp on me.

"Is this all your defiance amounts to?" Cythymau asked me. "After all this time? Tis embarrassing. It is time for you to concede now, yes?"

I screamed, putting my whole being, my whole soul into my next actions.

Looking within, I triggered my own tattoos. Deliberately. Consciously.

And wrestled control of my Sense back from his network.

I pulled the rune slab from under Robert, letting him settle gently to the floor. Then summoned the carved rock directly above Cythymau.

And dropped it.

The demon deflected it with a superfluous flick of his hand. I gathered the rest of the empty stones in the room above him. Twenty-plus slabs, stacked all the way to the ceiling of the cavernous room and avalanching down toward the demon.

In the split second Cythymau's attention was elsewhere, I turned my focus and yanked on the power network we were plugged into. I stole all the power to myself.

It smashed into me. My tattoos brightened into radiant blue flames across my skin.

The power coursed through me in a rush. Exhilarating. I felt juiced up, invincible—as though all my fear and rage had just turned into useless cobwebs and burned away.

With this new strength, I wrenched myself out of Cythymau's grasp. I turned the link we shared against him, copying what he had done to me so many time in the past. The demon's tattoo's flickered, dimmed, then faded as I cut off his access to his network of batteries. For the first time since I'd met him, his skin looked plain, weathered and leathery, no tattoos in evidence.

Cythymau let out an expletive in a language unknown to me.

If this was the only way to leave, so be it. I would embrace it. Whatever I was.

I reached out, grabbing onto Robert. Held my Sense around him like a protective bubble until we were like one being. I refused to lose hold and leave him here.

Then I slammed all my stolen power into the teleportation runes under my skin. They flared even brighter, casting brilliant blue shadows on the walls. Just for a fraction of a second.

I flung us away from here. As far away as I could possibly get us. Clutching desperately onto Robert's semi-conscious weight in my Sense the whole time.

Reality folded with jarring abruptness.

The next moment, cold wind buffeted at us both. We fell through darkness toward rolling waves I could barely see. I reached out with my Sense to slow our descent, peeling energy away from us, seagulls crying overhead.

We plunged into the waves. I came up gasping and choking as a ship's horn sounded. The waves shook me as I struggled to keep afloat, head above water, with no shore or ship within Sense range.

Robert tried to keep sinking.

I floundered after him.

Piss and shit, but we were fucked six ways to Sunday.

ROBERT

I DON'T REALLY REMEMBER the impact.

That's probably a good thing, really. I've no idea exactly how high above the Puget Sound Andrea summoned us—and she refuses to tell me. What I remember is suddenly being very, very cold.

You see a lot of jokes about being awakened from a deep sleep with a bucket of ice water. It's one of the more dramatic forms of waking up—and it makes for a good video on the internet. Something to sit about with one's buddies and have a chuckle at.

Well, when it's an entire *ocean* into which one is dropped whilst still unconscious, it *certainly* has a stimulating effect. My body grew half-numb in the frigid water before I even *felt* the pain from slapping against the surface tension of the Puget Sound in the most dangerous bellyflop of my life.

The second thing I remember is the taste of seawater as I tried to gasp for air.

There's a moment in between when the lungs register their need for oxygen and when the brain registers ... anything at all, where your body runs on instinct alone. Without my brain fully engaged, my lungs just sort of did what they thought was best—inhale. Lungs, on their own, are sort of stupid that way, and the gagging didn't start until after the overwhelmingly salty taste of the sound hit my mouth.

I panicked.

I'm not proud of it, but I couldn't help it. I knew, with absolute certainty, that I couldn't breathe ... and that sort of thing rouses instincts in a person I didn't know about until just then. Not *good* instincts, either. I locked up and thrashed about with my hands, trying to find something to grab and pull myself up with. My brain had no control over it—none. I simply let my body do what it could to try to keep me alive whilst my brain screamed its despair.

And then I found something.

I pulled on it. Hard. I mean, I absolutely reefed on whatever I'd managed to grab onto, because my body *knew,* instinctively, that pulling something *down* meant pulling me *up,* and at the moment up was the only thing that mattered.

And ... it worked, for a second. My face broke the water and I gasped, sucking much-needed air into my lungs in a joy, but only a single breath before I began to sink back down. *No!* screamed my lungs. *Not enough!*

But whatever I'd managed to grab was now beneath me, and I couldn't grab anything else, and so I splashed wildly at the water once more, knowing that one breath to be my last.

Which is when Andrea shot out of the water from where I'd pushed her down and punched me squarely in the face.

The shock of it—of taking *concussive* damage—engaged a very different part of my instincts for a moment, which gave her just enough time. She grabbed one of my wrists and twisted, rotating my body as she pulled me in close to her, then hooked her other arm under one of my armpits before transferring her grip to hook her second arm underneath my *other* armpit, gripping me from behind in what would have been a full-nelson, had she locked her hands together.

She didn't, though. Instead, she leaned back in the water, taking me backward with her, if above slightly, and I could sense us begin to move as she kicked under the surface. "Calm down," she said ... and it sounded like she was *trying* to be calm and soothing, but the edge in her voice didn't quite get there. "I have you, Robert. Calm down."

And ... I did. I felt the warmth of her body through our shared, thin clothes, and the strength of her arms holding me against her. And I stopped coughing ... as though the seawater in my lungs had simply ... left. It took me a moment to realize that's *exactly* what had happened —she'd managed a summoning on top of her aquatic maneuvers.

"Where ... " I asked, but didn't get any further than that.

"We're in the Puget Sound," she said. "Not sure exactly where, to be honest, but it's better than where we *were*."

"How—" I'll admit I was still pretty out of it, and formulating full sentences seemed to be far beyond me. Fortunately, she picked up what I was asking without more words than that.

"Same way we got out of the van before they blew it," she said. "Which is to say, summoning. Of course, we're still in the middle of the Puget Sound, and while I'm a *good* swimmer ... "

She left off there, and I nodded. The Sound represented a tiny fraction of the Pacific Ocean, but in terms of distances to swim in frigid water after being abducted ... we had some problems. My brain finally started to engage again. "Can you ... teleport again?"

"I'm pretty tired already, and it's not really long-range. I don't think I could get us back to shore, if that's what you're asking, and *you'd* have to carry *me* after."

Damn.

"So ... did you have a plan?" I asked.

"Um," she said. "Sort of. I tried to teleport us somewhere Cythymau couldn't follow immediately. *That* seems to have worked."

I chuckled weakly—then half-grinned in amazement. This was, perhaps, the most conversation I'd had directly with Andrea without an argument recently, and for some reason she seemed far more relaxed with me than she'd been before. It figured that as soon as things got absolutely terrible, that's when she'd feel at home.

"Well," I said, "I suppose it's better to drown ..."

"Yeah," she replied in a quiet tone. "Though I think hypothermia might get us first."

I nodded—the water was *cold,* and I still didn't have the strength to bring up my Sense. Andrea undoubtedly had hers raised, as she always did—but heating that much water would be a monumental effort and would probably accelerate the drowning portion of the evening.

"Damned if we do, damned if we don't," I said, and she nodded.

And then ... we didn't talk. She continued to kick us towards the shore, as though willing us to make it—but we wasted no further effort in speech. I closed my eyes and allowed my weakened body to be dragged futilely onward.

And even so, it felt ... right. To be in that place, with Andrea. We'd fought next to each other before. We'd risked our lives for each other before. And if we were going to go ... well, there was something sort of nice in the thought that neither of us would die alone. I leaned my head back against her shoulder, and a small smile crept over my face as I took what comfort I could in the closeness of her.

I don't know what went through her head. Rage at the situation? Despair? Did she share my odd acceptance of the inevitable? I couldn't know—nor could I see her face. So I chose to believe that she and I were of like mind. If it wasn't true, at least it was a comforting illusion.

There's a quiet beauty to the moment you accept that you're going to die. A sort of stillness comes over you, and you become afraid of nothing at all because you've already accepted the worst. I have experienced this sort of tranquil acceptance probably more times than is actually healthy, but in the moment, I have to admit that it's as peaceful as I've ever been.

The thunderous blaring of a ship's horn sort of wrecked that, though.

A great deal of western Washington is marred by the Puget Sound. It's this body of water not quite significant enough to create any sort of political divide greater than a county line, but still massive enough to be difficult to traverse with a bridge. There's one spot where that's not true, at the Tacoma Narrows, but other than that, commuting from one side of the Sound to the other involves a rather lengthy drive around it.

Or over it.

I hadn't really known about the ferries, when I'd lived in Spokane. But it turns out that the State of Washington maintains a robust fleet of ferries. Massive, green-and-white floating chunks of highway onto which the commuters drive directly from terminals set up at various locations throughout the Sound ... the most central of which is directly next to downtown Seattle.

I hadn't ridden the ferries ... yet. They intrigued me, sure, and the fact that they kept running even after Cythymau had taken over the state was a testament to the importance of their function to the people of the Sound. But being in an enclosed space with literally nowhere to run but the sea hadn't really appealed to me.

Being in the Puget Sound already, though, my groggy mind struggled to come to terms with the massive beast bearing down directly at Andrea and me. The wide-open front of its carport gaped like a hungry maw ... but even that was above our position. The ferry had sounded its horn, but in the dark it had only spotted us at the last moment ... and we, being confused and looking in the wrong direction, had managed to *not* notice a massive, well-lit ship sneaking up on us on a relatively flat body of water until we had no time to swim out of its way.

Hypothermia's a trip, people. I don't recommend it.

I remember feeling a vague sense of irritation. Here I was, all nice and tranquil, consigned to a slow death by hypothermia, and this ferry had to come along and ruin it by killing me in an entirely *different* way. It felt ... rude. Like one last nut-kick from the universe on my way out.

And then I felt the jarring feeling I'd come to recognize as Andrea's own, weird version of summoning, and suddenly the two of us were dripping wet and laying on a steel deck in-between the front bumper of a maroon Pontiac Grand Prix and the back end of an old, faded-blue Vanawagon with a massive bumper sticker that read "Shaggin' Wagon" in psychedelic colors.

And that's when I began to shiver.

So did Andrea. The wind whipping through the ferry's carport hit our wet clothes. We hadn't been shivering in the water—I'm no medic, but I'm guessing our bodies just didn't see the point—but as soon as the windchill hit us, we both started shaking uncontrollably.

We heard footsteps on metal, then a door opening and people shouting to each other in voices long used to being raised over the hum of an engine. Andrea, still shivering, got up for a moment.

To this day, I'm not sure what it is, exactly, that Andrea did to the old Vanawagon. It could have been an application of her Sense. It could have been some criminal trick learned in days long gone. It could have been the thing was never locked. Whatever it was, she popped open the rear hatch, raising it upward.

I could hear the footsteps on the deck in the carport, but none seemed to be walking betwixt the cars, yet. The boat crew likely were looking for bodies in the water, not stowaways, but our sopping-wet status would certainly beg many, many questions ... and at the moment, I was content that any radio message being sent out by the ferry's crew involved running over people in the water, not stowaways. Chances were that Cythymau would figure it out eventually ... but the ferry itself continued its movement away from Seattle, and if we could just make it to shore in one piece, that would be ... something.

And so I stood shakily, bracing myself against the van. My whole body trembled with cold and exhaustion, and my left leg began to twitch as though it *really* wanted to cramp up on me, but I clenched my teeth and pushed myself up into the back of some stranger's van with what little physical effort I had left.

The smell hit me before anything else. The smells of marijuana, both fresh and burnt, permeated the interior. The back seats of the van had, in classic hippie tradition, been removed and replaced with an old mattress, and a mesh laundry bag that *had* to be uncleaned added a sort of stale, sweaty undertone to the weed. In my muddled state, I couldn't resolve whether it was the most disgusting smell I'd encountered in my time on earth, but I at least figured it had to be top ten.

Which—combined with that "Shaggin' Wagon" bumper sticker—

did *not* say pleasant things about the mattress upon which I now lay. I tried not to think about it too hard.

Andrea began ... stripping. Somewhere in the back of my mind, the part of me that was still a hormone-driven boy approved heartily. But hypothermia, pain, and exhaustion had me at the point where most of me just wanted to do the same. So, I removed my own drenched clothing. Once we were down to our undies, she reached for me, enfurling me in her arms, and pulled the rank sweat-blanket up over the top of both of us.

It felt ... right.

THE NEXT THING I remember was the door to the Vanawagon opening.

How long had we been asleep? Couldn't have been long. Hell, the ferry only crossed the Sound, it couldn't take more than an hour to do it. My head swam in groggy confusion, aided only slightly by my adrenal glands kicking out the last bit of whatever they could after their long night of work. Andrea lay next to me, entwined with me in an embrace, and she looked up groggily as well.

Neither of us were fast enough.

The head that poked into the van looked almost exactly like what I'd expected when I saw the van itself. An older man, late sixties, early seventies. John-Lennon-style circular glasses. A long, braided ponytail of silvery-sheened hair, and an almost equally long, unkempt grey beard. He wore a tie-dyed shirt with nothing more than a peace symbol on it.

He looked at us for a moment, taking in the picture of two young, mostly naked bodies intertwined atop his mattress.

One has certain cultural expectations for moments like these. Rage, normally. A sense of violation. We'd broken into his property, after all—the man was entitled to be pretty pissed off at us. I still had no energy to fight, nor did I have a desire to hurt this old hippie, but I couldn't be sure that Andrea wouldn't react in her normal, efficient— and ofttimes lethal—manner. Damn.

But after a moment, the old hippie just cracked a big smile and said, "Far fuckin' out, man."

My expectations and reality jammed together in my brain like two cogs with misaligned teeth. "Um," I said, fighting to bring myself to cognizance. "Sorry about …."

"No, man, spreeeead that love. I get it," he said, sliding himself into the driver's seat. "Gotta find the right place when you're young, my brother and sister. My home belongs to everyone who enters with love in their hearts."

Now, I don't like religion, generally. My experiences with it came up largely from the foster system, and religion had generally been the cover story people used when they wanted to abuse someone. Faith, as a concept, had always seemed an illusion. But every once in a while you meet someone who truly practices what they preach. Francene, for instance, had done so when she stepped between me and a demonic wolf-creature.

This wasn't that … but it felt similar. We'd violated this old man's property, but he seemed … happy about it. I'd always made fun of hippies, but in this moment, it felt like I stood before a man of profound faith. Even if he lived in one the worst-smelling vehicles I'd ever been in.

"I have to drive this love bus off the ship in Bremerton, though," he said. "You two need to turn arooooound, or are you free to journey?"

"Uh," I thought, then shook my head, trying to bring my brain more fully online.

"Our wings are wide, my brother," said Andrea next to me … in a tone that almost exactly matched the old hippie's. "Where are your winds blowing to?"

I looked at Andrea, gawking. She barely noticed.

"Right on, sister," he said. "Right on. I plan on driving the coastline, cruise the one-oh-one, hear her mighty crash upon the waves and see the sun set down behind the blue."

"Mmm," she said. "Groovy, man. I could dig that. We'd planned on exploring her hidden parts, down in the little bays and shallows. See if we can get her to give us some of her nourishment from the beaches, but if the wind's blowing—"

"No, man," he said. "That sounds like a vibe I could dig. Chill in the hidden places, right on. South we go, then." After a moment, he added "Names don't matter, much, but you can call me Blue Mole. I see the whole earth, and I just dig it, man."

"I'm Willowbreeze," Andrea said without any hesitation whatsoever. "And this is Robert," she added, not even bothering to assign me a hippie moniker. I didn't know whether to be insulted by that, or relieved.

Just then, the overhead announcement allowed for the starting of engines, and the Mole turned back toward the front of the van, turning the key and letting the little engine whine itself to life. "Far out," he said. "Far fuckin' out. What a great day to be blessed with company, my brother and sister. Let's go see what the day has in store for us as we walk this life-path."

As the van began to roll off the ferry and onto land, I sank back down into the mattress and into the warm arms and embrace of my companion. We were in a stranger's van, naked, vulnerable, and too exhausted to use our powers—and yet somehow I felt safer than I had in months.

ROBERT

"YOU SURE YOU two love-birds don't want to just continue in flight with your buddy the Blue Mole? Doesn't look like whatever you're heading into has a chill vibe, and might be that floatin' on the wind is a better path for you two earth-children."

I had to admit that, sitting in the passenger seat of the Shaggin' Wagon a block and a half away from the house, there was a certain pull to Blue Mole's words. The rank smell of the van had long since normalized itself into my nostrils, and the last hour of listening to him and Andrea talk hippie philosophy to one another had notes of nostalgia for a time I'd never been in.

We were both wearing clothes that were ... not borrowed, as we'd likely never get a chance to give them back, but communally shared with Blue Mole. I was in all denim—including the jacket, covered with old patches denoting the places of his travel. She was wearing another tie-dyed shirt, long enough to reach her knees even after being belted like a dress. Our own clothes had been, well, communally shared with Blue Mole, not that he'd ever find much use for Andrea's. Or, hell, maybe he would. Who knows?

To ignore the plight of the world and just venture down the Pacific

Coast Highway, enjoying the world with the simple love Blue Mole tried to show everyone ... it had appeal. In a different life, or a different time, I might have taken the old hippie up on it. Lived a life of nothing but love for my fellow man and ignored the need for a home outside of a beaten-down old VW bus. Blue Mole had shown me a glimpse of a different way to live, and I envied him his joy in life.

But.

I looked back, and Andrea and I locked eyes. The simple fact remained ... Blue Mole's way of life was an illusion. A pleasant one. It beckoned with a siren song ... but the only way a man like him could live free was if we kept up our fight to hold the universe in one piece. It was sort of nice to know that he would be out there, taking it easy for the rest of us, though.

"Sorry, man," I said with a genuine note of regret for the might-have-been in my voice. "But we have some things we have to do."

"Sounds like a drag, man," said Blue Mole, but his tone was more empathy than argument. "You want to live a free life, cut them ties and just love the world as it comes."

I smiled at him weakly. "Yeah," I said, as I opened the door and slid out. I turned back to look at him. "Hey, thanks. For the ride, I mean." Andrea, stepping out the side door of the van, nodded.

"We're all children of the earth, man," he said. "I help you, who knows? Maybe someday someone helps me. Whole point is to put as much love into the world as we can. All of us do that, we'll all be groovy."

I laughed a bit and nodded to him. "Yeah," I said. "Guess I'm trying to do that in my own way, really."

"You do you, my man. You do you."

Andrea said her goodbyes as well. I'd forgotten, really, that Andrea had grown up in the sixties and been taken by Cythymau in the seventies. In a way, both she and Blue Mole had been suspended in time—her by being magically removed from it, and him by a simple, stubborn refusal to surrender a philosophy that the world had moved past.

But walking back toward the house, I felt the weight of the world begin to settle once more on my shoulders. Exhaustion, held at bay for an hour by the conversation with Blue Mole, combined with a sense of what was to come and dragged me downward. I opened the door, walked back into my life, and braced myself for the next step.

The first thing that hit me when I walked through the door was a high-velocity mother-figure in the form of Francene. How she'd managed the acceleration to achieve her velocity the moment I swung the door outward I'll never know, but my intended "I'm home" turned into "I'm ho-oooof" instead.

I've been hugged by Francene many times. Her hugs came in flavors, really—the short hug hello, slightly longer goodbye. I'd held her in my arms for an eternity when I finally got a chance to talk to her about her husband's death.

None of them—not *one* of those prior hugs—prepared me for the fierce, mother-bear protectiveness that came with this particular embrace. I really lost my sense of time, as the force of the hug seemed to affect my perception. It had to have been mere seconds, though, as nobody else reacted in the moment.

Then my foster mother released me and kissed me on the cheek. And before I could say *anything,* hit Andrea with a hug *just* as fierce as the one she'd laid on me.

Andrea's face froze in shock, then slackened into a passive sort of acceptance, then darkened a bit further into something unreadable. But she returned the hug gamely, and in due time Francene released her.

"So," I said. "I take it you know what happened?"

"*Know?*" said Francene. "You think we *know* where you were? All we had was Matt telling us something about you being taken—there's been some chatter on the net—and Rick looking like a loyal dog whose master had left him. We didn't *know* anything, all we had were the things we *feared.*"

"I ... Mom, look. I'll tell you the whole story, I promise. But it's been a hell of a night, and right now what I need more than anything is to slee—"

"No," said Andrea from behind me. I'd never heard Andrea give a *command* before, but that firm, cutting tone of voice couldn't be called anything else. "There's things, Robert. Things I learned while you were out. We need to talk with everyone, and we need to do it now, and it doesn't matter a bit how tired we are."

I looked at her—this mad woman had freed me from captivity. Had pulled me from the waves and had sheltered me in the safety of the Shaggin' Wagon. I'd saved her life once, but surely she'd repaid that favor over and over enough. She owed me nothing ... and something in my brain clicked.

I'm not proud of this. Maybe it's all the bad fiction I used to read, maybe it's growing up in the town of Spokane. But even after she'd rescued me from my confines in the Spokane County Jail, Andrea had always been *the girl I'd rescued.* My crowning achievement. My damsel in distress. A walking symbol that I was ... what? Some kind of knight in shining armor, riding about and performing deeds of derring-do?

But she stood there, every bit as exhausted as me. Hell, probably more so, as it'd been her magic and not mine that had saved our asses repeatedly over the last night. There were bags sunken in below her eyes, and her hands shook a bit, if you knew to look for it.

And she spoke with an easy authority. The exhaustion stripped away her nerves, her dislike for social interaction, and left her bare and exposed ... and the thing underneath was *steel.*

That's when I looked back at how I'd been treating her. How I'd been thinking of her. And all I could feel, in that moment, was a deep and resounding shame. Andrea was the girl I'd rescued—and I was the boy she'd rescued. And that meant precisely nothing. She wasn't a symbol, or a possession—and while I'd known that consciously, I knew I hadn't admitted it to *myself.* But now ... she was none of those things. Hell, she wasn't even the girl I was afraid to admit that I had a little crush on. She was my *partner.* And damn, but I was lucky to have her.

"Right," I said. "Coffee. And get everyone roused, Mom. We've got some things to talk about."

~

" ... the Puget Sound. Which wasn't terribly safe, but was the only place I could think of to put us that would only kill us *eventually* instead of *immediately*," said Andrea, finishing her little story. I looked down at my cup of coffee, still three-quarters full and lukewarm, by now.

It's funny. I've been in mortal peril more than most people. There's only so many times you can think *this is how I die* and be wrong before the thing becomes almost blasé. Our harrowing escape from the Puget Sound didn't even make my top five. But listening to Andrea describe what had happened while I was knocked out gave me the absolute willies. On one hand, there's something to be said about dying in your sleep, peacefully. On the other, learning about it after the fact is the sort of thing that causes one's anus to form a completely airtight seal for a moment or two.

Andrea stood before the rest of us. Phineas and Francene had the two recliners in the living room, the rest of us deferring those positions to them almost by instinct. Matt and I shared a couch, and Amy draped herself over the loveseat. Andrea had ceased talking but stood there without giving so much as a concluding statement. A bit of awkwardness passed as we all realized she'd finished.

Phineas broke the silence first. "So," he said, "you're telling us that you are an intelligence asset for our greatest enemy." He put no malice into his voice, no blame, no recriminations.

"Yeah," said Andrea.

"What's this bond between the two of you like? Is it consistent? Intermittent? How does he use it, exactly?" The way Phineas fired off the questions reminded me of nobody so much as Grace. He had a problem in front of him, and he'd begun to spin the thing about in his mind, looking at it from as many angles as he could.

Andrea, though, had never known Grace. A year prior, she'd have simply retreated into herself at the barrage—now, she faced Phineas with the same cold desire to exchange information.

"It's ... " she said, then stopped, her brow furrowed. "It's similar to the bond Robert and I have with Rick, actually. Same sort of magic. I have ... some of his power. It's how I've been able to do some of the things I've done. But in return, he has some control. Access. To me, to what I know, how I feel."

"Hmmm," said Phineas. "Which means Cythymau knows about the summit. Knows where it's happening. Knows where, when, and who. Knows where we are, too. Right now. In fact, could be listening in on this very little tête-à-tête. That's a problem."

".... Yeah," said Andrea. "I'm sorry."

"Oh, honey," said Amy from the loveseat. "No. No, you don't need to—"

Phineas cut Amy off with a look and a gesture of his hand. "And how long have you known about this bond?" he asked. He kept his voice modulated, down-to-business. No sense of blame or accusation —but no sense of forgiveness, either.

"I ... I'm not sure," said Andrea. "I think a part of me's always known. But ... "

"Very well," said Phineas. "You understand that this makes you a security risk? While I don't believe that he is paying attention twenty-four-seven to whatever information you're sending to him, we have to assume any given conversation with you is being listened in on by our enemy. And any location you know about—including this one—is at risk of being attacked."

"I know," said Andrea, hanging her head a bit. "I'll ... go pack."

The room fell quiet as Andrea walked out, defeated not so much by Phineas as by the circumstances. I wanted to say something. To do something. But ... she was right. Phineas was right. We were all at risk. The summit. The resistance. Andrea had saved me from Cythymau's clutches ... but she'd been the reason I'd fallen into those clutches in the first place.

"What are you people doing?" asked Francene after a beat. She looked around, meeting each of our eyes in turn. "*What the hell* are you people doing? Are you just going to let her leave like that?"

"Ma'am," said Phineas in that same, formalistic tone. "She is making a decision for the good of us all. And it happens to be the correct decision."

"Like *hell* it is," said Francene. "She is a *child.* There aren't that many of you. Of us. She has rescued my *son* on multiple occasions. She has saved the lives of almost everyone in this room before. If she walks out, vulnerable as she is, and all alone ... you all know what happens to her. She hasn't got a prayer. You may as well put a bullet in the back of her head right now, for all the chance she has if she walks out that door."

"She'll lead him back to us," said Matt quietly. "He knows where we are."

"And he's done what with that information so far? He waited until you were *separated* before making his move. Because when you're not separated? You've kicked the hell out of his people. God, you people keep making decisions out of *fear,* and that's no way to live your life."

It was probably the exhaustion. I could barely string two words together, but when Francene started talking about how to live our lives, I couldn't stop myself from picturing Blue Mole for a moment. *Whole point is to put as much love into the world as you can.*

"She's right," I said quietly. "I know it's a risk. I know she's a danger. But she's also one of us, and that has to mean something. Groves haven't managed to survive this long in the shadows by fracturing."

"Well, when someone turned State's ev—" Phineas began.

"Shut up," said Amy. "Andrea's not a rat, selling us out. She's someone with a bug on her. That's a different situation. And Robert's right—we're more than just a Grove, here. More than just a scrappy group of dissidents. It's been us against the world so long... " She shook her head. "We're a family," she said. "Sometimes dysfunctional, I'll grant. But what families aren't? Still—home is where, when you have to go there, they have to take you. And this is Andrea's home."

Francene nodded. "That settles that," she said, dusting her hands off each other as she stood from her recliner. "Now. I'm going to go try to convince *her* that she's being rather silly in getting herself killed this way. You all figure out what you're going to do about it."

And with that, Francene exited the room, leaving me, Amy, Phineas, and Matt alone.

"Dammit," said Phineas. "There's too much on the line for this kind of sentimentality. We're looking at the first actual summit between summoners and mundanes. We're finally on the brink of forging an alliance to stand against this demon that's invaded our world. Everything's on the knife's-edge, here, and we're going to just let our adversary have a camera into our planning? You *know* he's going to move to break up the summit. He has to."

"Doesn't matter," I said. "Amy's right. It is what it is. Andrea's saved my life at least three times that I count in the past twelve hours. I can't cut that tie. So we need to move past this first idea and assume she'll be here. Assume that Cythymau has a camera and knows all our plans. So, now that's decided, what do we do?"

"I don't know," said Phineas.

"I don't either," said Amy. "God, I love the girl, and she's staying, that's settled. But what we do with her is a different question."

"Well ... Francene is sort of right, isn't she?" I asked. "Cythymau's known where and who we were this whole time, and it's not like he's gotten up in our grill about it. We beat the hell out of his strike force in Missoula—maybe he's scared to mess with us."

Phineas snorted. "You beat a small unit designed to take out mundanes," he said. "It was well and cleanly done, but it was a fraction of the resources available to the Seattle Grove. And Cythymau knows damned well what he has to work with. No, if he decides to descend on us in force, the best we could hope for is to make it cost him—but he'd win, in the end. And he knows it."

"Sure, but we'll have additional Groves defending the summit, right?" asked Amy. "I mean, maybe we can hold against him."

"And protect the mundanes? No. There might be a chance in a straight fight, if we didn't have people to protect—but where his victory condition is the death of a couple of mundanes he's going to get it. If Andrea stays with us, the summit is off."

And that's when Matt inhaled. We'd all sort of forgotten him— Matt had the natural talent of true nerds for folding himself into the scenery, becoming unnoticed in a social interaction. Maybe it was instinct, maybe it was conscious, but he'd been quiet this whole time. Yet when he inhaled, preparing to speak, we all fell silent.

Because Cythymau was wrong. I had raw power. But *Matt* was the most dangerous opposition he had. The Turing to Cythymau's Hitler. And we all knew it.

"The interesting thing about cameras," he said, "is how much they *don't* see."

ANDREA

I FOUND THE OLD, ratty, thrift-store suitcase that Matt had gotten me last time we had to move. Throwing it on my bed, I then proceeded to take all the clothes from my closet and throw them in. Sure, I could have summoned them from wherever I ended up, but packing is a ritual, a parting, a way to say goodbye to where you have been and ready yourself to pull up your roots.

It gave me something constructive to do with myself while I was too exhausted to think. I was going to have to be on my own. Eventually, if I walked out that door, the ultimate result would be that Cythymau would find me and control me. Again. Because this whole time, my escape had been an illusion. Walking out of this house was the same as admitting I would walk back into his, because hiding was laughable. But if I stayed, I would just pull the others into captivity or death with me.

I wadded up a t-shirt and threw it with more force than needed into the pile, then groaned.

"Piss and shit!" I yelled, flailing my hands. I *had* to leave. I knew I did, but it felt like a betrayal of everyone who had helped me in this Weave. Even that prissy Thad who was working so hard to bring the summit to fruition.

I laughed without humor. Nothing could doom the summit to failure faster than me. I wasn't even sure anything could be salvaged at this point. I might be leaving much too late to save it.

That demon's voice twisted through my head, and hell if I knew if it was real or imagined. *Remember, you chose this. You begged me. You summoned me.*

Yeah, yeah, I had. And I regretted it. Deeply. And apparently I would never stop paying the price for it.

I sat down on the bed and sighed, sweatpants destined for the pile twisted up in my hands.

Someone knocked on my door, and then opened it without waiting for a reply. Probably predicting that I would've told them to go away if they gave me any time.

Robert's foster mom, Francene, peered at me through the doorway. Then let herself in, one hand still on the knob as she closed the door gently but firmly behind her.

"Andrea, dear, I need to talk to you," she said.

"Now isn't a good time—" I said, putting the sweatpants I held onto the pile.

"And when will there be a good time?" Francene answered placidly. "Never, I would guess, given the state of your suitcase, but I have some things I must say to you. For us, everyone, and for myself. So I will try not to take up much of your time, but I will say them now."

"Be my guest," I said snidely, not meaning a single word.

"Thank you, I will," she said, and sat down next to me on the bed, her gaze levelly meeting mine.

"I understand why, after all you just said, you feel like you have to leave." Francene picked up my hand and held it between both of hers. I resisted the urge to pull it away. Once I left, who knew if I'd ever have the chance to hold onto someone again. I didn't think she could change my mind, but her clasp felt warm and comforting.

"I will not force you to stay, if after we've talked, you really believe you must go. But Andrea, let me tell you what I see here." Francene squeezed my fingers earnestly as she spoke.

"Uh, that's not necessary. I'm pretty sure I know," I said,

deliberately turning my head and breaking away from her gaze to look out the window.

"I'm pretty sure you don't. You're so sure that demon's got his hooks into you."

"How can you say he doesn't?"

"I'm not saying he doesn't, actually. But I doubt it's as simple or as cut and dried as you appear to believe. Would you at least agree that, where Cythymau is concerned, he's got your head so twisted up that you generally can't see the forest for the trees?"

That characterization rankled, but I supposed I couldn't really debate it. Put me in the same room as that demon, and my survival technique was act first and think about it later, or hold very, very still and do nothing at all. "I suppose that's fair," I said grudgingly.

Francene nodded. "But I can see you and how you react under pressure, whether from Cythymau or elsewhere. And what I see is a person who is trying her best to protect those around her, even when she doesn't know the right thing to do, or make the best decision all of the time." Francene gave me slight smile. "What I know is this: my son wouldn't be in the next room if you hadn't already put your life on the line to rescue him. Multiple times. You kept him alive, and in one piece, and brought him back home to me. None of the others in there could have done what you did."

"He wouldn't be tangled up with Cythymau if not for me either, though, so I'm not sure that actually counts for much." I said, immediately discounting her words.

"Really?" Francene said. "Let's think about that assertion for a minute – that is, your thought that, if not for you, Robert wouldn't be tangled up in this mess with Cythymau. How does that follow?"

"Well, he and Grace tried to rescue me, and—"

"So, the first time Cythymau became aware of Robert was when he came to rescue you, then?" Francene asked.

"Well, no, that was actually the second time Robert had been to Cythymau's Weave. The first time was while he and Grace were trying to defeat Rick—"

"Ah, so if you hadn't been there at that time, when Robert first went to Cythymau's Weave, Cythymau wouldn't have been interested in Robert at all?" Francene persisted.

I groaned and pulled my hand away from hers so I could use it clutch my forehead. "That's not—I can't say Cythymau didn't already have an interest in Robert, but my presence didn't help anything. I only made the situation worse. And I'm not really sure I *didn't* compel Robert to come back for me. It turns out I've compelled Rick to do a few things when I didn't mean to. Piss and shit, I could be compelling you to come talk to me, because I really don't want to leave!"

"Well, I'm happy to hear that you don't want to leave us, but I assure you I am here on no one's volition but my own." Francene said, ignoring my agitation with a placid chuckle. I glowered at her.

Francene bumped her shoulder into mine and then continued, "I don't even know how you're supposed to have laid a geas on me, when I had every intention of holding onto you as fiercely as I could before you even walked back through the door alive tonight."

I started to protest, but Francene shook her head. Then she looked up at the ceiling as she said, "You have no idea how many prayers I said while you both were missing!" Her voice trembled, her heart speeding up at the remembered anxiety, and I could feel the pent-up emotion behind her words.

Francene finally looked back at me, her gaze uncomfortably direct. "Plus, Robert is quite capable of falling into his own messes without help from anyone else," she finished crisply. "From what I've heard, Robert actually attracted the attention of this demon before *anyone* with his clumsy, ill-advised summoning."

I looked at her stunned. I couldn't even argue with that. From what I remembered of Cythymau's interactions with Robert, she was probably right.

Francene continued, "Even Grace only found Robert because he was about to be murdered in that horrible mall massacre," she said firmly. "You have to stop believing that everything that happens with *that* demon is your fault. Do you somehow *control* Cythymau's actions?"

No. I pressed my lips into an annoyed line, refusing to voice the word and shooting Francene an irritated look. She seemed to take that as encouragement.

"Oh," she said innocently, opening her eyes wide, "Well, if you're not controlling him, then perhaps you praised all of those ruthless exploits and encouraged him to do more? No?"

I scowled at her. "It doesn't change the fact that I originally asked him for help, for power. I didn't know what kind of pact I was making, or what he would do after, but I really did do that. I made that choice. And I don't want anyone else paying the price with me or because of me, not if I can help it."

"I don't know if this will help, my dear, but we all make bad decisions. It's impossible to go through life without having one or two truly disastrous choices in your past that you have to learn to deal with."

"Those bad choices don't usually have the potential to end the world," I said.

"No, but they can and do kill people. Even those made with the best intentions originally. I chose to foster a child. But for that choice, my husband would be alive. Does that mean I killed Donald? Or that Robert did? No."

Francene recaptured my hand and squeezed it firmly. She stared earnestly into my eyes as she said, "You can't foresee the consequences of every decision ahead of time, you can only make your best guess given the knowledge at hand, and then try to make a better decision that takes into account your past experience and any new knowledge the next time."

She leaned toward me conspiratorially. "The trick, one that so many have to learn, is not to let a bad decision become the only thing that you are. It's true that some decisions can't be undone, but what did you do and learn after? That decision is just part of circumstances as they are now. That decision is *not* all that you are."

"I get what you're trying to say, I think, but doesn't stop the fact that Cythymau could be eavesdropping on everything we say right now. Piss and shit, for all I know, he could take control of my Sense and use me to murdercute you—everyone—and I wouldn't be able to lift a finger to stop him. It's just not safe for me to be here."

Francene shook her head. "This is just my opinion, but I believe it's just as unsafe for us—if not more—for you to go. You're the only one who truly knows how that demon operates. You say he has a link, a bond to you, that you struck a bargain, and you can't get out no matter what you do."

"That's right! I did. I thought it was the best option at the time, and I agreed. But I regret it. I regret it so much."

"Well, but, my point is, what are *you* going to do now? Not regret, because that's really a pointless emotion, except as a prod to something else. I've been watching the bond you share with Rick, with my son. It fascinates and mystifies me, to be honest. You can tell if they're alive, injured, what they're feeling. Now you say you share a similar bond with Cythymau. What does he share with you?" She paused, considering. "I'd guess it's uncomfortable, negative. I'd likely want to block it out myself, if I could."

I blinked at her. Why didn't I feel anything from Cythymau's end of the tether? Was that on purpose? Somewhere, unconsciously, had I blocked it out for my own protection? I could definitely feel when he used my Sense to fuel his magics, but I'd never tried to reach out or find him, like I could detect Robert or Rick. I could clearly feel those two through the link we shared with very little effort ...

"The other thing that really bothers me," Francene continued, "is that a pact is a contract. Robert and you have both said that this demon has a business-like demeanor. He likes transactions. And a pact or a bargain is nothing more than a fancy contract between two parties. It's binding for both sides. So, my question for you, Andrea, is what did Cythymau agree to? What *can't* he do by entering into an agreement with you, and why did he do it?"

"I-I don't know," I stuttered.

"Speaking of which, why did he pick *you*?" Francene was apparently on a roll now, and I couldn't even get a word in-between her barrage of questions. "Are you sure it's just because you have a large Sense? I mean, you and Robert both have fairly big ones from what I've heard, but surely they're not so big that it makes you or Robert unique?"

"I think I was just there," I said. "And conveniently stupid enough to strike a bargain with him."

"Really? This demon who—from everything I've heard—is a consummate manipulator, a mastermind who sets pieces in motion before anyone else is aware a game is afoot, just *happened* to pick you up because you were conveniently there and available? He didn't plan it at all? He had no reason to hold onto you other than you just *happened* to be there?"

I sat there, stunned. Francene had no magic of her own, had only tangentially been present when Cythymau had been, once, at Robert's graduation. And yet she had flipped my paradigm on its head with those questions. *That* demon never did anything without a reason. If he picked me up as something 'convenient,' he would have no problem disposing of me just as conveniently and with no fuss. And yet, at least so far, he had done the opposite.

So, just what was I to Cythymau? Why did he even care if I went off and did my own thing? Surely he could find a replacement for me easily if he tried, and I assumed with him collecting new batteries, he had. But in that case, there was no reason to kidnap me and Robert in the first place. What exactly was his interest in me? In Robert? Why us in particular?

"No," I told Francene slowly, testing the words out as I said them. "You're right. It doesn't fit. Cythymau doesn't do whimsy, as whimsical as he may try to appear to others. If something has no use, he discards it. Or ignores it from the beginning. But I summoned him. I asked him for help. He warned me, and we struck a bargain," I said, unconsciously repeating back the words he'd said to me earlier.

"If that's true, what exactly did you get out of it? What did he get?" Francene asked mildly. "Why is Cythymau so fixated on you and my son? Are you *sure* you're not the best hope my son has of living through whatever this demon is ultimately trying to do to our world?" Her eyes earnestly searched my face. "Are you certain that walking away from us isn't the worst thing you could do right now, for both you and us?"

"He knows where we are. He could attack us anytime."

"But he's apparently known that this whole time, and he hasn't. He's always waited for you and Robert to be isolated to attack. So why? What is he gaining by waiting? Because there must be something."

"Robert and I together aren't that powerful, and certainly neither are the rest of the Grove members, so I really don't know—"

"But there must be a reason," Francene repeated, "You just said yourself that he never does anything without one. So, what's been holding him back all this time? And are you really sure you want to break whatever it is up? Without understanding it?"

"You'll all be in danger."

"Oh my. Dear, we already are. And that doesn't change whether you leave or not. You just wouldn't be here to see it through with us."

"Greater danger then," I said, somewhat grumpily, since Francene was not buying into my self-sacrificial plan at all. Had poked it all full of holes, in fact. I was grateful, but I somehow started to feel like I looked just a little silly. "But my concerns about Cythymau and his abilities really aren't silly at all." I said out loud before realizing I was going to. "With me here or wherever, he could attack us anytime," I reminded her.

"He could, but he hasn't. From my perspective, the only thing your departure buys the rest of us is the ability to move to an unknown location that Cythymau doesn't know—yet. And we'd be giving up an asset who knows the most about him, his magic, his abilities. We'd lose the Maiden of Missoula, whom the mundanes *love*. Not to mention you're one of the Grove members with the most raw magical oomph from what I've seen—after my own son, of course. So, you're Cythymau's unwilling spy. So what? Stay with us Andrea. And help us figure out what to do about it."

I found it somewhat amusing that she still managed to throw a boast about Robert into her impassioned plea for me to stay. There were holes in her logic; there were definitely things she had put in their best possible light.

But when it came down to it, she was right that there was a lot that I didn't understand about Cythymau's actions. That I'd never thought to examine closer until now.

My brain hurt from exhaustion and too many questions. "I still don't know that staying is the best thing, but I can't deny that leaving only leads to one outcome for me, if not everyone else. I'll stay for now. Until it's clearer whether my presence is still detrimental or not. But I don't even know where I need to start. I don't know how to keep everyone safe."

"What you need right now," Francene said in a no-nonsense voice, "is sleep. Don't you dare go anywhere without telling me or the rest of us." Francene gave me a one-armed hug, then stood up. "And unpack the suitcase. You don't need it." She quietly exited, leaving me to fall into an exhausted, dreamless sleep.

I would deal with all the problems and disquieting questions tomorrow. After all, Francene had decreed it.

ANDREA

After my discussion with Francene, I slept long into the next day, not waking up until late in the afternoon, judging from the sun slanting in through the windows. I felt groggy and sluggish, as if my body really wanted to hibernate for several days more.

When I finally poked my head out of my room, no one was home. I'd been scared that it would be awkward; I had no idea what more to say. Everyone else was well into their day and likely much too busy preparing for the summit to have much free time. Even Francene appeared to have run out somewhere. I had the house to myself, and too many things crowding my head to know what I wanted to do.

My stomach growled in protest, and I tried to remember when I'd last eaten. Not last night, and not any time during our kidnapping. I padded into our shared kitchen and rummaged through the cupboards until I found the peanut butter. As I prepared myself a peanut butter and jelly sandwich, I debated my options.

First and foremost, I needed to keep everyone alive. Second, I needed to not blow up the summit by accident, which meant I needed to stay as far away from the preparations for it as possible. Third, I needed to figure out what Cythymau was thinking, at least when it came to me and Robert.

Ha. That was the hardest of the three.

Those all seemed like pretty broad and laudable end goals. Also pretty intimidating, since my opponent was a millennia-old demon that had more knowledge in his pinky than I had encountered in my whole extended lifetime thus far.

I sat down at the empty dining table and chewed my sandwich thoughtfully. Francene had asked me what I wanted to do with my experiences besides regret, what I wanted to accomplish with everything I'd learned.

That got me thinking that Cythymau wasn't the only one I'd learned from lately. Francene, Robert, Thad, Matt, Amy, Phineas, all of them had taught me something. Even those community college classes that Matt had insisted signing me up for turned out to be useful.

One of my first challenges with the blood-pact I'd made with Cythymau was that I'd been too young and naive to require its terms be written down and a copy be provided to me.

I mean, it was a blood pact. The universe witnessed it and all. As soon as it'd been invoked, it instantly became binding with all its terms and conditions. But it wasn't like I could go over to the local recorder's office and demand a copy.

I had no doubt the demon remembered what had been said and promised word for word, but I was only human, and that had been an awfully long time ago. The details were ... fuzzy.

I remembered my mom, my gran ... vanishing. They'd gone to investigate strange deaths in the town nearby and never returned. I had tried to find them, failed, then gone to enlist help from the rest of our small Grove community, and found broken chaos, emptiness, and rumors of demons instead of the people I'd hoped for.

I'd been alone, barely trained, ill-equipped, and certain I needed help to prevent more deaths. I'd tried to summon ... some guardian spirit. I couldn't even remember its name anymore; it had been so long. And instead, somehow, I had summoned Cythymau. He'd offered his help for a price. And I'd accepted, thinking I had nothing to lose, and therefore could pay any price.

But I hadn't conceived anything that would come after. So together, we had banished the Lycaon pack that had killed my family, my friends. And I'd returned to Cythymau's Weave with him.

I squinted my eyes shut, trying to remember *exactly* what he'd said, what *I'd* said. But I couldn't see anything Cythymau had gained from that encounter—except of course, me.

I sighed. I needed a trigger. Something to catapult me back into that moment. Just like meeting Blue Mole. I hadn't missed the hippie brethren I'd grown up with until talking with Blue Mole. Hadn't even remembered them. But as soon as he spoke, I'd answered in kind, and I'd felt more at home than I'd ever managed to be, since my return to this Weave.

Blue Mole had spoken to a piece of me and brought forward the memory, nostalgia, and words from me by just existing next to me. His way of life, his philosophy, welcomed me home and introduced me to myself in a way I still held somewhere, but that I'd forgotten.

I wept a bit inside that I couldn't just travel with him, letting life flow around me, eating off the land, and letting fate take me wherever it willed.

But for me, while Cythymau still held on to me, that lifestyle could be nothing more than warm nostalgia.

Francene told me that the relationship between Cythymau and I had been an exchange. That sounded right in a way I couldn't explain in words. I'd given up my freedom—I thought in return for his help banishing the Lycaon all those years ago—but in hindsight that had been incredibly small potatoes to him. It hadn't needed to be near as flashy as he'd made it appear at the time, with lightning, and barriers, and warded artifacts. And he certainly hadn't needed *my* help to banish a few Lycaon.

So, what had we really done that night? What had been *his* aim? I'd gone to his Weave briefly, we'd rummaged through his storeroom, equipping ourselves for the fight. He'd asked me to solve a puzzle, testing me, and I had. Even looking back, I could find no significance to that, though.

None of this answered why he'd wanted the pact in the first place. So, what he had gotten out of the exchange?

The easy answer was me, but that didn't seem quite right .... And even if so, why, then?

What *did* a millennia-old demon mean when he promised to "aid me"? And what had I truly gotten in return?

He'd told me something yesterday ... What was it?

Why must I always dwell on the negative aspect of an action.

So, what was the positive aspect he thought I was missing? That we were linked? That I literally had access to his whole library, even if most of it was gibberish to me?

I wiggled the idea that our arrangement had value for me like a sore tooth. I had to admit, Cythymau liked deals that he could crow about having a mutual benefit. So where was my benefit here? If he was thinking of my perplexing, unchanging age, he could shove it. I hadn't wished to live like this forever.

But one of the things those college professors kept harping on in my courses included breaking broad goals or big problems into smaller, more manageable tasks so you weren't overwhelmed in front of a deadline. I was dubious whether that could be applied to my current situation (it felt a little weird to assign myself homework in front of a possible battle-to-the-death), but since no one else was currently around to bounce ideas off of, I decided to give it a try. I could only hope that, as I muddled along, I'd figure something out. I wasn't crazy enough to start experimenting with my link to Cythymau, but ...

I felt for my link with Rick, and was able to tell he slept in the forest on the outskirts of Shelton, not far from where I'd hid Cythymau's library. Hazily, I could feel Robert, awake and frustrated about something, but I purposely didn't try to find out more. If I needed to know, he'd tell me.

∼

It wasn't hard to get Rick riled up into a rousing game of force-ball catch. His spines ruffled up in competition. the Cornuprocyon hurled yet another ball of force at me. I spun, flinging it up and back at him. He sneezed in the torrent of wind, not bothering to dodge, laughing at me with his tongue lolling out. His big club tail twitched back and forth in dangerous glee.

"Hey, watch the trees buddy," I told him. "You're gonna crush ... well, more of them." The big racoon bounded up to me and swiped me with a big, rough tongue that left my t-shirt and face sticky with overgrown-racoon spit. Over the link, I could feel his contented pleasure. He felt deforestation and dodging falling limbs were supposed to be part of the fun of the game. He seemed disappointed he had to point that out for me. Earth-conscious, Rick was not.

"I know you're excited, but down boy! Chill your jets," I told him. He bounded away and then bounced right back with a series of *woomphs* that shook the surrounding foliage. The next ball he hurled at me came with the force of a freight train. Had I not been expecting it, it would have flattened me and created a culvert that would have held a small creek.

Fortunately, my Sense was large enough that I had a little lead time to dissipate and divert it before swinging it back in his direction. Rick shook his head, unsure why I kept returning a softer pitch than he'd expected. *I'm being nice.* I wasn't sure this game was as fun as Robert and Rick both seemed to believe, but I was here to gather data and experience anyway. Besides, even if I wasn't enjoying the game as much as advertised, Rick sure was.

Rick's joy in the day, my presence, and the match came to me clearly through the link. Along with his confusion that I apparently thought force ball was 'just okay.' Which caused the big galoot to double down in an attempt to make it more to my liking.

It took all of my effort to not die in the next few seconds.

"I wasn't complaining the game was too easy, Rick," I wheezed. "Truce, I call truce. I need a break."

I flopped into the shade of a large, bushy hazel tree and spread my arms wide while I looked up at the clouds.

Rick huffed, a little put out that I hadn't found his extra efforts rewarding, and circled a few times before laying down himself, his head on his forepaws as he stared at me dolefully. I was finding if I concentrated, I could actually track where he was pretty well, even when I couldn't see him through the forest. It wasn't pinpoint by any means, but it pretty much meant I could predict where the next "playful" onslaught was going to come from.

I closed my eyes and concentrated on the link between me and Rick. I knew Robert "fed" Rick part of his Sense through the bond they shared. I'd never done that, preferring not to become snack food, no matter how friendly Rick appeared.

Cythymau had turned my Sense into his own instrument, using it how he saw fit at his convenience, the whole time I'd known him. Until our most recent encounter, I thought it'd been a function of being on the runed table where I'd been strapped. Certainly, he used the runes on those tables to augment his link between those trussed-up summoners or the tables would be pointless. But it appeared, at least in my case, he didn't actually *need it* to fuel his own magic.

I'd been conscious and walking around when he'd easily snatched away my Sense to beat up Robert. We'd been in pretty close proximity, but I couldn't guarantee that was a requisite for anything. I knew from my own experience that all it took to activate the link between Rick and me was concentration. And my Sense was, conveniently, always up. I was about ninety percent certain that that was just one more thing I had to thank Cythymau for.

Which led me to believe Cythymau didn't need the help of any device to feed off me, steal my Sense. Not unlike how Robert voluntarily fed the Cornuprocyon, but in reverse. He already had everything he needed. In fact, with the way summons worked and the copious amount of compound rune tattoos currently hiding on my body, I had to assume he could get me to do just about anything at distance.

The only question, then, was why he hadn't yet. What was he waiting for? After all, once he stole control of my Sense, he knew much more about what my tattoos were for than I did. I was going to need to draw out a list of my tattoos and start looking them up in my hoard of Cythymau's tomes. That could be tomorrow's task.

A thought came to me.

"Rick," I said, "What do you think about trying a game of tug of war or keep away? I'll give you treats later," I promised. Who was I kidding? That big lout was up for trying anything. I'd had him as soon as I thought the word "game."

❧

SEVERAL WEEKS LATER, I stood in front of Matt's van-du-jour and glowered at the beach and sprawling hotel before me, with a sick feeling in the pit of my stomach. There was no way Cythymau wasn't going to hit this summit. And here I was, giving him a really good look at it thanks to my requested presence here with all the other fools.

Robert stepped out of the van, Matt close on his heels. He came over with a jaunty step that I found *completely* inappropriate and clapped me on the back.

"Lighten up, Andrea," Robert said. "Matt and I, we got this. Cythymau's a goner if he hits this Summit."

Ugh, were there any more famously doomed last words? Hold my beer, perhaps?

I crossed my arms over my chest, knowing my irritation came from worry, but unable to leave it unvoiced. "Look, I came because you all convinced me it was a bad idea to stay behind. But I don't know that it's such a great idea to have me accompany you all to the summit venue," I told them, hugging my arms nervously. "I can see all the wards you have set up outside the hotel to keep unwelcome Vistors out waaaay too well. I'm going to try to just stay out of the way. You guys go on and do what you need to do."

"It doesn't matter if you see the wards, or not," Robert said, "because we've put up so many protections on this place. We've brought in so many Grove heads, their security experts. Plus the military bigwigs, the leaders they represent, and prepared absolutely everyone all to the gills. If Cythymau is dumb enough to still attack while the delegates are here, he'll just get bitch-stomped. Those wards are just the tip of the iceberg. Right Matt?"

"It's true we've done everything possible to make the summit hotel impregnable. There's *nothing* here for Cythymau to exploit. This place is more secure than Fort Knox." Matt said, his bragging tone obvious.

I quirked an eyebrow.

"Or the summoner's equivalent to that," Matt corrected. "You know what we mean. Cythymau's cruisin' for a brusin' if he tries to get our delegates while they're here. So it's better to have you here where all the security is anyway, rather than off by yourself. We all already agreed we're not going to leave any of us hanging out there as easy pickings for Cythymau, and that absolutely includes you."

"Oracle has spoken," Robert intoned in a deep voice. I wanted to punch him. I settled for glaring at him instead. He had the gall to grin. It did not improve my mood.

Matt shook his head before continuing. "I made hotel reservations for you and the rest of us next door, for obvious reasons. The official government and Grove delegates start arriving soon. Amy and Phineas are already helping the hotel staff get everything set up inside with the aides that were sent ahead. I need to get in there and start assisting them." Matt waved and loped off toward the entrance.

"Seriously, Andrea," Robert said, "I know you're trying to keep your eyes focused elsewhere, but don't go too far okay? The last thing we need is one of us getting caught unawares by that bastard somewhere outside our safety perimeter, where our defenses are less tight."

"I'm worried, not stupid," I said.

"I know. Same."

"I brought several books to read. I'll just go down to the beach and keep my eyes on those. I'm trusting you all that you really have this under control. I don't want to know anything else."

Robert saluted and jogged off. I sighed, and shrugged into the backpack I'd brought that contained many of Cythymau's books. Next, I pulled a beach chair out of the back of the van that hadn't been there a moment before. I was getting pretty good at this covert summoning shit. Too bad there was no one here to show off to.

Except, of course, the demon looking over my shoulder.

Somehow, that thought was less comforting. I plodded down to the beach and settled in with my book to wait, one ear and my Sense primed to leap into action at the first sign of mayhem. I couldn't help but think this all just represented the calm leading up to the storm. I knew Cythymau, and I feared that Matt and Robert underestimated him this time. But my hands were tied.

I studied the waves as they rolled in toward shore, the wind whipping around me from down the beach in a cold torrent that brought mist and rain with it. The morning wind flowed through the freezing, grey, dreary day while everyone was arriving. December was a cold and stormy month on the Washington coast in general, and even though I was wearing sweats and a fluffy down parka, the wind still managed to stick its cold fingers down my spine. But I much preferred being out on the beach by myself than up where the activity was happening.

Still, it was hard to miss the parade of shiny black cars dropping off public officials and dignitaries, their security details clustered tightly before escorting their charges into the summit hotel. Marked and unmarked patrol cars circled the hotel on both the roadside and beach side.

I closed the book. This was my cue. Time for the Maid of Missoula to help greet people. I plodded back up to the hotel.

For a "secret" summit, the site was practically humming with activity, but I had to give it to everyone that at least all civilians had been cleared for blocks around the event site, as far as I could tell. Everyone here had something to do with the summit. And it just made me even more certain that Cythymau wouldn't be able to let such a juicy fruit go without plucking it.

As I stepped back out to the parking lot, I heard revving engines, and then hooting laughter on the wind, and a shiver shimmied down my spine. Adrenaline jolted through me.

I skidded to a halt next to Robert, my heart hammering in my throat.

A wall of military-style vehicles blockaded the parking lot from the avenue in front of the hotel, preventing anyone from leaving. Summoners, rune-boards on their arms, bandoliers of vials crisscrossing their chests, poured out from the vehicles in a swarm that felt just as vast as the sea at our back.

And at their head, watching with a gloating expression, was the demon who'd declared himself my teacher, whether I willed it or no.

"You've been expecting me, yes?" Cythymau said, grinning merrily. "Andrea, I did tell you I wished to be invited, did I not? Robert Lorents too, I believe our unfinished business awaits still."

Have I mentioned that sometimes I love being right, and sometimes it's just fucking awful? I'm just saying, I should've put up a sign as a soothsayer. One of those sandwich board, doomsday-crier types. That felt about right.

ROBERT

As soon as Cythymau's forces moved on us, our allies began summoning. Visitors from unknown dimensions appeared in the parking lot of the old hotel. One appeared to be a massive platypus and another an eight-legged beast resembling a centaur whose horse bits had been replaced with millipede. And coming at us, the Lycaon and Cornuprocyon of Cythymau's home world, combined with the Visitors summoned in by his own Groves.

It *really* needed a soundtrack.

Striding before them was the small, lethal form of the demon himself. A face that haunted my worst nightmares. He made a little gesture with his hand, and the kinetic force of his voice amplified, sending it booming across the incipient battlefield of a parking lot.

"Robert Lorents! Come, speak. Perhaps a deal is to be struck here, yes?"

I looked to my left, to Andrea and Phineas. "What do you think?" I asked.

Phineas shrugged. "Not sure what sort of deal he wants to strike but couldn't hurt to speak with him."

Andrea, next to me, shuddered. "Make no deals, Robert. None. You can't afford it."

I nodded. "Well ... best go see what our wannabe overlord has to say," I said with bravado I didn't come even close to feeling, then strode down to the parking lot. Cythymau, leaving his own forces behind him, stepped out to meet me. Two generals, discussing terms before the battle. Though what made him think *I* was a general in all this, I didn't know.

"Hello again, Robert Lorents," he said. "This is all very wasteful. No reason for your power-wielders and mine to slaughter each other. Wasteful, and one should never waste power, yes?"

"Agreed," I said. "I accept your surrender."

"Whuft!" the demon said, and began to laugh. "This is why I admire you, Robert of Lorents. But this is not a fight you can win, yes? I know your defenses. I know your strength. I know you yourself are aware you're not strong enough to hold me back. And you are right, yes? Andrea spoke to you what she was, and you could have sent her back to me. It's her destiny, that her power merge with mine. Only way things can happen. Bargained for, even. Yet you keep her with you, next to you, watching all you do. Would I appear here if I thought your defenses equal to their task, hmm?"

"Maybe," I said, tossing the word off like I'd seriously considered his last question. "You've always been sort of tricksy. Could be you're running a bluff."

"Do you see a bluff behind me, Robert Lorents? You are outnumbered and outpowered. Stand down. Submit. Allow me to take you and Andrea. Allow me to take the mundane leaders you have gathered here. Join your forces with mine. Let there be one power on this world. One power on which we all prosper or fall, yes? Efficient. Strong."

"And if I tell you to fuck off?"

"Then we break you, and those who stand with you. I will take what is mine and what is needed, and you lose all. Not a pleasant prospect, but our purposes do not run at cross. This does not need to occur. Do not oppose me. Join me. I need strength, yes?"

I tried to think of something pithy to say. Something diplomatic. But this conversation hadn't gone any different than it had in my head, and Cythymau had made a single mistake. I was a frontline shock troop, not a general. I had no terms to surrender by. Talking had, as always, been pointless.

So I kicked him in the balls instead.

It caught him completely off guard. My hiking boot came up squarely between his legs. He didn't crumple, or clutch at himself, or any of the other overstated reactions to that sort of assault that I'd hoped for in my secret fantasies. But he did bite his lower lip, and he had to inhale deeply. I took some satisfaction in that.

Yes, it was juvenile. But I figured hell with it—I'd always wanted to, and the opportunity had presented itself. Plus, I think the gesture was the sort of thing that could easily be interpreted by both sides of the line.

He took a moment to steady his voice before saying. "Very well. These deaths are on your head. I tried to do this in a less wasteful fashion, but I can make this work as well."

And then he turned on his heel and began walking back to his lines.

I'd seen this scene in the movies, of course. I knew that the parley was an honorable conversation between opponents, and the path back to the battle lines was sacred. I knew that any aggressive move against Cythymau would be highly dishonorable. I knew that, were I a soldier, I'd be violating any number of assorted Rules of War if I did anything to him. I knew all that.

I just didn't *care.*

What I did instead wasn't a summons. I didn't even bring up my Sense. Instead, I simply whispered, quietly. "*Sic him, boy.*"

The ground beneath Cythymau erupted as Rick attempted the cheapest of cheap shots at our demonic opponent. He attacked Cythymau with one of his best force-blasts from below, throwing chunks of parking lot sky-high. Cythymau, unfazed, simply shimmered as some sort of shield came up around him. He staggered back a couple of steps, and Rick pressed him, launching another blast.

Grace had effectively nuked Cythymau, and it hadn't killed him. I'd never held out hopes that Rick's cheap shot would, either ... but anything one can do to disrupt enemy command at the beginning of a fight, right? I couldn't make him dead ... but I'd hoped my buddy could make him *hurt.*

Or at least take his attention. Rick had managed that, before.

Which meant things could kick off without him in control. Even as he and Rick faced off against each other, the demon's collected army surged forward, one great mass in a frontal assault without orders from their commander.

They'd taken the bait.

The only problem I had left—and it seemed minor, in comparison—was that, regardless of what happens to a mouse when it triggers a trap, it still seldom ends well for the *cheese.*

I sprinted like a madman back for my own lines. I'd managed to kick things off early, to disrupt enemy communications, but looking at the size of the force charging straight at us, we were still screwed. Cythymau had known our defenses when he launched the attack—he'd never have done it if he'd thought for a moment he'd lose.

I brought up my Sense as I ran and felt a Lycaon closing on me. I kept running, not wanting to slow. Instead, I summoned a Buick from the parking lot/battlefield and placed it directly in front of the sprinting Lycaon. Newton's First Law did the work from there. I Sensed the Lycaon's impact, but after running out of Sense range, any further assessment of damage was impossible without turning.

Once back with our forces, I turned. The line of Visitors was hot behind me, a wave of monsters coming to kill us all. Our forces sent our own Visitors out to meet them.

Thad looked at me as I took up my position next to him.

"Why the nut-kick?" he asked in a calm tone—the sort of tone one uses to pretend they're not currently in mortal danger.

"Why not?" I replied with an impish little grin.

Thad shook his head, and that was all the time we had for banter.

Staring at the oncoming wave of Visitors charging across the long parking lot, I readied myself. Those of us on the ground were defense—our job was to cover the hotel. Phineas commanded the action from the hotel roof with his offense team. They had the fun of summoning attacks over and behind the enemy and protecting our flanks. My job boiled down to making sure no enemy made it through my Sense to attack the hotel.

Simple, right?

Let Phineas worry about the big picture ... I was here to fight, not command. That cold, calm feeling I get swept over me and took my fear and my panic with it. I began to move almost automatically, Sensing and dealing with threats as efficiently as I could. The terrified parts of me sat in the back of my head and watched, as though they'd signed up for the Saturday night thriller double-feature.

Two Lycaon burst into my Sense from the front, and I calmly put cars in front of each of them. The one to the left impacted, crashing into the car. The sounds of crumpling metal and shattering glass joined the general chaos.

The Lycaon to my right dodged, moving for me.

I didn't mind that ... I had a plan B. The mid-sized sedan I'd summoned to block it fell back down, and I seized that energy and sharpened it, driving a spike of pure force up into the surviving Lycaon's skull just before it got close enough to bite. The hot blood of the Visitor spattered over me, but in my passionless state I did not care.

Then I felt the tiny air currents of warded bullets entering my Sense. I summoned the Lycaon's corpse around to fully block me and heard a chattering *thuck-thuck-thuck* sound as the wave of ammunition hit the meaty flesh—but at least it wasn't *my* flesh.

The terrified bits of me in the back of my head screamed about the carnage going on around me. The bullets flying overhead, the massive battles of Visitor on Visitor. The platypus-thing spitting some sort of acid onto a Cornuprocyon. The Millitaur taking a series of bullets from some automatic weapon and falling onto the asphalt. Death, destruction, and pain reigned around me.

I ignored it all.

Hot on the heels of the Visitors, the first wave of enemy summoners charged. Three of their Sense-bubbles entered my own. They fired their weapons—warded bullets. Not tranquilizer darts; we were in kill-or-be-killed territory, but my giant wolf corpse continued to shield me.

And then I, being the complete idiot that I am, *hesitated.* My battle-trance faded as I remembered the face of the kid I'd killed the last time Cythymau and I came to blows. Remembered thinking how stupid and pointless his death was. And so I didn't do ... any of the things I could have. Didn't kill anyone. They'd believed Cythymau, but a part of me knew they didn't deserve what I could do to them ... and so, for just a split-second, I didn't do it.

If ever you find yourself in a battle? Don't hesitate.

Their magics suddenly extended past their Senses in small, focused shots—Rune-based summons, reaching out for something. One felt like pure heat ... I deflected it upward, wrestling my Sense against my opponent's. A second summons came in on its heels, though, and I tried to stop it cold, not sure what its effects would be. But pitting my Sense against two summoners at once put me near my limit. So the *third* summons I could only *partially* deflect.

The concentrated force-blast took me in the leg and not my chest as a result. My knee bent backwards with a sickening, cracking sound, and I screamed at the excruciating pain. My Sense dropped, and I fell backwards, covered by Thad.

I have taken a lot of injuries in the course of my time as a summoner. I've been cut, burned, electrocuted. I've had bones broken. I've even been shot. Nothing, and I mean *nothing,* compared to the pain of having my knee forced to bend the wrong way.

Andrea appeared, then, pulling me backward. I bit my lower lip as the pain of getting dragged out of the line of fire sent streams of agony up from my shattered knee, but she lugged me back through the hotel, to the beach, where we'd staged our wounded. Behind us, I watched our lines begin to crumble, falling back against the onslaught.

"I'm sorry," said Andrea. "This is my fault. I'm sorry."

"Shut up," I said, gasping in pain. "Chose this. And I don't hear any fat ladies, yet."

Andrea gave me a confused look, but I shook my head.

Rick bounded to join us. His coat of quills was ... smoking, a little bit, though I'd no idea why. He'd blood about his muzzle and a lot more on his giant, chitinous club of a tail. Other than that, though, he simply seemed worried about his people. As Andrea flopped me onto the sand, I grinned at him. "Watch our back, buddy," I said.

"We're losing, aren't we?" she asked, putting my leg into a makeshift splint. The medical summoners from the other Groves ... the few that we had ... were seeing to more severe patients, and even more were on their way. "They're going to get in. They're going to kill the summit."

"Yeah," I said. "We're losing. They're getting in. But we're making them pay for it."

From the hotel, Thad emerged, leading the last of our forces back out and through. He began forming a defensive perimeter along the beach. From the top of the hotel, our fire support summoners slid down the ropes pre-set for that purpose. Together, they formed the sort of circle typically referred to as a 'last stand' around us wounded people.

They weren't followed. Of course they weren't. Cythymau didn't care about *us* right now. He'd come for the summit—and that meant he didn't care about the things happening on this side of the now-unguarded conference room. So our guards stood, ready for the last assault ... but hoping it would not come.

And then a portal opened within the circle, and Phineas stepped through. He had a small smile on his face.

"Are they in?" he asked, in a completely casual tone of voice.

Thad looked back over his shoulder at Phineas and grinned wildly. "Damn near. Give it a couple seconds, let them all get in there."

Phineas nodded. Andrea glanced about, confused. I took a moment to look at her and smiled. "Andrea ... don't take this one personally," I said.

"Don't take what personally?" she asked, looking a bit confused.

"Hey, asshole," I said to her ... but the words were meant for the person I *knew* was looking through her eyes and hearing with her ears. She nodded, understanding. "I have another counteroffer for you."

And with that, Phineas removed a small remote-control from his suit coat and unceremoniously clicked a button.

I'd always thought there'd be a dramatic pause. Of course, in the movies, a good bomb has a countdown. Turns out that's not the way electrical impulses actually work.

The moment Phineas pressed his little button, the entirety of our beachside hotel turned into a shockwave and flying rubble.

Explosions ... real ones ... aren't really like the big fireballs in Hollywood. There wasn't a lot of orange flame when the ANFO we'd stacked under the floor of the conference room went up. Just the most horrendous noise and a fountain of rubble. The summoners around us shielded us with their Senses, but the hotel and its parking lot went from being a slightly run-down grand dame of a beach resort to a cloud of dust and rubble. What it had done to those inside that blast was unthinkable.

Of course, as a medic finally got around to getting me some really good painkillers, I stopped thinking about much at all. I'd done my part ... the cleanup belonged to someone else, and I let the euphoria carry me off to darkness.

ANDREA

I WATCHED in frozen shock as the reverberation of the explosion shook the beach where our ring of survivors stood. Debris pelted down before being deflected by the summoners around us. I couldn't help but wince at the damage being done to the sandy ecosystem. At some point, if we lived through the next few hours, this was going to be a hell of a cleanup project.

I didn't know what had just happened, but ... the summit had exploded with all of the government delegates inside. How many summoners had been killed or injured fighting Cythymau? How many top decision makers died after all Thad's assurances of their safety?

Countless diplomatic relations had been destroyed along with the hotel.

There was no way a blast like that had taken out my nemesis, either. Knowing Cythymau, he'd probably come sauntering out with some mocking commentary in a few minutes. I only knew two things: this was a fiasco of epic proportions. And everyone around me appeared much too calm about blowing up their only hope. None of it made sense to me.

Black despair sat on my chest like a physical weight. Robert lay unconscious in the sand, knocked out by the medics. His knee already looked gnarly and swollen. Matt's face had been smudged with blood and grime, and the shoulder of Amy's tunic was a ragged, bloody mess. This. This is where keeping me next to them had brought everyone. They were alive, but the summit wasn't. The peace between summoners and the public wasn't. My hands clenched into futile fists.

Next to me, Thad started cackling with what I could only describe as manic laughter.

Piss and shit, but either the shock had gotten him or he'd gone off the deep end. *This* was the loss that finally broke him? Well, he had given himself up as a political captive. Seeing all that work shatter into nothing had to be devastating.

Thad threw his head back and shouted, before looking around until he could find Matt. Then, of all things, he grinned from ear to ear. I had never, ever, seen an expression like that on Thad's perpetually stiff face. My world tilted on its axis. Something was seriously wrong here.

"We did it. That bastard actually took the bait. Ah, it feels so good to finally get one over on that prick," Thad said.

Thad held his hand up, and Matt smacked it in congratulations. Phineas came over and clapped them both on the backs in an informal group-hug. The three of them huddled there, in the middle of our wounded, filthy, tired, but looking somehow pleased. Phineas had a lot of sadness behind that smile. Thad and Matt outright grinned at each other.

I stared at them, bewildered. Had everyone gone crazy? Or was I the one off her rocker?

"Uh ... so what's going on?" I said finally, totally at a loss to make sense of their reactions. "Who took the bait? What's even remotely happy about all this?" I gestured at the destruction surrounding us.

"I think it's safe to say it now," Thad said, his face still gleeful. "Phineas? Matt?"

"As far as I can tell, we achieved a hundred percent of our goal," Matt answered, pulling a tablet out of his pocket and checking it. "According to my drones, there's only one target still alive onsite, and it's the one we expected."

Phineas chuckled. "I don't think there's any benefit to trying to hide it now."

Thad turned to me and said, "None of the delegates were on site. They're fine. We've accomplished everything we hoped so far here today."

Part of the debris shifted with a rumbling clap, raising a plume of dust.

Out of that miasma, definitely worse for the wear, staggered Cythymau. His face was rigid— whether with pain or fury, I honestly couldn't tell. He had a cut under one eye, and blood dribbled down his cheek, spotting his dust-encrusted clothes. His tattoos glimmered through all the dirt.

"There's just one last hurdle left— how to capture or incapacitate that demon before he starts it all over again. For better or worse, we need to end this today, or eventually we'll be back where we started," Thad said, his tone suddenly all business, his face grim. He reached for his pistol, turned, and fired before I even knew he was going to reengage.

Cythymau blinked out of the path of the warded bullet, reappearing closer to us, shaking his head reprovingly. "It would be best to put away your little toys. It appears everyone is set on trying my patience today. I grow weary of this constant defiance, though I applaud your persistence. You have struck a blow—I suppose if I include Lorents' crude attack, two blows—on me today. Quite the feat. But it ends here. You would be wise to accept defeat gracefully. Even alone, I am more than capable of—"

"Hold it right there," I said, throwing up a hand. I stepped to the front of our little group.

I still made my own choices. Cythymau had taken my freedom, he could control my magic, but not my mind and not my free will— even if I'd been hard-pressed to tell the difference many times.

Cythymau paused, then looked at me expectantly, his lips quirking in that mocking smile. "Since it is such a rare request, my *plentyn*, I will wait. Though I will not tarry for long. Do *you* wish to negotiate on their behalf?"

I'd made a blood pact, and that was something I couldn't change. Been there, done that, ended poorly. But I had people to protect. People who had stood by me when they had every reason to throw me out.

I looked at Cythymau and did something I'd never done, not since the disastrous end of my very first meeting with him.

I accepted where I was. When I was. Who I was.

What I had become.

I accepted the younger me who had turned to an unknown Visitor for help. I accepted the blood and death I'd been a part of as that demon's right hand. I accepted the sacrifices that Grace, Robert, and this small Grove had made to give me a safe haven. I accepted that I would forever feel connected to them for that. And I accepted that I would never again be the optimistic, bright-eyed girl who'd bargained her life away for strangers without worrying about consequences.

I'd already survived and found a way to persist, time and time again. *I* had stuck by Robert. I'd *chosen* to stay when I could have left. These people mattered to me.

In that moment, it all became so clear. No matter what, I was not just some powerless pawn.

The relationships I formed were mine, even those ill-advised or doomed. No matter what painful humiliation I endured next, what I did would be up to me.

All the fear and terror I'd become so accustomed to fell away. A strange tranquility filled its place as I owned all the pain, all my many failures, all my horrific experiences—and let it form my resolve.

I let go of all the things I'd been telling myself I couldn't do, couldn't look at, couldn't deal with. I faced myself head-on and let the knowledge, the skills, the power I'd gained over my long life with Cythymau flow through me. For once, I allowed myself to consider *all* the available options.

I knew what I *must* do. Even stranger, I felt I could do it.

"No. No negotiations," I said to Cythymau. "We fight, you and I. Now."

"You have challenged me before," Cythymau said. "Why do you

expect a different outcome? You have been on my side for ages, both now and past, no matter how much you deny it."

I didn't answer, I just smiled. I met gazes with Cythymau, I heard him, and I did not flinch. *Today* would be different.

I looked at Cythymau anew, as he stood in front of the destroyed hotel, and found myself wondering if he'd always been such a small creature?

Pieces of that destroyed building behind him began to lift into the air. He hurled them toward us, monstrous chunks of cement mixed with rebar and broken glass. He snapped his fingers, and a portal popped into existence behind him. Around me, the summoners scrambled to deflect the debris and protect the wounded.

"Get them out of here; I'll handle this," I told Thad and Phineas. "I'm sure there are people waiting for you to report."

I turned to Rick. "You go with and guard them, guard Robert," I told him. The overgrown racoon whined at me, wanting me to come with, but I felt his reluctant acceptance.

"I stay here. Alone." I told everyone.

Phineas and Thad looked at me, then each other, before nodding.

"I'll back you up if I can," Thad said.

"Be careful, Andrea," Amy said as they all moved to put more distance between themselves and us.

I dropped to one knee, pulling a runetag from my backpack and blooding it. The stone dagger I summoned felt strangely comfortable in my hand. It felt right that I wielded the knife that began our blood pact all those ages ago for this fight.

For the first time, I opened the link between that demon and myself from *my* end. Cythymau's eyes flared open, his expression bemused for a moment at what I had done.

Thad chose his moment of distraction to fire a second warded bullet, but Cythymau blinked out of the way easily.

I reached through my link with the demon and yanked with all my might on the tethers Cythymau had to his batterized summoners. Cythymau and I fought for control, but I kept pulling on them anyway until they finally gave, coming toward me.

I fed that power into the network of tattoos that coated my own skin, stealing the reserved magic for myself. I infused it into me, expanding it through the runes etched through me. My tattoos blazed to life as lightning lanced down, cracking open the sky with thunder and the smell of ozone.

I felt electrified myself, as if I suddenly stood ten stories high, all that power crackling through my nerve endings and giving the world I saw a hazy, blueish sheen. My Sense practically vibrated against the Weave with the extra energy.

Then I cut the tethers off their batterized sources, sealing those summoners from Cythymau, away from our open link. It meant I couldn't use them anymore, but neither could he.

The summoned lightning hit Cythymau square-on. It vanished, absorbed into the shields I knew he must have. He'd already withstood the collapse of the hotel, but the runes marking his skin began to fade.

I teleported next to him and swept my leg out, catching him behind the knees, then summoned a chunk of concrete from the hotel to pin his falling body.

Cythymau blinked away from me. He turned and threw a warded knife at me, but I could feel the air it displaced and dodged it. I nicked a finger with the stone dagger and blooded a charm from my rune bracelet. Through the runes, I stole some of the vast power of the ocean, sharpening it into a focused lance of kinetic force. Aiming for his heart, I released it. He dodged, dropping to a crouch, rather than catching it with his Sense and returning serve.

Interesting.

I followed him, teleporting again, the runed tattoos glowing brilliantly against my white skin. The power, amplified by all those tattoos, crackled through me, heady and invigorating.

I lunged at Cythymau with the dagger, and he caught my wrist, spinning me away from him and throwing me high into the air, towards the retreating summoners. I caught myself and used the momentum from the ocean's constant wind to bring myself back in front of him. I peeled velocity from my fall, hurling it at him in a sharpened blast of force that allowed me to gently settle back onto my feet. Through the link, I felt Cythymau teleport away from the onslaught toward his open portal.

I activated my tattoos, summoning lightning to lance down from the grey clouds overhead, crashing down into the small demon just as he blinked into position. I teleported, following, not giving him any space.

Wisps of smoke or steam rose gently from Cythymau's skin, and he visibly winced, his laughing eyes uncharacteristically somber. His jaw clenched and his lips pressed into a grim line—he actually looked *concerned*.

I swung the knife down, and he dodged to the side, stumbling a little as he deflected my momentum. He watched me, his face whitening, his eyes flaring wide as his tattoos dimmed.

I couldn't help it. I grinned, my stolen power buzzing through all my nerve endings. Gods, but it felt good to have him on the ropes for once.

Cythymau quickly stepped backward into the portal, but I wasn't about to let him escape so easily.

I grabbed onto his shoulder, falling through the portal with him. We rolled and I found myself pinned under his wiry strength, my shoulders prickled by the dry grass and rock of our new surroundings. He grappled with me, trying to pin my arms.

But the power still crackled through me. There was little he could do I wouldn't be able to counter in his current state. That didn't mean I was going to concede any of my advantages, though.

The runed dagger I still clutched cut my palm. I jabbed upward, expecting the dagger to bounce off his wards, but intending to create an opening to get out of the grapple.

Instead, the knife gashed into his chest, raining blood across me as we struggled. He groaned, then hissed with pain and banged my hand brutally against the ground, prying the dagger from my tingling fingers, his normal laughter completely gone.

I threw an elbow into his wound, launching myself forward while he dealt with the pain. Then I blinked out of his grasp in a flare of blue tattoos. He caught up to me at the last second, flinging me backward.

We rolled downhill. Even though I could Sense it coming, tried to slow my momentum, I still crashed painfully, pinned between him and several large rocks.

It wasn't until then, dazed and staring up at the orange sky that I realized where I was.

I immediately turned and dry-heaved onto blood-splattered rocks where we'd just crashed. This was Cythymau's Weave. I was back in the Weave of my captivity.

It was just as dry and devoid of life to my Sense as the last time I'd been here. But now. Now, I was back with my jailer.

I shook myself. No. I couldn't think like this. Cythymau may have brought me back to the place of my worst nightmares, but I'd make it a place for his, too.

"Whuft, *plentyn*! This is already a place of my worst nightmares. There's naught you could do to me here."

I rewarded him by dropping a downed tree on his head. He deflected it, a cloud of dust rising from his grimy clothes with the concussive force. I looked at his face critically. Every time I forced him to use his tattoos, they grew fainter, less distinct. It was taking him more and more effort to keep them active.

There was no constant wind or waves to take of advantage of, here. Stealing from Robert's playbook, I teleported the tree high above us, peeling its velocity away and letting it settle gently back to the rocky grass around us. I sharpened and aimed that force at Cythymau's back. He turned to deflect it. I launched forward, lodging the dagger in his back.

It dug deep and stuck. Cythymau let out a gasping cry of pain.

Then the dagger vanished out of my hands as he teleported away with it still embedded in his shoulder. I swore, concentrating on my runes to teleport and follow him. I reappeared just outside of the cave and ran, wanting to close the distance between us, but almost fell into a void of nothing.

I stood on the edge of a crumbling precipice, my Sense reaching out into emptiness. Where the mountain and cave should have been had become a vast, sucking hole. Wind whipped past me into the void, and I stared into its blackness stunned. The only color came from the streamers of my hair, caught by that otherworldly gust. The nothingness had grown much bigger since the last time I was here. It remained closest to experiments I'd seen with a vacuum.

The dirt under my feet began to crumble and flow toward it, like a gruesome parody of sand art.

I teleported backwards in the nick of time, feeling like I'd escaped being lost to the void by seconds. My head pounded with the effort of multiple teleports in quick succession.

Cythymau teleported to my side, his tattoos appearing like faint-blue spiderwebs under the dust and dirt covering him. Blood coated his front and dripped down from the dagger lodged in his back. His strength and power reserves appeared almost depleted. I shielded as hard as could with my own tattoos, bracing for attack.

"Now you witness what I'm up against," Cythymau said instead, staring out at the vast maw where his home had been, "and what I am willing to do to fight it. This unraveling which will eventually overtake all Weaves."

"I'm sorry, what?" I said. "This is bad, yeah, but you've been torturing me for centuries. I don't know why a giant hole in your dead-ass Weave has anything to do with me."

"*Whuft*, child! You fail to see what is before you, yet again."

I frowned, "I'm looking at a demon who's had his ass kicked. Just so we're clear."

Cythymau looked out into the void, his customary cheer gone, his voice level. "This Weave is dead because it's unravelling; it is not unravelling because it's dead. Therefore, you fail to see the significance of what you witness." He paused and the corner of his mouth quirked up maddeningly. "Just so we're clear."

"Your ends justified your means, because you were fighting—" I gestured toward the gaping emptiness "—whatever this is?"

"The end of the universe, and everything in it," Cythymau said, his tone grim.

"I don't believe you."

"Whether you believe me or not, it's there in front of you, yes? Why wouldn't I use any means at my disposal to stop the destruction and unravelling of the cosmos? After all, if I don't succeed, there will be nothing here and no one to decry what methods I used in the first place," Cythymau pointed out.

I gaped at him and then at the blackness. This was not how I had expected this fight to go.

"Therefore, I will do whatever is necessary, yes?" Cythymau lunged, his expression focused, fanatical. He tackled me, yanking on my Sense through our open bond, intent on stealing my Sense, my magic, for his own use. But I threw an elbow up into his wounded chest and yanked back, refusing to cede my power to him.

Then I felt it. I felt the moment he left himself open, the heartbeat where he overextended his Sense in our wrestling match, exposing himself to mine.

As soon as he'd passed the fulcrum of no return, I reached in and pulled with all my might. I whisked his weakened Sense out of his control like a lever pops a rock out of the ground, and then held on for dear life.

I had done it.

I had his Sense under my control, with the flow of power through the link running in reverse of usual. But I didn't know how long I could hold it.

"My *plentyn*, this is not the time for this. You see with your own eyes what a dire situation we face," he gasped, sweat running down his face, his tattoos barely visible.

I summoned the runed dagger to my hand using my tattoos and held it at his throat. "Yeah, that's what you say, but you have yet to prove it. And I gave up believing everything you tell me a long time ago. It's never the whole truth, you know?"

"Every time you cut yourself with that, you but reinforce our blood pact. This is not a way out. You must truly join me, or kill me and take my power, child. Those have always been your choices, since the very first day our bargain was struck," Cythymau said.

"Wrong," I said. "Because I found out something you did to me all those years ago. And I figured out your price in all this. What you gave and exchanged with me. For a 'fair' bargain."

I leaned in and whispered close to his ear, "And I'm betting that which can be permanently opened could also be permanently closed. And well, if this kills you, I guess sometimes I do listen to what you want." Yeah, it was a petty and vindictive thing to say. I acknowledge it.

While I still had control of his Sense, I cut my arm and used the runed dagger, my Sense, and the tattoos to rip his Sense away from his body, slicing it from him cleanly. Then I closed our link permanently, and sealed it for good measure, using the last of the borrowed power I'd stolen from his network of summoners.

It felt so good, so right.

Cythymau sagged to the ground, his skin chalky and pale under all the dirt. No tattoos showed at all. If anything, he just looked like a tired, little old man. Nothing worth writing home about. Frail even.

I'd expected his Sense to dissipate when I let it go, cut off like the severed limb it was. After all, I'd sliced it off from everything, I thought. Instead, it curled around mine, swirling and merging into me with in a flair of tingly energy that felt like I'd stuck my hands on a Ven de Graaff generator.

I looked down and saw the faint-blue webbing of rune tattoos standing out on my skin with no direction from me. Just what exactly had I done?

"*Whuft!* Child, you never do anything easily, do you?" Cythymau whistled softly to himself. He looked around as if shocked to find himself here.

"What's your problem?" I asked him, still a little suspicious that I'd really managed to strip and seal his Sense away from him. But to my Sense, he came across as a normal ... well, not human ... but non-summoner.

Cythymau scratched his head, then winced as the action pulled on his wounds. "*Whuft, plentyn!* You continue to confound me. In this circumstance, I didn't expect to continue on. I have some reevaluating of implications, yes? Shall we go before we are devoured?" He gestured toward the vast void encroaching on our position before saying, "I find I'd rather not get unmade, since against all odds, I live. I applaud your ruthlessness, though. A bargain well-struck, I think."

"Oh, shove it. I need you because I have too many questions. I don't believe you, but I can't afford to assume you're lying, either," I said. "You have to come with me, this time. Don't think you can escape. And don't try any tricks."

"Wouldn't even dream of it," the demon said. "After all, I *respect* a bargain. Unlike some people."

I trudged back to the portal, my head pounding. "Well," I said as I opened it, "let's go shock some people. This ought to be fun."

ROBERT

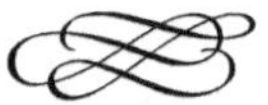

VICTORY USED TO BE EXHILARATING. This time, it just felt profoundly empty.

When I woke from my painkiller-induced haze, the medical summoners had done quite the number on my leg. Oh, it still hurt like hell, and I still had weeks in a cast to look forward to, but at least I'd walk again.

Which was more than I could say for the Seattle Grove.

When I finally limped through the door to our little home in Shelton, Francene led me in and sat me down in one of the recliners, then took her own seat on the nearby sofa. "How are you?" she asked with that motherly smile.

"Honestly?" I said. "I ... don't know. The leg hurts, but ... "

"Yeah. Well, how much do you know about the rest of the world?"

"Matt gave me some briefings," I said. "I know the *actual* summit—the one we teleported all those people to—went well. I suppose having already won the war helped with that. At least we're going to see things change a bit with the legality of what we do. Amnesty and a whole system of licensing, run by the Groves. Gonna be a new world."

"Mmm," said Francene. "Yeah—though you know most people will still hate you for what you are."

"Well, I didn't expect people to stop being idiots," I said with a little half-grin. "I mean, if there's one thing humanity's good at, it's collective stupidity. But at least I won't have to cover up from the police. No more 'reality terrorists.'" I paused, thinking on it. "That is, if I can get someone to license me. No idea what sort of a bureaucratic headache that's going to be."

Francene laughed a bit. "I don't think you'll have a problem with that."

"You're my mom," I said, smiling to her. She got that glow she always got when I applied the term to her. "So you're biased."

"Maybe," she said. "How much do you know about ... us?"

I shook my head. "Not much. Matt kept things pretty terse. Phineas and Thad visited the hospital once—as a pair. That felt more obligatory than anything, though, not a lot of information shared. I haven't seen Amy at all ... which was really weird. She's usually so—"

"Amy's had a rough time," said Francene, cutting me off. "She ... well, as I understand it, she had a lot of friends and family in the Seattle Grove. Some of them, maybe all, I'm not sure..."

Francene trailed off, but I'd gotten the picture. Amy had helped us kill off people she'd once worked with. That probably *did* take a toll. Damn. I kicked myself a little for being so wrapped up in my own head that I hadn't thought about it.

"Didn't see much of Andrea, either," I said. "I'm not sure she likes places with large numbers of people. Like, say, a hospital."

"I'm pretty sure she doesn't," Francene said, though she had a bit of a different pitch to her voice. I stared at her for a moment, trying to place where her nerves were coming from.

"What else?" I asked.

"Andrea's been training. Out in the woods. With, um, Rick. A lot."

That made sense. Hell, it's what I liked to do when I had things on my mind. Andrea'd always been a bit on the weird side, so I didn't blame her for her lack of visits. "Oh," I said, then looked at Francene. There was something else there, something I couldn't place.

"And?" I asked, letting the implication hang.

"And the rest ... you should learn from her," Francene said. "Some things aren't my place. I love you, and I love her, and this is one of those situations you need to work out for yourselves."

I flushed. "What?" I said. "I don't—I mean, look, it was *her* idea to get naked in the back of that van, not mine!"

Francene blinked at me. "Robert! What? Naked? I ... no. I didn't mean—"

"Oh," I said, and I could feel my cheeks glowing beet-red. "Um. Do you know where she is? I suppose I need to talk to her."

"You do," said Francene, though the frown on her face told me we weren't *entirely* done with this particular line of inquiry. "About more things than one, it seems."

I waited, holding her gaze. She let that hang in the air, a not-so-subtle instruction to get my shit together. I left it, saying nothing further, letting her break the silence.

"She's at Mo's," Francene said at last.

For some reason, after great and terrible events, there's a strange comfort in the things that haven't changed. Maybe it's the proof that we did, in fact, manage to protect the world. Maybe it's just a piece of the subconscious finding comfort in the familiar.

Whatever it is, stepping into Smokin' Mo's once more and taking my first breath brought a smile to my face instinctively. The rich, smoky-sweet smell of barbecue continued to infuse the restaurant, a heady, mouth-watering constant in my life. True before, and true now. No matter what battles I fought, or injuries I took, or world-threatening demons I cheap-shotted in the scrotum ... Mo's would be here. A bastion of barbecue, a motte of meat.

The hostess gave me a little nod. It wasn't quite an entire room shouting my name as I walked in, but I still got the distinct, welcoming impression that I'd entered a place where everyone knew my name.

And not because it had been showing up on newscasts, for once.

She approached me, but before I could tell her why I'd come she said "Robert? Your party is waiting for you. Back this way."

My ... party? I was here for Andrea. Had Thad and Phineas decided to join her? They'd never really been big on Mo's—or doing anything social outside the house, for that matter. Still, maybe with the war over, their sphincters had unclenched slightly and allowed for a night of barbecue. A bit of me felt ... disappointed?

Had I been looking forward to having dinner alone with Andrea? The emotion surprised me, and I began to pull on it, examine what it meant ... but then I saw who 'my party' was. Andrea, yes ... and next to her in the booth, a small man who, for a moment, I didn't recognize.

Until my memory overlaid a web of blue, runed tattoos over his now-unblemished face.

In a flash, I raised my Sense. The world stilled around me. I may have had one leg in a cast, but that didn't mean I wasn't at least the third-deadliest thing in the restaurant. My Sense began picking up on the potential weapons within its range—there are a *lot* of steak knives in a barbecue joint, it turns out.

And Andrea's Sense, omnipresent, met mine. At a larger range than she used to have.

"Robert," she said quietly. "Don't do whatever you're thinking."

"Andrea. What has he done to you? Get up from the table slowly, let's see if we can't get the restaurant to evacuate."

Andrea sighed, then said, "No, Robe—"

At that moment, a waitress arrived at the table carrying a massive platter. The social convention of restaurants kicked in on all three of us, deferring the floor to the waitress.

She'd brought the Family Meal—a giant mix of barbecued meats and sides served family-style for a group of people. An awkward tension hung over the three of us as the waitress placed basket after basket of meat and sides on the table. I kept my standing position, but the waitress simply turned to me and said, "And what will you be having to drink, sir?"

I looked between Andrea, Cythymau, and the waitress, jaw hanging for a moment. Then I said, "I'm thinking I'm going to need a decent beer. Bring me the darkest one you've got on tap."

The waitress smiled and nodded, then stepped away from the table, freeing us to resume our conversation.

"No evacuating," said Andrea after she'd gone. "And I'm perfectly in control of myself, Robert. Now sit down."

Cythymau very calmly carved off a rib, coated it in spicy barbecue sauce, and began eating it. In all my time contesting him, I think this was the first I'd seen him actually eat food. "*Whuft,*" he said. "You were right, my *plentyn*. The food here *is* delicious."

My Sense remained up, though it met no challenge from Cythymau.

"Robert," said Andrea again. "Sit down. Eat. We need to talk about some things."

And there I stood, Sense up, battle-ready, and heartily confused. "Andrea?" I asked. "What in the actual *fuck* is going on here?"

"He's harmless," said Andrea.

"I've never wished harm," said Cythymau, his voice a pillar of indignation.

"Maybe," said Andrea calmly. "But he can't *cause* harm, now. Well, not magically, anyways. He has no Sense anymore."

Around us, I caught the looks from our fellow barbecue patrons. Some showed fear, some anger—but nobody called the cops. We were legal. Hated, still, just as Francene had predicted. But legal. Speaking of Senses and summoning right smack-dab in the middle of a restaurant. This was going to take some getting used to.

"Quite right, her. My *plentyn* ripped my power away from me," he said, grinning.

"And you haven't tried to kill her for that?" I asked. "No great fallback plan for vengeance?"

"Robert Lorents! When have you known me to be *vengeful?* When a bargain is broken, then, perhaps. But Andrea has fulfilled hers, at last. Or is fulfilling it. Do you not get it, boy? I have *won.* There is no ill feeling here, yes?"

"Everyone who followed you into battle was killed," I said, trying to feel out what I was missing, here.

"Yes, true, though some of the Grove remained at headquarters. I did beg you *not* to waste lives, yes?"

"You are now ... entirely powerless?"

"Say rather that I have no more magic than a mundane. I *am,* in fact, like a mundane now, though my years of knowledge and accumulated wisdom, I would like to think, add some degree of value."

I blinked. "And ... that means you *won?*"

"Sit, boy. Maybe now that my teeth are less sharp you will actually listen to my words without attacking me. I won, yes. The *plentyn* has accepted her role, and in time I am hoping you will accept yours. After all, existence itself lies in the balance."

"I—" I shook my head, less to deny anything he said and more to simply try to clear the cobwebs from it. "But that's why we were fighting *you.* To save our existence."

"*Whuft.* No. You fought me to save your *way* of life. To stop me from ruling, from changing your idea of justice, as though either were goals worthy of being my ends. You fought to stop me—*I* have been fighting to preserve existence. Do you never *listen,* Robert Lorents?"

Something in his tone of voice reminded me so much of Grace that it took me aback. Stunned, I slid into the booth next to the demon—if that's what he still was—that I'd tried so hard to kill just weeks ago. That Grace had *died* trying to kill. The one responsible for all those bodies in Missoula, in Ocean Shores, and in so many other places across our continent.

Did the government know the demon still lived? Did the other Groves? How could we trust him? I had so many questions, but one thing seemed certain—I Sensed no power from Cythymau. His rune-tattoos were missing from his face, and that buzz of power I'd always felt from him was simply gone. Or, rather, it felt like it came from Andrea, now. I had so many questions, for him, for Andrea, for the universe in general.

Then I thought about Grace, and wondered what *she* would do in this situation.

I sliced off some of Mo's smoked meatloaf and coated it with sauce, then added some beans to my plate. "So ... I'll at least listen. Why is it, exactly, that you think all of existence is at stake, again?"

EPILOGUE

GRACE

I DRIFTED over the gentle waves on a giant, red, inflatable floatie, my legs draped in the water, a tray of queso-smothered street tacos balanced on my stomach. A mojito sat, waiting and ready, in the floatie's cup holder.

Outside the sheltered lagoon where I reclined, I could hear waves flirting with the shore, a constant cheerful murmur. And over that, in the distance, I could pick up laughter as other spirits played on the beach, mimicking their living counterparts.

The sun reflected brilliantly off the surf. I lay there, basking in my swimsuit, sunglasses, and wide-brimmed hat. I just soaked in the sun's rays—my mood perfectly content, my mind a bit drowsy.

One perk of being dead: there's no one to call you out for how many mojitos you drink or how many tacos you eat. I mean, what's one more going to do? Kill me?

Already been there, *so* done with that.

Tacos would have been a delicious way to go, but I couldn't actually say they would've been better or less painful than what I'd done. Turns out making yourself the epicenter of a nuclear explosion takes you out pretty damn fast.

Gone in a flash.

Literally.

I chuckled at my own dark humor and lifted a taco from the tray, biting into it. I lay, lazily relishing the citrus and spice that burst over my tongue.

Let's be clear, here. I'm not really complaining. Turns out for me, the afterlife became a pretty cushy gig. Each day passed much like the last one, no emergencies, no tough calls, no paralyzing fear that all my decisions would someday prove to be the wrong ones.

I'd left that all behind me in my old life. Today remained another great day in a long chain of similar ones.

Only one thought niggled at the back of my mind, no matter how I tried to squish it down: what trouble had my foolhardy apprentice found to embroil himself in recently? No way could that boy stay quiet for this long.

I admitted to curiosity there.

I'd seen Robert once since I died, and I'd yelled at him pretty roundly for yanking me out of my heaven with no warning. So far, my lecture on the grave incivility and danger of summoning someone who hasn't agreed to become a guardian spirit must have stuck. He hadn't put on a repeat performance, yet.

I was *almost* disappointed about that.

I'd taken some time from my peaceful days to figure out how Robert had managed to find my soul in this Weave without a Visitant pact. He'd tethered it to his summon without my consent. Guardian spirit pacts were pre-arranged, formal affairs that were invoked before death, with the summons being left behind with a person's last effects.

I hadn't signed up for any of that crap. I'd had enough of being at a Grove's beck and call during my short life, thank you very much.

It had taken some experimenting and some trial and error, but I was reasonably confident I'd figured out how he'd done it. I'd only tested it minimally, though. As a spirit, I didn't have blood. But I'd discovered I could put myself—my spiritual energy—directly in the runes if I wanted to power them. My new theory was that while we were mortal, blood held the highest concentration of spiritual energy to interact with the runes. As a spirit, there was no need for all that mess.

But I'd also discovered, unlike blood, my spirit essence didn't seem to replenish. The more I tried to use runes, the less of me there was. So in the end I hadn't tested the "Robert's-a-reckless-idiot" summon fully.

I'd just seen if I could reach out to Hyctea, my owl familiar, in her Weave outside our usual Visitant pact without actually expending the *oomph* needed to bring her here. It had still cost me, but not nearly as much.

There weren't many spirits I was on good enough terms with to pardon the rude yanking of their soul into a different realm as an experiment, anyway. And I couldn't go around yanking on Robert's spirit willy-nilly, even assuming I'd been sure of the ultimate results on his mortal flesh.

Which I wasn't.

Either way, though, the kid really would be incorrigible if even I tried something like that.

So I held onto my high ground, and my new knowledge about summoning, with no use for it. But I'd figured it out. I snorted, amused—even in death, I couldn't let go of my curiosity about how things worked.

Shaking off my nostalgia, I took a long pull from the damp, frosted glass holding my mojito.

Even with sunglasses, I squinted at the brightness. The sun danced off the water in a dizzying display, the sand glittered, and light wind kept the temperature pleasant. Seagulls screeched overhead, other spirits laughed in the distance, and the waves whispered soothingly.

Then the Weave shuddered around me, vibrating against my Sense. It felt like tremors through a trampoline, and then everything went quiet.

Sudden shouting startled me, a zing of concern prickling along my skin and cutting through the pleasant day.

Multiple voices hollered in a confusing cacophony, but I wasn't able to discern words. I pushed myself up on my arms to try to see better, the floatie lurching underneath me unsteadily. At the lip of the lagoon, I could see people running, their knees lifting high, their arms clutching their beach towels, umbrellas, day bags. One of them dropped something, the object rolling away from the cluster of runners, but they didn't stop to pick it up.

I hadn't seen anyone run flat-out since arriving here— I'd seen frolicking, gamboling, or cavorting, sure. But a no-holds-barred, dead-ass terror-sprint up the beach? That was out of place here.

I hadn't seen something like this since before my untimely demise.

But I still recognized panic when I saw it.

I guess we'd better see what's up, Gracie, I told myself, sighing. *If this turns into a working holiday, I'm gonna file a complaint with upstairs.*

I scanned in front of me for anything obviously amiss. The ocean separating me from the beach glinted blindingly, and I squinted, trying see farther down the sand.

I looked behind me and up into the sky, and saw what looked like a jagged line standing out against the sky's blueness like a crack through porcelain.

Well, that definitely wasn't natural.

I didn't think one crack warranted full-blown panic time, but I'd lived through a lot more than most people. I jumped down into the water off my float and began swimming my way to shore, dragging the float behind me.

Of course, with not being able to summon using blood, even fixing it would be a challenge. But then, when was that anything new?

A moment later, the shaking resumed and the sky split open above the lagoon wall, becoming a giant, gaping hole, frayed around edges.

The tear started unraveling from my left, widening quickly. The gap in the Weave expanded so fast, it looked like something stripped the weft away from the warp, leaving the warp hanging like discarded strings.

Okay, *that* I couldn't fix. Everyone's panic suddenly felt like a much more reasonable response.

The tear widened and lengthened, descending and slashing into the rocks around the lagoon's edge. The rocks that had been there just ceased to exist. It destroyed lagoon's sheltering barrier, creating a gap. I swore.

Stranded in the middle of the water, I doubted that was going to be good for me.

I expected waves to rush into the lagoon, but the opposite happened. The lagoon's water flooded toward the new gap, immediately changing the water's nature and ferocity.

In the fraction of a second, the placid waves became a sucking torrent, cascading toward the massive hole in reality. It swept everything in my little refuge up along with it. Including me.

Just my luck.

Again.

My time in the afterlife had lulled me into forgetting that my fortune had a way of turning to absolute crap. I cursed, then choked and spluttered on a mouthful of salty seawater as the current tried to drag me under.

I struggled, the water sucking at my limbs, pushing me downward, sweeping me toward the rocky lagoon wall. It was as if the ocean had been tipped on its side, or—in a much less elegant phrase—flushed toward the widening void. I threw an arm over my floatie, trying to keep my face above water.

Whatever had happened, this was a much bigger catastrophe than any rip I'd ever seen before. And due to my particular apprentice's lack of control, I'd seen really messed up holes in reality before. Something here had gone very, very wrong.

Okay, Gracie. So what now?

I didn't have any blood. I didn't have my rune board. I didn't have rune tags, or a surface to write runes on, even if I could. I had just me, and whatever crazy plan I could think of in the next few seconds. Even though I'd bragged I couldn't die again, I didn't immediately want to test how true that was.

"Little sister!" A low bass voice called. I looked to see Redwood, my massive tree spirit friend on the shore. His roots dug deep into the sandy beach, balancing him precariously against the drag of the current.

A root snaked out next to me and I grabbed it. My old friend had bought me some time. He did not try to run from the massive, sucking wound in the Weave. He'd stayed for me, my lifeline, making himself my anchor.

Struggling against the rushing water, I clung to that rough, feathery root as Redwood towed me toward him. Released from my grip, my red floatie vanished into the ever-widening maw behind me, taking my mojito and half of my tacos with it.

Finally, I dragged myself up onto the beach next to the giant tree spirit and sat, gasping and coughing water out of my lungs.

But we didn't have long to delay—the spirit world frayed and disintegrated in front of us as we watched, separating, leaving dangling, dissolving warp. It unraveled as easily as if someone had pulled a string on a sweater.

The lagoon emptied, leaving wet rock and sand, that quickly fissured as the void came toward us. We backed up as sand began to crumble away from the beach's edge.

Maybe ten yards down the beach from us, still in its path, a beach bum who'd woken late from all the commotion stared at it expanding with wide eyes. Not moving. Not trying to get out of the way.

I winced, yelling for him to run. But he didn't.

The spirit put a hand out in front of it, as if to fend off the tear. The moment his hand touched that void, it unraveled like all the rest. The spirit stared at the stump where his hand had been. Then something snagged him and pulled fine spiritual threads from his essence. His form collapsed and he vanished with the rest into the inky nothingness.

I swallowed, unsure of what I'd just seen. In my experience, rips in a Weave formed from an imbalance. Encountering a gash, things might get sucked into a different Weave, but I'd never heard of something dismantling spirits and surroundings like this.

"Have *you* ever seen anything like this before?" I asked Redwood.

"No, little sister, this is beyond my ken," the ancient tree answered in a hushed tone. "I have nothing to compare this to in all my long years."

I tried to keep my panic wrapped in a tight little ball at the pit of my stomach.

I squinted at the destruction. At the rate it was going, there was nowhere in this Weave that would be safe. Absolutely nowhere we could run in time.

Redwood watched the doom coming for us with me, his limbs swaying in the gale of this world's demise. I sat in his branches, hugging his trunk, my curly, wet hair whipping around me in an obnoxious riot, trying to blind me.

We were witnessing this Weave's end. I couldn't say how or why. There was no collision or imbalance with another Weave I could conceive of to cause this. It felt cold, methodical.

If it sprang from a demonic incursion, it was beyond my reckoning.

Something was pulling the Weave apart, along with all the spirits inside, reducing it all to threads and filaments, separating and spooling the threads away until there was nothing left. And the implications of that made me cold all the way down to my toes.

Spirit or no, I would be unmade. Redwood and I would both cease to exist. We'd already been reduced to the core essence that made up our souls, and that was about to be pulled apart.

As the unmaking approached—I couldn't think of anything else to call it—Redwood suddenly spun, putting the back of his massive trunk between it and me. The tree plucked me off my perch and held me suspended in his branches.

"You find your way out," Redwood said. Threads started spinning away from his far branches, fine as a spiderweb, reminding me of smoke with no flame.

The massive tree continued, "I promised your great grandmother I'd always look out for you, when you were barely any bigger than an acorn."

"I—what are you—" I stuttered, already appalled and heartbroken that he'd put himself between me and what appeared to be an inescapable fate. If I'd had any breath, it would have left me.

"I believe in you, little sister," the tree said, "You have always been clever and resourceful. Don't let your growth end here." He released a torrential gout of wind, blasting me away from him, flinging me head-over-heels up the beach, buying me what I guessed would be mere minutes.

I landed hard on the sand, bouncing and rolling, then spun back to look at him. Redwood stood at the edge of the void, his branches and bark peeling away into long strands that vanished into nothing. He turned away, hiding his expression from me. What did Redwood expect me to be able to do against something like that?

Dammit. If I did *nothing*, it was all over anyway.

I crouched on the sand, biting my lip and hurriedly drawing runes. I needed to get a better look at what was really happening to my old friend. Who cared if I would be weakening my essence by infusing myself into them? I took a deep breath and sent a piece of myself into the runes, then through them.

I could feel pieces of Redwood splitting away, cascading into the anomaly behind him. I followed and found myself caught in the tines of a vast, primordial machine. It methodically broke the Weave into the raw materials of existence, of all realities everywhere. It coldly, mechanically consumed all in front, not caring if what it broke apart had been sentient just a moment before. I shuddered.

It started pulling apart the piece of me that I'd sent through the runes. The sensation frizzled along my whole being as part of me was dismantled, reduced to the basic building material of all reality. Had I been alive, I would have died, then. But I wasn't. From this close up, I could watch the process, see when the essence that had been me joined with the essence that had been Redwood and everything else in this world.

I watched the threads unspinning and I saw how they fit into the underlying pattern, how they bound one another, together and yet distinct until they were broken apart.

I could see the pattern making up my old friend. I looked down at my own hands on the sand and saw a similar pattern underpinning and running through the glittering grains.

Finally I turned my Sense inward and found the twined strands making up me, my soul, my person. I recognized the essence, the pattern that was solely mine in my gut.

And with that came a heady, reckless plan. I *could* do something. I could fight to preserve myself, however temporarily, against whatever this was. But then what?

I remembered Robert's summons.

I hastily started scribbling the rune formulas out on the beach. My forehead wrinkled with tension, and my stomach filled with rumbling fear. It was entirely possible this was crazy and all for naught.

But hey, if I was wrong, the worst thing that could happen already stared me in the face, right?

I stepped back and gazed at the section of the beach I had coated with runes. Then I glanced at the giant blank where Redwood had been moments before.

Now or never Gracie.

I said a prayer to the universe, knelt down, and put all that I was into the runes I'd drawn.

Through them, I gathered the universe's flaxen threads and looped them around the giant spools tearing apart the Weave. Sliding in, I hijacked them for my own purpose, coaxing them into the looped curlicues of my own tiny pattern.

My strength faded like a weak battery. I tried to get them to form the knotted, twisted, gnarly pattern that made up Redwood, but they refused to budge any farther.

I wanted to scream and cry, to rant at the uncaring universe. But there was no time, and I couldn't waste Redwood's gift to me.

My consciousness became fuzzy as I powered the next-to-last part of the summon, reaching out through many Weaves.

I found the distant beacon of my apprentice's soul in his Weave. I tethered myself to that spark, then hooked in, reeling myself toward him.

The summons took hold, feeling like a punch to the solar plexus, and jerked me out from the middle of chaos.

I powered the last part of the summon, and felt air exchange itself for me, sealing up the Weave behind me. I sprawled onto the pavement by my apprentice's feet. I could only hope Robert wasn't in the middle of some large crowd.

I'd landed on a quiet street next to a restaurant. The smell of barbeque hit my nostrils and my stomach rumbled. It smelled heavenly. Still wet, barefoot, and wearing a swimsuit, I shivered in the cold breeze.

Then I stood, dusting myself off, and noticed my hands and knees stung, and appeared scraped and bleeding. Huh. I poked at the scrape, and winced with pain as my finger came away sticky and red. It appeared I'd actually woven myself a new body? That was new, and not entirely intended.

A throat cleared loudly above me. I looked up, and found Robert, Andrea, and a wizened little man who I couldn't quite place staring at me.

I immediately zeroed in on the large white takeout box Robert held. I took the box out of his unresisting hands and opened it to take a deeper whiff.

Then unable to resist, I slapped Robert's back, grinning at him cheekily before asking, "So, did you miss me?"

END

ABOUT THE AUTHORS

Frog and Esther married in 2002. For a decade, they swore not to read anything the other wrote, lest catastrophe befall their marriage. Then, the stars aligned in the heavens. In a moment foretold by prophets, they broke their own rule. The result is their critically-acclaimed *Gift of Grace* urban fantasy series. Since then, they spend their free time watching anime, playing board games, and writing. Their short stories can also be found in several high-profile anthologies, such as *Straight Outta Deadwood* published by Baen books, and alongside Brandon Sanderson, David Farland, and Todd McCaffery in *Dragon Writers* published by WordFire Press. They also run the small genre press, Impulsive Walrus Books, that published this book and the rest of the Gift of Grace series. Their next big Kickstarter project will be *Cthulhu FhCon,* a Lovecraftian anthology set at a fan convention, which is scheduled for September 2022. The submission call will close on April 15, 2022, and can be found on the Impulsive Walrus Books website.

Follow along with Frog and Esther's projects at:
https://jonestales.com/
https://www.facebook.com/frogesther
https://impulsivewalrusbooks.com/
https://www.facebook.com/impulsivewalrusbooks
Twitter: @EstherImp @Frog_Jones @ImpulsiveWalrus

ALSO BY FROG AND ESTHER JONES

Grace Under Fire: Gift of Grace Book 1

Coup de Grace: Gift of Grace Book 2

Falling From Grace: Gift of Grace Book 3

www.ingramcontent.com/pod-product-compliance
Lightning Source LLC
Chambersburg PA
CBHW071246190726
48292CB00007B/2436